MURDER AT THE OLD ABBEY

Murder, mystery, and suspense in South Wales

PIPPA McCATHIE

Paperback published by The Book Folks

London, 2019

ISBN 978-1-0998-7603-5

www.thebookfolks.com

To Jeannie

Prologue

The old house was never totally silent, not even in the darkest hours of the night. Maybe the ghosts of the monks who'd inhabited the nearby ruins all those centuries ago walked the corridors. Maybe the ancestors of the present occupants roamed around, re-enacting old quarrels. Or perhaps it was just that the ancient walls and wooden floors contracted and settled as the cold crept in after the warmth of the day. On this dark November night, only one window in a downstairs corner room showed a glimmer of light, but there was no-one in the garden to notice it.

The kitchen clock ticked away. Ten to ten. His usual night time drink was ready; plenty of whisky, lemon juice and honey – good and hot. It must be right, particularly with the mood he was in. One last stir, best to be sure. This done, the tray was picked up and footsteps echoed down the corridor and across the cavernous hall to the study. The door was pushed open.

The old man glanced up from his desk and said, "Thank you. Put it down over there."

A moment later the door was softly closed. He was alone again.

He picked up the mug, decided it was too hot and put it down, then went back to staring at his computer screen. After a few minutes he picked up the mug again and sipped at the drink, muttered occasionally between mouthfuls, swore once, and then saved what he'd been working on. The mug drained, he turned the computer off.

As he mounted the wide staircase, he stumbled a little, but the house was quiet, no-one noticed. When he got to his room, he stumbled again, grabbing at the back of a chair. There must have been more whisky in it than usual. He managed to get undressed and put on his pyjamas before he fell across the bed, out cold.

In the early hours of the morning, the door opened soundlessly. The curtains had not been drawn and the moon, half shrouded in cloud, lit the room. As the clouds drew back, the light of the three-quarter moon, just for a moment, shone straight on to the syringe held in a trembling hand.

Chapter 1

The atmosphere was not good. The high-ceilinged, shabby old dining room in White Monk Abbey, with its dark beams and threadbare tapestries, had seen many a family confrontation over the centuries, but this was building up to be one of the worst. As she ladled soup into bowls and handed them round, Rhiannon Giordano, known to the family as Nonna, watched the faces of those round the table. Caradoc Mansell sat in his carver chair at the head of the table, drumming his fingers on the ancient wood, his face thunderous. He'll burst a blood vessel if he's not careful, she thought. To his right, Megan, glancing nervously at her father, fiddled with the scarf around her neck and the bracelets on her arm.

"Stop your damn fidgeting, girl," Caradoc snapped. Her hand froze, and she turned to gaze straight ahead.

On his other side sat his daughter-in-law, Delma, dressed in jodhpurs and riding jacket, her dark hair shining, her make-up immaculate. Something about her was a little too sleek, a little over-done for a family lunch. She gave the old man an occasional nervous glance but said nothing. Beside her was an empty chair; her husband, Rodric, Caradoc's son, was late. He'd suffer for that, particularly after the dreadful row he'd had with his father earlier that day.

Next to Megan sat Delma's brother, Mike Cotter, an unwanted visitor to the Abbey. His heavy features showed little awareness of the undercurrents, a sneer hovered round his mouth as he leant back, one hand resting on the table, the other draped over the back of his chair. Nonna noticed the dislike and contempt in Caradoc's eyes whenever he looked at Mike. That was another source of conflict.

The door opened and Rodric rushed across the room, apologising as he did so. He was followed by David Harris, the estate manager, who seemed quite calm in the face of the atmosphere.

"Sorry, sorry," Rodric said. "We got caught by Ted Marsden, he wanted to talk about the top fields again–"

"I'll not have you consorting with the enemy, damn it," Caradoc growled.

"We weren't, Father." Rodric's response was stiff as he sat down. "He just wanted to know if you'd made a decision yet, perfectly reasonable."

David sat down without speaking and gave Megan a quick reassuring glance as he did so.

"Reasonable!" the old man shouted. "I will not sell any of my land to that jumped up Englishman, do you understand? I thought I'd made that abundantly clear."

"You did, and I understand how you feel about it, but the money would mean we could do so many repairs. For a start we could sort out the foundations. If we don't do that soon, parts of the house are going to collapse. Added to the production company's fees it would make all the difference."

"What unmitigated nonsense. I won't hear of it. I've given in over those dreadful filming people, but that's final. The only other thing I'm willing to consider is selling the horses."

Delma looked up, a sharp protest ready on her lips, but Nonna intervened, "Here's your soup, Rodi. Now, how about we eat and stop quarrelling?"

She held Caradoc's gaze for a second and he subsided. For a while, all that could be heard was the clink of spoons on bowls, and the sipping of soup.

Megan helped Nonna remove the bowls and bring in the roast lamb, roast potatoes and vegetables. Caradoc rose to carve the joint and Nonna noticed that the portions put on the plates were in strict relation to his feelings about those around the table, one slice each for Delma and Mike, two each for his children and David, three for Nonna and himself. She smiled grimly – *he's certainly in one of his worst moods today, but that's hardly surprising*. Vegetables, gravy and mint sauce were passed round, then the heavy silence continued as people began to eat.

Only halfway through the food on her plate, Megan laid her knife and fork down, shot her father a nervous look, and took a deep breath. "Da–" Maybe she thought to soften him by using the diminutive. "You know the new book I'm writing, the Welsh folk tales?"

He grunted but showed little interest.

"Well, I've found someone to illustrate it. I met up with her – in fact, she came to stay the weekend you were away in London."

Caradoc still didn't comment. He hardly seemed to be listening.

"I thought her an impressive woman," Nonna said, "and we enjoyed looking at those sketches she brought with her. Did you see them, Rodi?"

"Yes, I thought they'd suit Megan's book very well."

"Seems a bit strange to me, going from the police force to being an artist," Delma said. "Wasn't there something iffy about her retirement? I thought she was involved in some corruption scandal."

"Bent coppers, eh?" said Mike with a sneer. "I didn't realise that was what she was."

"She isn't!" Megan exclaimed. "She was completely exonerated."

Her raised voice seemed to break through her father's preoccupation.

"So, you're inviting visitors to my home behind my back now, are you?"

Nonna intervened. "Is there any reason why your family can't invite their friends to visit, Caradoc?"

He glared at her under his brows, then shrugged and went back to his food.

Megan rushed on, "Her name's Fabia Havard, she's an artist who lives in Pontygwyn; she's good, just the right style for what I want. I really need to go through it all with her in more detail. I was thinking I might invite her to visit again, maybe next weekend or the weekend after, so that we could discuss things in detail." She gazed at him anxiously and Nonna could tell how tense she was. His response wasn't long in coming.

"What? More bloody visitors invading our peace?" He shot a venomous look at Mike. "What do you think this is? A damned hotel?"

"Of course not, but it's important that we work together. You've actually met her and I thought you might—"

"Did you say Havard?"

"Yes."

His attitude had changed. "I used to know a Havard at Christ's in Brecon, ended up as a professor of law at Swansea University, brilliant brain but totally impractical, good chap though. So, is this artist related to him?"

"She's his daughter," Megan said, palpable relief in her voice. "She used to be in the police, but she retired early and now she makes a living as an artist. She's just your sort of person, Da."

"And what does that mean?" Caradoc glared at her, but he no longer seemed to be angry.

"Well, she's very attractive, lots of curly red hair, and a good figure, and she's, well–"

"I've come across her in the past," David said quietly, with a smile for Megan. "She was pretty high-powered when she was in the police, a superintendent, I think. An interesting woman."

Caradoc glared at him and Nonna came to the rescue. "I think what Megan and David are trying to say is that she's a good-looking woman with a brain. Like Megan said, your sort."

He shot her a look that was hard to interpret.

There was a pause, then Delma intervened. "But wouldn't that mean more work for Nonna, having weekend visitors?" She gave Megan a malicious glance. "You're always saying how we should help her out more."

"And so you should. Nonna isn't a servant, she's a member of the family," Caradoc snapped, but her intervention had tipped the scales in Megan's favour. "Go on, invite the woman if you must. If she's Tudor Havard's daughter I'd be interested to meet her."

As Megan relaxed and began to eat the rest of the cooling food on her plate, Nonna almost felt grateful to Delma for unwittingly pushing the old man into agreeing. That'll teach her to put her oar in, she thought. But the more relaxed atmosphere didn't last long. Having eaten his way through his plateful and helped himself to more vegetables to compensate for his meagre meat ration, Mike took it into his head to stir things up.

"I've been looking round the Abbey," he said, smiling as if he was convinced his opinion would be of value. "It's a fantastic old house, lovely place but, like Rodi says, it's in great need of some TLC. Had you thought of selling off some of the artwork and antiques? I know about these things, and I know of a great chap who could give you a fantastic deal, particularly on some of the paintings."

What evil genius had persuaded him to propose such a thing, Nonna could not fathom. Had he learnt nothing in the time he'd been staying with them? She sat at the end of the table, fingering the crucifix that hung round her neck and waiting for the explosion, but Caradoc's reaction was very quiet, and somehow that was worse.

"You do?" he asked, his tone icy. "And who is this great chap?"

"Friend of mine, he's an auctioneer and he's got a good business going in London. He'd be more than willing to come and have a look, give you some estimated prices."

Delma tried to intervene, "Mike, I don't think–" and Rodric, having shot an anxious look at his father, also opened his mouth to speak, but they were both ignored.

With great deliberation Caradoc put his knife and fork down on his plate, made sure they were exactly side by side, then, his head bent, he placed both hands on the edge of the table. The silence in the room was full of tension. It was probably only a few seconds, but it seemed like longer to Nonna before Caradoc looked straight at Mike.

"You are a foreigner, and a visitor in my home. For that reason, I will attempt to forgive your extreme ignorance of the ways of our family." Caradoc's voice was low and trembled very slightly. "We do not sell our birthright for the sake of mere expediency, we do not allow any *o'r tu allan* to trample all over our family history."

He pushed himself up from the chair and swept an arm around as his voice rose, his Welsh accent becoming more pronounced with the emotion of his words. "You will find out, all of you, that I'll not be bullied. I'll preserve this for my children," he paused then said, with deliberation, "and my grandchildren, my granddaughter, in spite of you. Soon enough you'll find out I'm still in charge, by God you will."

Thrusting his chair back so hard that it rocked back and forth on its legs, he strode from the room and slammed the door behind him.

Silence reigned in the room. Delma glared at her brother but said nothing. Megan and David exchanged glances, anxious from her, reassuring from him. At last

8

Mike gave a cocky grin and said, "Well, that's me told. What does 'or ti allen' mean?"

Rodric gave his brother-in-law a contemptuous look. "It means outsider. For Christ's sake, what possessed you? As if this morning wasn't bad enough, you've really screwed things up now." In a pale imitation of his father's actions he pushed his chair back and stalked from the room. Delma followed in her husband's wake, Mike shrugged and walked out, and Megan and David left the room together.

So, Nonna thought, not much point in bringing in the apple pie.

* * *

Rodric had intended to go to the estate office to go through some paperwork after the disastrous family lunch, but now he'd changed his mind – he needed to do something physical. He went through to the kitchen where he knew his old lurcher, Mabel, would be dozing in front of the Aga, shrugged on his battered wax jacket and took her lead from the hook by the door. Immediately her ears pricked up. She lumbered to her feet and trotted towards him, her long tail waving slowly back and forth.

"Come on girl, let's go and check if the top stream needs clearing."

But he wasn't going to be able to escape quite that easily. His wife came in as he got to the back door.

"Rodi, where are you going?"

"Out," he said curtly.

"I can see that, but I have to speak to you. What's this about selling the horses?"

"Father says that would be better than an invasion from your film people. He's never been that keen on that side of the business."

"But he can't!" It was a wail of protest. "I've put so much into those stables. If I didn't have them to look after, what the hell would I do in this god-forsaken place?"

9

"Thanks, Delma." He looked at her anguished face and relented a little. "Okay, I'll see what I can do."

"Was that what the row with your father was about this morning?"

"Yea, and money generally."

She grasped his wrist with hard fingers. "You have told him you've said they can use the Abbey, that you've signed the contract?"

He looked at her wearily. "Yes, I have. And do you know what he said? That I've betrayed him, that I'm selling us down the river and he's damned if he'll co-operate in any way at all when they invade. His words."

"But he has to. The amount of money they're paying, they'll expect to have proper access. And it'll mean we don't have to give up the stables. Rodi, I know them, that's why I recommended them – he could ruin the whole thing if he starts being high handed."

"Do you think I don't realise that?" Rodric glared at her. "And he also told me I'll regret this when I find out about the will. He's been making these dark hints about changing his will for weeks, but I thought it was just his usual wind up, now I'm not so sure."

"But the land is entailed. He can't leave it to anyone else but you and Megan, can he?"

"That's as may be, but he can leave the contents of the house to whomever he chooses. I wouldn't put it past him to find some distant cousin or other and let them have all the valuables just to spite us."

"What?" It was almost a screech. "The silver, the porcelain, the – the stamps and paintings, your mother's jewellery?"

"Exactly."

"Oh my God! You must speak to him, Rodi. He won't sell anything and use it to repair this ruin of a house and he won't let me wear any of the jewellery, which is ridiculous, that sort of stuff needs to be shown off, and then there are my horses – stupid old bastard."

"No, he wouldn't get rid of the jewellery, and don't talk about him like that."

"Can't you persuade him to take up Mike's offer?" she pleaded. "He's not kidding, you know, he's good on antiques and he's got some really solid contacts. He asked me to try to persuade–"

"Delma, I think there's a snowball's chance in hell of Father taking him up on his offer," Rodric told her.

"But Rodi," she sounded frightened now. "If he doesn't, I don't know what Mike will do."

"What do you mean?"

Her glance slid away. "Ah, nothing, it's just – well, he's very keen to help. And he says it's not fair for me, us, to be stuck here in this ancient ruin with so little money, having to dance to the old man's tune."

"This ancient ruin, as you call it, is our home, Delma," he said. The weariness was gone, he was angry now. "I thought you understood we'd be living here for the foreseeable future."

"Yea, yea, but, with all this land, and the way the locals kowtow to your father and seem to bloody worship 'the family'," she wiggled her fingers to indicate inverted commas, "I thought there'd be more–"

"–in it for you?"

Before Delma had the chance to respond to this, Nonna came into the kitchen with a tray of dishes from the dining room. She gave them a sharp look but said nothing, just started to load the dishwasher. Delma gave her a glance of acute dislike, then stormed from the room.

"What's up with her?" Nonna asked as she closed the dishwasher door.

"Nothing," he looked down at the lurcher who'd stayed close, patiently waiting for the humans to stop arguing. "I'm going to take Mabel out for a walk, she needs the exercise."

11

"Good idea. And when you get back you can tell me what that argument was about this morning, and why your father's talking about grandchildren."

He glanced at her but said nothing, just clipped on Mabel's lead and left the room.

* * *

Caradoc was very angry indeed. Admittedly it wasn't an unusual state of mind for the old man, he seemed to spend a large part of his time in a simmering rage, but this was different. For the second time in his eighty years, he felt as if he'd lost control.

The first time he'd felt as bad as this had been way back in Mauritius, in 1965, standing to attention in front of his CO, sweat pouring down his body; yet inside he'd felt cold to the bone.

"You'll cut off all contact immediately, understand?"

"But, sir, she's my—"

"I don't think I gave you permission to speak, Captain. Good god, man, it's not as if you were having a tumble in the hay with a village girl. Do you realise her father's one of the most important politicians on the island? This could rock the colonial – Christ Almighty, man, what the hell did you think you were doing?" The man's voice was full of anger and contempt. "No, don't answer that. There's a Dakota leaving at 18.00 hours, get your arse in gear, you're going back on it, Nairobi first then London."

"But what will I do? Sir, I have to tell you—"

He was cut off yet again. "You'll be escorted back to your quarters to pack your kit and at no time will you be left alone until you leave, understand? I'm pushing my luck letting you go without a disciplinary, but you've been a good officer until now so I'm willing to be lenient."

Caradoc had no choice. He'd gritted his teeth and remained silent.

Back in his rooms he was in the middle of throwing things into a holdall when his batman, Dewi Jenkyns, came quietly into the room.

"I just heard, sir."

Caradoc didn't respond, just asked, "Is he still out there?" referring to the military policeman he knew would be standing outside his door.

"Yes, sir. Here, let me do that." Dewi took over while Caradoc fumbled for a cigarette and lit it, stood with his back to the room, gazing out of the window at the parched ground and the scarlet flame trees. After a few minutes of tense silence, with just the sound of Dewi pacing about the room as he packed, Caradoc turned.

"She doesn't know, Dewi."

"I realise that, sir."

"Can you get a message to her?"

"That I can, sir."

"You're a good man, a good friend."

"Thank you, sir."

"I must write to her," Caradoc said. He sat down at a small table in the corner of the room and, for a while, the scratch of his pen and the rhythmic whoosh of the ceiling fan were the only sounds that punctuated the silence. He folded the letter and put it in an envelope, pulled his signet ring from his finger and put that in too, then he handed the envelope to Dewi.

"Tell her I'll write again directly I get to the UK. I have to know when the baby arrives. Oh God, Dewi, what am I going to do?"

His batman had had no answer.

But all these years later, the situation was different because he knew, if he'd been younger, he could have dealt with Rodric's plans and the other problems. Now age was against him, and Dewi was long gone, killed in a motor accident years ago. And it wasn't just his age, it was this feeling that all those around him were against him – family, so called friends, neighbours. This was a war he couldn't hope to win, the grim reaper would see to that, but he could certainly win a battle or two. Oh yes. Only once before had he gone down without a fight, and he wasn't about to do it again. What was the family motto? *Ymladd yn ôl!* Fight back! The English translation didn't roll round the tongue in that satisfying way the Welsh words did, but still, the meaning was clear, and it was exactly what he was going to do before it was too late.

Deep down he realised Rodi was right, they'd got to find money from somewhere, that's why he'd given in about having those bloody film people invade the place. Getting that money, and the amount had staggered him, would mean they wouldn't have to sell any land, or any of his precious possessions. He had much better plans for them.

He sat at the leather-topped desk in his shabby study, his arms spread as he leant forward. If only Bella hadn't moved up north, they could have had a game of backgammon and talked it all through. But suddenly his heart lifted as he thought back to that meeting in London. No, not everyone was his enemy. He lifted his fists, thumped them down on the shabby leather surface and smiled grimly. Not everyone.

Chapter 2

"Is Father down yet?" Wrapped in a shabby old dressing gown, Megan wandered into the kitchen at half past nine. She stroked Mabel's soft head and looked round at Nonna.

"He's a bit late this morning," Nonna said. "I'm just doing a tray to take up now." She placed a mug of black coffee on the tray with a plate of toast, some butter and marmalade, and tucked a folded copy of the Western Mail on the side.

"Do you want me to take that up?" Megan asked.

"Don't worry, cariad, I'll do it. You get some breakfast. Rodi's been and gone, up to the north field he said; Delma's in the stables, and there's no sign of her brother yet."

"Okay." Megan took two slices of bread, put them in the toaster, and stood daydreaming as she waited.

Nonna made her way to the hall and up the staircase, then turned to take the right-hand branch to the gallery. She glanced across to the left to check if there was any sign of Delma's brother – there wasn't. By the time she got to the end of the gallery, her arms were aching from the weight of the tray. She placed it on a small table by the door of Caradoc's rooms and knocked. There was no

15

answer; she knocked again. Still no reaction, she turned the handle and went in.

The curtains were open. Windows looked out on the grounds to her right and either side of the bed opposite the door. Caradoc was sprawled on the bed.

Nonna rushed forward and shook him by the shoulder, but he didn't wake. She reached over to feel his heart, there was a slow, hesitant beat. She picked up his flaccid wrist and felt for a pulse, yes, it was there. She shook him again, but still he didn't wake. She rushed to the gallery bannister and shouted down, "Megan! Megan, come quick!"

A moment later, she heard running footsteps and Megan was looking up at her from the hall, fear in her face. A second after that, Delma appeared behind her.

"What's the row?" Delma asked irritably.

Nonna ignored her. "It's your Da, Megan. He's collapsed, I can't wake him. Call an ambulance!"

Megan stood frozen, unable to take in what Nonna was saying.

"Megan, call an ambulance," she repeated urgently.

Delma just stood there goggling and her brother appeared from his bedroom.

At last Megan reacted, plunged her hand into her dressing gown pocket for her mobile and punched in 999 while Nonna rushed back to Caradoc.

When the operator asked what service she needed, Megan found herself saying, "Police," and couldn't think how to change it to ambulance. Her voice shaking, she told them her father had collapsed and they couldn't revive him. The operator asked her if they needed an ambulance and she said yes, they did, maybe that was better, but the voice on the other end of the line told her it was probably best to inform the police as well, just in case. In a panic she agreed and blurted out what had happened yet again. Finally, she ended the call and rushed up the stairs to help Nonna, who was bending over Caradoc, trying to lift him.

"Get me a glass of water," she said to Megan, who rushed to the bathroom and filled her father's tooth mug, brought it back to Nonna who tried to persuade Caradoc to drink, but he just groaned and slumped back.

Once again Megan rummaged in her pocket for her mobile and phoned her brother. "Thank God," she said when he picked up. "Rodi, where are you?"

"Up at the north field. Why? What's up?"

"It's Father, he's collapsed, I think it's a stroke or something."

"Christ! Have you called an ambulance?"

"Yes, and–"

But he cut her short. "I'll be back as soon as I can."

* * *

"I've actually been to this place once before, but that was in the summer, not in this lousy weather," Sergeant Dilys Bevan said to her companion, PC Dave Parry, as they drove towards White Monk Abbey. "We were asked to investigate some missing silver, I think it was." She frowned. "But they decided it hadn't been stolen after all, it had been sent for restoration, seemed a bit odd to me."

A moment later she said, "You know it's rather strange."

"What is?"

"It was only yesterday I was talking to Chief Inspector Lambert about the Mansells; well, one of their connections, at least."

"Who was that?"

"This bloke who's come down from London, Mike Cotter, his sister is married to the son."

"And what's he done, this Cotter bloke?"

She didn't answer immediately as she negotiated the narrow road, frowning in concentration. Up ahead, just visible through the rain, was a battered wooden sign pointing to a lane to the left. She crawled forward – yes, it said Castellgwyn, two miles. Dilys gave a sigh of relief and

17

made the turn. Almost immediately the road dipped steeply down between high banks. There was a threatening feel to it, particularly where the trees stretched long branches across to each other, twig fingers touching in the middle. It was only three in the afternoon, but in this dark green tunnel an early dusk had fallen.

"Bloody hell, this is like something out of Tolkien," she muttered.

"What's that?"

"You know, Lord of the Rings, haven't you read it?"

"Seen the films, they were okay. But I leave the reading to the wife."

"The wife? Hasn't she got a name?"

He grinned.

"You're such a throwback, Dave!" Dilys told him. "Men read too, you know?"

"Yea, but not me. Rather watch a good game of rugby with a pint in my hand."

Dilys laughed, then she picked up on their conversation. "The counter-terrorist chaps in the Met are interested in Cotter, and so's the border force. We've received some information about a company he's involved in, so-called antique dealing, and he's also been importing wine from Eastern Europe. Those businesses appear to be tidy, but they think he might be using them as a front to smuggle artefacts back and forth. He's also wanted for his involvement in a fascist group they think is responsible for some pretty unpleasant activities, beatings and arson for a start, and Islamophobic attacks. They know he's visiting his sister in Wales and we think he might be lying low as it's also rumoured he's fallen out with some of his London pals. Anyway, they've asked us to keep an eye on him, see if he contacts any fascist groups round here."

"On our patch, Sarge?" Dave was scornful. "Can't imagine anything that heavy's going on round here. What do they expect, The Pontygwyn National Front? The Newport Nazi Party?"

"Come off it, Davey. You should know there are some nasty outfits in this area, quite apart from your old-fashioned 'free Wales from the English yoke' type stuff." A moment later she said, "Ah, I think this is it."

To their right was an entrance made imposing by two tall gate posts topped by fierce looking dragons carved in stone, their tails curling down round the pillars they crouched on, their wings half spread and menacing. A couple of claws were missing, and a wing tip or two, but this made them no less threatening.

There were no longer any gates to bar the way, so Dilys drove carefully through and up the long driveway, overgrown with grass sprouting down the middle and more trees looming either side. At the top was a wide courtyard bounded on three sides by buildings from various different eras. To the right was a tower next to a long ruin with tall empty windows, straight ahead was what looked like a long gallery from which a small amount of light shone through leaded panes, and at a right angle to this a three storey structure with steps up to an enormous oak door in the centre. Either side of the door were sash windows. Light streamed out onto the cobbles from one of these. White Monk Abbey seemed to be the most extraordinary building – untidy, gloomy, but impressive.

Parked in the courtyard were two cars: a turquoise Porsche, which looked completely out of place, and an ancient Volvo, which didn't. Dilys parked to one side of them and, as they got out of the car, Dave looked up at the building and said, "Not my idea of a cosy home."

"No," said Dilys, "give me a two up, two down in Newport or Cardiff any day. Okay, so let's see what's been going on."

They mounted the steps to the oak door and rang the bell.

* * *

Megan reacted to the bell first and rushed to the front door, hoping it was the ambulance. It wasn't, although she was relieved to recognise one of the police officers.

"Oh, it's you," she said.

"Yes, Miss Mansell, Sergeant Dilys Bevan." She indicated her companion, "and this is Police Constable Dave Parry. We attended when you had... a theft. Now, can you tell me what the problem is?"

"Yes, oh yes, it's my father, he's collapsed, but I'm not sure I should have phoned you, it's rather an ambulance we need, you see–"

At that moment, a battered old Land Rover lumbered into the courtyard and came to a juddering halt. A man jumped out and strode towards them.

"This is my brother, Rodric," Megan said nervously.

He gave the police officers a curt nod. "I've no idea why you're here. My sister should have called an ambulance, not the police." He turned to Megan, "Where is he?"

"In his bedroom, Nonna's with him, and I did call an ambulance," she said in a protesting wail. "See, here it is now."

"And have you phoned Doctor Nash? He saw Da a matter of days ago, said he was fit as a fiddle."

"No, no I–"

"For Chrissake, Megan!" he snapped, hardly taking any notice of the vehicle that squeezed itself into the remaining space between his Land Rover and the police car. Turning his back, he strode across the hall and up the stairs.

Two paramedics jumped down from the ambulance and rushed forward. Megan said, "Up there, where my brother's going," and pointed towards the stairs. With a curious glance at Dilys and Dave Parry, they followed in Rodric's footsteps and Megan turned to the sergeant.

"I'm sorry, it's all so dreadful," she said, and burst into tears.

Dilys Bevan took her arm and led her to an armchair which stood by the enormous stone fireplace in the hall. "Come and sit down. Can you tell my constable where the kitchen is, he could get you a glass of water, make a cup of tea?"

* * *

The Mynach Arms in Castellgwyn was full that lunchtime and the news was spreading from person to person like an eager virus, as each new arrival was brought up to date by those already there. Little groups had formed to discuss the tragedy in hushed tones, as they felt was fitting in the circumstances.

"They do say he's not got long."

"I heard it was a stroke, probably in one of his rages."

A woman joined in. "That's not very kind, he's had troubles of late, what with that daughter-in-law of his and her brother – nasty piece of work he is."

There was a murmur of agreement.

"Says he's interested in antiques," said someone else. "Probably got his eye on all those treasures in the Abbey. But then, I don't know why the family don't sell a few and get the place fixed up."

"It certainly needs it; falling apart, it is."

"I heard there's some TV company interested in using it for one of those dramas, you know, like a Welsh Downton!" a young woman said, eyes bright. "That'd bring in a few pounds, wouldn't it?"

"I doubt the old man would want a pile of luvvies wandering about the place."

"Maybe that's what pushed him over the edge. The very thought. Disgraceful I'd call it," one elderly man said.

"But still, they pay loads those companies."

"And we could be extras, couldn't we?" said a youngster with ambitions to be on television.

Garan Price, the publican, did not join in the speculation. Occasionally he'd pull a pint, mix a gin and tonic, or pour a glass of wine, but his mind wasn't on the job. A worried frown on his face, he wiped down the bar and stacked glasses, his movements automatic as he went over and over the news. What if the old man died? Caradoc Mansell owned the pub and the land all round it, and he'd always been good to Garan, said he'd make sure he was okay. But who would inherit? It was well known Rodric didn't get on with his father, partly because of that wife of his, partly because Rodric wanted to bring modern methods to the running of the estate. And what about Megan? She'd always been a bit fey, floating about in all those scarves and draperies and writing fairy stories. What sort of a job was that for a grown woman?

He turned as his wife, Sheryl, came up behind him. "You'll wear that glass away if you go on polishing it much longer," she said, giving him a sharp sideways glance. "They still going on about Caradoc?"

"Yup. Wish they'd lay off the poor old sod."

"Poor old sod!" she said, with a touch of irritation. "He's not done you that many favours, has he?"

"He set me up here."

"So he should in the circumstances."

"And he's been a good friend to Mam, in spite of everything."

"I'll give you that," she conceded, "but you've worked damn hard, pulled this pub up from nothing to a bloody good business, and I've not heard him thank you for it, and you his—"

"Don't start on that," he snapped, his tone unusually sharp.

"But we've got to think about it, Garan. It's our future at stake."

"I know, I know, but there's nothing we can do until we know if the old man's going to live or die. A stroke at his age, it's not good, is it?"

"They sure it was a stroke?"

"Think so, although why the police should be involved if that's all it was, I don't know – that's another thing that's worrying me."

"Police!" Her voice was sharp enough to turn a few heads. She lowered it quickly. "How do you know?"

"I saw that sergeant go by, the one that came when they had that trouble with the silver. She was on her way up to the Abbey; nowhere else she could have been going up the Cwmbach Road – it doesn't lead anywhere but to the Abbey – except perhaps Ted Marsden's place by the back road."

She gave him a hard look under her dark brows. "They could have been going there. Anyway, there's no point in speculating, so let's just concentrate on selling a few more drinks to this lot, take advantage of the crowd." She turned to greet a customer, put on her practised smile, and said, "The same again?" as she took the glass from him. She was halfway through pulling the pint when a sudden hush descended on the room.

The man who'd just come in was stocky and powerfully built, with a boxer's nose. He looked about him as he crossed towards the bar, but before he got there, someone shouted across the room.

"That car of yours, Mr Cotter, you got it sorted yet?" The speaker was a mechanic from the local garage.

"Yes. I took it to a specialist in Newport," he said, his London accent at odds with the softer Welsh ones of the locals.

"And was I right, was it the hydraulics?"

"As it happened, it was." He didn't sound particularly pleased at being questioned.

"Ah, thought so. So, have they fixed it for you?"

Mike looked annoyed. "They have."

"You should have left it with me," the mechanic said, with a grin. "It would have cost you much less than some fancy garage in Newport, that's a fact, that is."

"Maybe it would, maybe it wouldn't." He'd arrived at the bar and turned his back on his questioner.

"And how's the gorgeous Sheryl today?" His eyes flicked down to her cleavage, lingered there, then came back to her face.

"Good morning, Mr Cotter. What can I get you?" she asked, her tone cool.

"Call me Mike, please. As I've said before there's no need for formality, and I'll have gin and tonic, a double, I certainly need it."

The buzz of talk had started up again, slightly higher pitched, but Sheryl could tell there were many straining to hear their conversation.

"Oh yes?" she said, "and why is that?"

"You heard about the old man?"

"The old man?" Her tone was even cooler. She may have her issues with the Mansell family, but that didn't mean she wanted this incomer to show any disrespect.

"My poor sister's father-in-law, Caradoc, he's had a bit of a seizure. Hardly surprising at his age, but what must they do but drag the local coppers in, God knows why."

"I hope it's not as bad as we thought?" Sheryl said, a question in her voice.

"I don't know, he's still with us, but they don't know for how long." He leant one elbow on the bar, turned and looked at the crowded room, his eyes flicking from person to person. "The family's in a right panic, so I thought I'd do them a favour and get out of their way."

Sheryl hadn't heard Garan come up behind her. "Very supportive of you," he said. She turned and realised he'd heard it all and he was very angry.

"Well, you know me, Garan, always like to help out."

Garan gave Cotter a look of extreme dislike, then turned to his wife. "We need some more tonics, I'll go down for them," he said before switching to Welsh, *"Don't let this shit distract you, there are others to be served."*

She nodded and walked slowly down to the other end of the bar. What a day, and what the hell was going to happen next?

Chapter 3

From her place at a table by the door of the Chapel Gallery in Newport, Fabia Havard looked around and wondered how on earth she'd got to this point in her life. Was she really the artist responsible for all these paintings? It was hard to believe, but yes, she was. She smiled and gave herself a mental pat on the back.

The gallery, which had once been a Baptist chapel, was an elegant building with white painted walls, tall windows and a ceiling supported by the sweeping curves of oak beams. All the pews had been removed, but the wooden floor had been retained, and there were several screens placed at an angle down the length of the room. On these Fabia's work hung, together with several of her larger works on the walls. She was delighted with the result.

As she sat by the entrance, she'd been busy asking all those who came in to sign the visitors' book, taken details for the occasional commission, and the money for any sales. So far there'd been a steady stream of punters and she was quietly pleased with the numbers.

She glanced up as the glass door opened once again and smiled when she saw it was her friend, Cath Temple, vicar of her local church in Pontygwyn. She was even more pleased when she saw that Cath was carrying a paper bag from a nearby delicatessen in one hand and a container with two cardboard cups of coffee in the other. Fabia hadn't realised how hungry she was until this moment.

"You're an absolute life saver, Cath, bless you."

"Well, it's nearly one o'clock and I thought you'd be getting a bit peckish." Cath put everything down on the table, then she thrust her hand into the bag and brought out several packages. "That's feta, pesto and tomato, this one is coronation chicken and – what was the other one? – ah yes, avocado and prawn with lime mayo, I thought we could have a bit of each. And I got you your usual latte, oh, and some Welsh cakes for later."

"Cath! It's no wonder the two of us have expanding waistlines."

"Speak for yourself," Cath said, grinning and smoothing her hands over her generous hips. "Anyway, I believe in being a comfortable size. I hate all those stick thin models, and it's about time you put on a bit more weight, you lost so much after that ghastly business–"

"Cath, let's not go there," Fabia said, her voice tight.

This was a reaction Cath had become used to. "Okay," she said, glancing sideways at her friend.

What she saw was a tall, statuesque woman who could easily carry a little more weight. She was an imposing figure, with a fine complexion and a mass of coppery hair, who used to strike fear into subordinates when she was a superintendent of police. Cath, on the other hand, with her short, rounded figure and curly hair clustered round pink cheeks, was the epitome of a kindly vicar ready to listen to all your troubles. The fact that she had a sharper, more unconventional side was only known to her closest friends.

"Has Matt Lambert been in yet?" Cath asked through a mouthful of feta and pesto sandwich.

"No, he hasn't," Fabia said, and there was disappointment in her voice. "But then, I hadn't really expected him during the day; he's more likely to come in early evening, maybe on his way home from the station."

"Is he very busy at the moment?"

"He's always busy. Since he made Chief Inspector he's been rushed off his feet. Once he – we – solved those murders in Pontygwyn and the case was wrapped up, he was involved in clearing up the aftermath of the Cwmberis fraud–"

"And clearing your name."

"Yes, bless him. Then he went straight onto a drugs case involving some Newport nightclubs, followed by god knows what else. Some weeks I go without seeing him at all," Fabia said.

"You would expect to see him every week, would you?" Cath's tone was a little teasing.

Fabia could feel her cheeks warm. "Well, I'd–"

"You'd like to."

She gave her friend a rueful grin. "You know me too well, but it's not going to happen, is it?"

"Oh, I don't know. It strikes me it's you holding back, not Matt. I think, deep down, you're still a bit angry with him for taking so long to realise the truth about your so-called sick leave, and he's still feeling guilty about not supporting you at the time. That's not a happy combination. One of these days you need to sit down and talk it all through, that's my advice."

"Easier said than done," Fabia said.

"And then, of course, there's the fact you're *so* much older than him."

"Cath! It's only seven years."

"I know, so I really don't know why you make such a fuss about it."

"I don't," she said, indignant. "It's– it's difficult."

Cath relented. "Never mind, Fabia, I'll stop teasing. But you do need to sit down and talk, the two of you, one of these days."

"I'll think about it."

They finished their meal without returning to the subject of Matt Lambert and, when Cath came back from disposing of the wrappers and coffee mugs in the gallery's kitchen, she remembered something else she'd wanted to ask Fabia.

"How was your trip to White Monk Abbey? Are the Mansell family as doolally as you remembered?"

Fabia thought for a moment. "More dysfunctional than doolally, I think. The tensions between them are pretty obvious, but half the time I couldn't work out what was actually causing it. One moment one of them would say something that would reveal some kind of background to the atmosphere, the next they'd clam up and nothing more would be said."

"Tell me about them. You were invited by the daughter, weren't you? Megan is it?"

"Yes, she's written this book of Welsh fairy tales, modern versions; they're rather good, and she wants me to illustrate it. It'll be a lovely job, right up my street, and my agent is interested. I'm planning to use just pen and ink, I'm really looking forward to it."

"A bit like the style you used for that sketch of Matt?"

"Yes, that sort of thing. Anyway, Megan's very sweet, but frightened of her own shadow, and I don't think she gets on with her sister-in-law, Delma, who's a very different kettle of fish. Determined, a bit brassy, but the funny thing is I think she's scared too, but of her own brother. I came across a lot of men like him when I was in the force – arrogant and, I wouldn't mind betting, a thorough misogynist, and that wasn't just the criminals, it was some of the policemen as well, as you know."

"And what about the brother, Rodric? He's the only one I've met, other than Caradoc himself."

"The old man was away at some Welsh Guards reunion in London, so I didn't meet him. And as to Rodric, a nice enough chap, but discontented. I don't think he's that strong a character and I got the impression his marriage isn't happy. I mean, talk about chalk and cheese when it comes to him and Delma – she's always perfectly made-up and very smart, and he's a bit shabby and down at heel, as if he can't be bothered what he looks like. What's more she's absolutely obsessed with their stables, to the exclusion of all else, whereas he has the whole estate to worry about. I gather Caradoc fights every single attempt to modernise, he seems to want to live in the past and won't admit their finances are in a parlous state, which, apparently, they are. A classic case of property rich and cash poor."

"But I've heard the Abbey is chock-a-block full of treasures. Couldn't they sell some stuff off and plough the money back into the estate?"

"That's one of the things Rodric was talking about, but he says his father won't hear of it."

"Difficult, particularly while he's still head of the family."

"You could say that."

"Is that everyone?"

"No, there's Rhiannon Giordano, known as Nonna."

"That's a name to conjure with."

"It's her married name. Elizabeth, their mother, was her sister, and she came to live with them when Rodric and Megan were small as Elizabeth was always rather sickly. When she died Nonna stayed on as a sort of surrogate mother. It's obvious she's devoted to the family and I got the impression Rodric's choice of wife didn't go down very well with her."

"That must make things rather difficult for Delma."

"Yes, I think it does, but she hides herself away in the stables most of the time. She runs them and has an office out there. She has a riding school for children and adults, and she also has a couple of stallions she puts out to stud. Megan told me her father hates horses, something to do with an accident he had as a child. That must make things that bit more difficult for his daughter-in-law, particularly as I believe the stables are one of the few areas that are making money."

Fabia sat looking thoughtful for a moment. "I have to admit I found the whole atmosphere rather disturbing. Staying there I got the feeling I was sitting on a powder keg waiting for it to explode. I was fully expecting to have one of those nightmares while I was there, but I didn't."

"Well, that's good, maybe you're getting over them."

"God, I hope so." She gave Cath a sideways grin. "Ignore me, I'm letting my imagination run away with me."

A moment later there was a flurry of activity with visitors to the gallery; then Cath had to get going, so they didn't have the chance to renew the conversation. But that didn't stop Fabia going over everything that had happened during her visit to White Monk Abbey.

* * *

Anjali Kishtoo sat on the train gazing out of the window as it made its steady way towards Cardiff and Newport. She wasn't really seeing the back gardens of the houses, the parks where people wandered with their dogs or watched their children playing, the warehouses and high streets they passed. She was thinking back a few days to the extraordinary meeting that had changed her whole life.

At his request, she'd met Caradoc on Sunday at the Cavalry and Guards' club in Piccadilly. He'd told her he always stayed there when he came to London. When she stepped down from the bus at Green Park, part of her had wanted to turn and run. Nerves made her stomach churn, but she'd forced herself to mount the steps to the impressive porticoed entrance and ask for him at the reception desk. She'd paced up and down as she waited, looking around at the vast paintings on the walls, and the sweep of thickly carpeted stairs with wrought iron bannisters. It felt like an age, but was only a few minutes later when a tall, elderly man, his mane of grey hair receding a little, made his way towards her. He was wearing dark twill trousers, a checked shirt, a tweed jacket and regimental tie, and through his glasses he studied her with hawk-like care as he crossed the tiled hallway. Over his shoulder was slung a canvas holdall.

"Anjali?" His deep voice hesitated on the name.

"Yes." She was surprised that her voice sounded normal. "I– I'm not quite sure what to call you."

His lips had twisted in a rueful smile. "How about just Caradoc for now?"

"Okay – just Caradoc."

"I've ordered coffee in the lounge, it's this way."

There was no hug, no kiss on the cheek, but, as he'd studied her face, he had briefly clasped her shoulders with large, warm hands.

She followed him, still looking around her. Where in the world would you find another place like this? It was so typically British, and yet she knew there was a similar club back home in Mauritius, in the capital, Port Louis, although that one also had ornate brass fans hanging from the ceiling, and there'd probably be others in New Delhi, Lagos and other Commonwealth capitals.

The room, when they entered it, was virtually empty, just a couple of men at the far end, heads together over a laptop. They didn't even look up as Anjali and Caradoc sat down. She put the briefcase she'd been carrying beside her chair and, as the waiter brought their coffee, they stumbled through an awkward conversation about the weather, their respective journeys, his from Wales, hers from her friend's flat in Streatham. Finally, the waiter asked if there was anything else they needed.

"No thank you, Tony," Caradoc told him, "I'll look after this."

Neither spoke as he poured the coffee, offered her a biscuit, which she refused, asked if she took milk and sugar. At last he sat back. Elbows on the arms of his chair, he steepled his hands under his chin and looked at her over the top of his glasses.

"How long have you got in London?"

"I'm here for a few weeks, going around with samples of my work. Sending photos over the net is all very well, but actually visiting the buyers works much better, making that human contact."

"The net," he said ruefully, "not a means of communication I'm that fond of, but it has its uses."

"It does indeed. Without it, my work would never have been noticed," she said. "I had a really good write-up in one of the Sunday supplements and, so far, the reaction has been very encouraging. Several people are interested and I'm hoping to get quite a few orders. Then I'm planning to take some time off while I'm here, but I'm not sure for how long, so I haven't booked a flight home yet."

"To Mauritius?"

"Yes."

There was an awkward little silence, then they both spoke at once.

"You have a look of–"

"I've brought the–"

Both smiled awkwardly, then Anjali took a small velvet pouch from her pocket and held it out to him. "Maman asked me to bring this with me, to show you; as some sort of proof."

He frowned and took the pouch from her, released the ties at the top and shook out a heavy gold ring embossed with a Welsh dragon and a motto. Eyes widening, she glanced up at her and then down at his hand. "My signet ring," his voice shook a little as he said it. "I– I remember giving it to Dewi that last day, made him promise to take it to Prabha."

"Which he did, and Gran-mère Prabha left it to my mother."

"Lord, lord," he said softly, then handed the ring back to her. "You must keep it."

"Are you sure?"

"Yes." There was a pause, then Caradoc leant forward in his chair. "I'm not good at this kind of thing."

"I shouldn't imagine any of us is. It's the sort of situation you see on those reality programmes on television, but you never expect it to happen to you." She doubted that he ever watched that kind of programme and rushed on. "I have to say, I'm very glad to meet you."

He looked as if he'd clenched his teeth. "It's– er– kind of you to say so."

She waited for him to go on.

"Well." He sat forward in his chair. "You told me in your letter that you have photos of your grandmother and your mother. Have you got them with you?" There was eagerness in his voice.

"Yes." She lifted the briefcase onto her lap, opened it and brought out two photographs. She glanced at him as she placed them on the table. His face gave nothing away as he stretched out and picked up the first, but she noticed his hand was trembling.

He picked up the first one. "This is your mother?"

She nodded. "When she was about twenty-three."

"She's very like her mother when I knew her." He put it down on the table, slipped his hand into his coat pocket and drew out a small envelope. "I'd like to show you this. I've never shown it to anyone, but, well, here it is." He took out a small black and white photograph and handed it to her.

Anjali glanced up at him then down at the photo. She took it from him. "Oh," she said, and swallowed as if there was a lump in her throat. "The two of you look so happy. Where was it taken?"

"At a beach called Flic-en-Flac, do you know it?"

She smiled. "Of course, it was my gran-mère's favourite beach."

"I know," he said.

"And this," she said, indicating the other photo she'd taken from the briefcase, "was taken of my grandmother last year." The elderly, white haired woman dressed in a gold trimmed sari, smiled into the camera. "It was taken a few months before she died."

It was when she said this that a look of deep pain crossed his face, as if he'd finally opened a door on something he was dreading to see. His head bent a moment and he put up a hand, rubbed his spatulate fingers across his eyelids. Again, she waited, said nothing. What could she say in the face of such obvious grief?

After a moment of gazing silently at the photo he said, "She was so beautiful, always beautiful."

"Yes," said Anjali, feeling tears threatening, "in looks and in character, one of the best. So is my Maman."

He picked up the other photo, glanced up at Anjali. "Do you think your mother looks at all like me?"

Gravely she studied his face. "I suppose there is a slight resemblance, she's tall like you. Gran-mère, my grandmother, was quite small."

"I remember."

"And that thing you just did, with your hands under your chin, she often does that when she's thinking hard, considering what she's going to say, and she looks at you over the top of her glasses, like you did just then. But I don't really know you, do I? I'd have to be with you for longer to decide whether there are any other similarities."

Caradoc sat watching her, and she found it hard to interpret his expression. He was bound to want to ask lots of questions, just as she did, but she'd made an effort to tread carefully. Like her, he was probably determined not to mess things up.

But then he began to speak and there was no longer any holding back. "You have such an air of your grandmother, that open, frank gaze, the wide mouth, the long neck. And your accent, yours isn't as strong as hers was, but it's similar. Inevitably your colouring is paler, you haven't the glowing caramel of Prabha's skin, and you're a good deal taller as you say. I remember your grandmother was just five foot, I used to call her my pint-sized jewel."

For Anjali the tears were very close to the surface. She put up a hand to press them back.

"I'm sorry," he said, "I've upset you." He gave her that twisted smile again and, in an awkward gesture, patted her hand.

She took a deep breath and smiled. "Tell me about your family."

"I have photos of my home, White Monk Abbey, and of Rodric and Megan – I suppose they'd be your aunt and uncle. Would you like to see them?"

It was Anjali's turn to sit forward in her chair. "Please."

He took an envelope from his canvas bag and laid some photos on the table before them. "Now these are of the house," he said.

She studied them in silence, then said, "It's very old, but impressive."

"The oldest part, here, goes back 800 years." Caradoc pointed to a photo of what looked like a church tower with narrow windows. "This" – he ran his finger along it – "was the abbey itself. Then, to the left, you have the more recent buildings where we still live." He chose another photo.

"This three-storey building was constructed in the 1700s by my ancestor, Daffyd Mansell, after he married – above himself as they say – a Lady Cornelia Morton. She was from Carmarthen and she brought with her a great deal of money, something that Daffyd sorely needed. It was her money that enabled him to pull down most of the old abbey buildings, which had been partially destroyed in Henry VIII's time, and build the present house. Then further additions, this portico here for instance, were made in early Victorian times by my great grandfather. A shrewd businessman, he bought up surrounding land as well as extending the house. He wanted to make an impression, but I'm afraid death duties rather crushed the family finances at the beginning of the last century, and, well, my son tells me my desire to hang on to the old ways and the history of the place hasn't helped, but what else do you have if not your ancestry?"

"Your family?"

Caradoc glanced at her and cleared his throat. The pain was there in his eyes again. Idiot! She shouldn't have said that.

He reached for the other two photographs. "So," he said decisively, as if to put an end to that part of the conversation, "this is my son, Rodric, and this is my daughter, Megan. I haven't told them about you yet. I shall do so when I get home. I would very much like you to meet them."

"Thank you," she said, touched.

He went on without comment. "Their mother, Elizabeth, died when they were quite young."

"When did you marry her?"

"In 1970, five years after I came back from Mauritius."

"I don't understand. How could you have done so when you were still married to Gran-mère?"

"But we weren't actually married," he said, his voice low and filled with regret.

"Oh. I thought you were."

"No, but as far as we were concerned it made no difference, we made our own private vows." His face softened, and a slight smile appeared. For a moment he said nothing, and Anjali waited. "We went to that beach, Flicq en Flacq. Your Uncle Nalen was there, and a close friend of your grandmother. What was her name?" He pressed a hand to his forehead. "Ah yes, that was it, Madhu."

"Tante Madi? Oh wow, I never knew!"

"You know her?"

"Yes," Anjali said, smiling broadly. "She was my gran-mère's closest friend. She's still around. She lives near my parents."

Caradoc returned her smile. "I would love to meet her again. We owed her a great deal."

"I'll talk to my mother."

"Thank you, thank you," he said, and she noticed, for the first time, there were tears in his eyes.

Chapter 4

Anjali stepped down from the train in Newport and pulled her coat more closely round her slim body against a nasty sharp wind. She hitched her handbag more safely onto her shoulder and, pulling her small case behind her, made her way towards the exit. The journey from London hadn't taken as long as she'd expected and her appointment to meet Caradoc at the solicitor's office wasn't for an hour yet, but she decided to take the taxi there now just so that she knew where it was. She could always find a café or somewhere to while away the time.

She made her way to the taxi rank and bent to the window of the first cab. "Do you know the office of Granger, Meredith & Llewellyn?" she asked. "They're solicitors, their address is 26 Hendre Avenue."

"I know where that's to, love, hop in."

"Thank you." She put her bag on the seat beside her and buckled up.

The taxi driver was chatty. "Your first visit to these parts?"

"Yes, I've come down from London."

"You from there then?"

"I'm just visiting, my home is in Mauritius."

"Aah, lovely place that. Been on holiday there a few years back, very hot it is."

She smiled. "Where did you stay?" she asked.

"Now where was it? A hotel on the east coast, near a town called Mahe something."

"Mahebourg?"

"That's it."

"There are lots of hotels in that area"

"You got family or friends round here then?"

"No, well, not exactly." She looked out the window, not wanting to say any more. Luckily the driver didn't ask any further questions but continued to reminisce about his Mauritian holiday and how much he'd enjoyed it. She let her mind drift as they passed a pedestrian area then turned into a roundabout and Anjali noticed an impressive modern sculpture, an enormous red circle towering up beside a river.

"What river is that?" she asked the driver.

"The Usk – comes all the way down from the Brecon Beacons."

"And the sculpture?"

"That's the Steel Wave, it commemorates the importance of the steel industry in Newport. Do you like it?"

"Yes, it's rather magnificent, isn't it?"

"Been there since the nineties. But the steel industry's been trashed in the last few years, it has. What's the main industry where you come from?"

"Oh, sugar, tourism, and textiles I suppose."

"I remember driving past the sugar cane fields, and my wife visited a factory that made women's clothes, it had a shop. Oh boy, she nearly bankrupted me."

Anjali smiled. If this man was typical of the locals, she thought she'd rather like it in Wales.

A few minutes later they drew up in front of a row of tall town houses, several with brass plaques by the door or lettering on windows indicating the nature of the business inside.

"There we are then, miss," the driver said as he drew to a halt. "This is the one." He leant over the back of his seat, his eyes bright with curiosity. "I do hope they'll have some good news for you, something to your advantage, as they say."

She smiled but just said, "How much do I owe you?"

"That'll be six pound."

She handed over the money with a generous tip and got out of the car. It had begun to rain so she pulled up the hood of her jacket. What to do? Although they'd passed a café a few yards back, she didn't really want a coffee.

Across the road she noticed an old chapel, but above the door was a board that said Chapel Art Gallery. She crossed over, curious, and mounted the steps. In a glass-fronted container, by the entrance, was a poster announcing an exhibition by local artist and illustrator, Fabia Havard. This could be interesting, and a wander round would eat up the time before her appointment. Anjali pushed open the door and went in.

* * *

Fabia looked round as the door of the gallery was pushed open. It had been very slow for the last hour. She'd got tired of sitting at the table by the entrance and had been wandering around the room. Now she was relieved to see someone come in at last. She studied the stranger with an artist's eye, looking at her as a thing of shape and shadow, form and colour rather than as a person. She watched as the woman walked slowly around, from painting to painting, studying each one carefully.

She was tall and slim, but not too much so, with high cheek bones and large dark eyes. Her coffee-coloured skin was clear of any blemish and her dark hair was cut short and close to her head. She could have passed for a top model straight from the pages of Vogue or a member of

41

some aristocratic Indian family. The richly embroidered hooded coat she wore, in striking peacock shades, somehow seemed to fit just right with her jeans and brown leather boots. Fabia returned to her seat by the table and asked her companion, "Cath, do you know who that is?"

Cath, who'd returned to keep her company after making a few calls, followed her gaze and frowned. "Striking isn't she, but no, she's not familiar. Fabulous figure."

"And an incredible face. I'd love to paint her. And she is vaguely familiar. Did she sign the visitor's book on her way in?"

"I think so."

Fabia reached out to the table beside them, turned the open book round, and looked at the last entry.

"Anjali Kishtoo, London and Mauritius. Interesting, and why does it ring a bell?" Fabia frowned in an effort to remember, then grinned. "I know, it was an article in the Observer magazine; a new designer from Mauritius, really original clothes and accessories – they were gorgeous. I'm sure that's the name. I wonder what on earth has brought her to Newport?"

Fabia continued to watch as the woman worked her way around the large room, her footsteps echoing softly on the polished wood floor. Sunlight from the tall windows shining down made her skin glow, and the colours of her jacket look even more vibrant.

"Do you think she'll buy?"

"No idea," said Cath. "I think she might just be browsing. It's raining, she's probably sheltering."

"Thanks a bunch!"

"Well, you did ask."

"Pity," said Fabia, who'd been a little disappointed at how few of her paintings had little red 'sold' stickers on them. Had it been a bad idea to set the exhibition up here? It was tucked away down a side street off the main shopping area and most of the other buildings were offices of one kind or another. But the gallery owner, Paul Hewitt, had been enthusiastic and wasn't taking an enormous commission.

"He fancies you, that's why," Cath had said to Fabia a couple of days ago when told of the easy terms he'd set.

"The feeling definitely isn't mutual. He stands too close, invades your personal space," Fabia had said.

"Who else has been in?" she asked now. She pulled the visitors' book towards her and ran a finger down the column. "There's still no sign of Matt." She couldn't keep the disappointment out of her voice.

Cath gave her a sympathetic glance but didn't comment.

"Ah," said Fabia, "John Meredith, he actually bought one of my watercolours, says he's going to put it in the reception area at his office across the road, bless him. He's a good friend."

Neither of them had noticed the tall, dark woman approach the table.

"Excuse me." The voice was soft, the accent half French, half something else.

Fabia looked up. "Sorry. Yes, can I help you?"

She sounded hesitant. "You are the artist?"

"I am," Fabia said.

"It's that painting over there," she pointed across the room, "Where – what is that house?"

Fabia glanced across at the watercolour. It was a small, atmospheric study of an old house, in greys and greens – half ruin, half three-storey building.

"That's White Monk Abbey," she told the woman, "at Castellgwyn, up the valley. A beautiful old place, there's a lot of history attached to it."

"Do you know the family?"

"Yes, I do, as it happens. I'm going to be doing some work for one of them, the daughter. I'm illustrating a book she's written. Do you know them?"

"I suppose. The father, Caradoc Mansell, I know him."

Fabia was curious. The hesitant tone of voice gave her the feeling she was only being told the bare bones of a bigger story. How on earth could this woman know someone as conservative and hidebound as Caradoc? But the woman didn't elaborate.

Fabia, never one to hold back when she wanted information, tried to probe. "Am I right in thinking you're a designer? I saw your name in the visitors' book and I remember seeing something about you in one of the Sunday supplements a week back. Some of the clothes they'd photographed were very much like that lovely coat you're wearing."

"Oh, did you read it?" Her eyes lit up in a proud smile. "Yes, my name's Anjali Kishtoo. And you are?"

Fabia held her hand out. "Fabia Havard." They shook hands. "And this is my friend Cath Temple. She's helping me keep an eye on the exhibition."

Cath gave her a kind smile. "I have to agree with Fabia, that coat is stunning."

"Thank you. So, all this work is yours?" Anjali asked Fabia.

"It is." Fabia grinned. "My first official exhibition."

"You're very talented."

"Thank you, and so are you, from what I remember of that article. You come from Mauritius, don't you?"

"Yes, but I'm in the UK promoting my designs. I was lucky enough to have a friend who works for the Observer, hence the article. It's all been a bit of a whirlwind, very exciting, but quite scary as well."

"I'm sure, and now you've come to promote your work in Wales?"

"Well, not exactly." She glanced away, biting her lip, and Fabia's curiosity increased. "I've got a meeting in Newport, and I must find a hotel to stay tonight. Can either of you recommend one?"

"I'm sure we can," Cath said. "But I suppose it depends what you have in mind. There's a Holiday Inn."

"And a couple of decent pubs that have rooms," Fabia added.

"That sounds more my style, I'm not dreadfully keen on hotels."

Finally, Fabia's curiosity got the better of her. "Tell me, how do you know Caradoc Mansell?"

Immediately she'd asked the question, she regretted it. The shutters came down and the smile vanished.

"It's a long story." Anjali glanced at her watch. "Oh dear, I must rush. I've enjoyed looking at your paintings, thank you." And with that, she turned and hurried out of the gallery.

Fabia and Cath gazed after her.

"Well, well, how interesting," Cath said. "I wonder what all that was about?"

"So do I," replied Fabia. "I must search out that Observer article and have another look at it. I wonder who her meeting is with, in Newport of all places. She's a tad exotic for this neck of the woods, wouldn't you say?"

"I certainly would," Cath said.

* * *

Half an hour later Anjali sat opposite John Meredith in his neat office, her eyes full of tears and a hand to her mouth.

"But how could that have happened? When I saw him in London, he was fine. A bit shocked by my news, but fine. No, no, I can't believe it."

"It only happened yesterday. I phoned to speak to him this morning and Rodric told me. I tried to get hold of you, but I got no response on your mobile."

"My fault, I forgot to charge it. I was going to do it when I'd found a hotel."

"You weren't to know. It was very sudden, they're not sure what's wrong, possibly a stroke. He's in hospital, but I'm sorry to say they didn't sound very hopeful. Rodric told me the police are involved, I've no idea why. Of course, this makes the situation very difficult for you, particularly as I don't believe he's told the family anything about you."

She was hardly listening. "I just saw a painting of the Abbey in the exhibition across the road. I went in because I was a bit early for our meeting and I met the artist. She knows the family."

"Fabia Havard?"

"Yes, she seemed rather nice."

"She is. She's an old friend of mine, used to be a police officer." For a moment there was silence as he waited for her to collect her thoughts. "Look, let me go and get us some coffee and then we can talk about what you should do. Caradoc made his wishes very clear to me, and the will is clear as daylight, but I think we're going to have to approach this carefully, in relation to the family, that is. I won't be long."

He got up and left the room and Anjali sat there, her mind in turmoil. What on earth should she do? Just go back to London? No, she couldn't, this had to be faced. She'd have to find somewhere to stay, but the thought of being on her own in some impersonal room with only a television for company made her feel sick. She leant back in her chair and closed her eyes, then opened them again quickly as John came back into the room, a tray in his hands.

"I'd like to visit him," she said. "Is he in hospital here in Newport?"

"Yes, but he's in intensive care so I'm not sure he's allowed visitors at the moment."

"Can you find out?"

"Of course."

"And I must find a hotel. I did ask – Fabia is it? Across the road in the art gallery? I asked her about hotels. She and her friend mentioned one or two." She drew a deep, shuddering breath. "But I do so hate hotels. Oh dear." She covered her face with her hands and muttered from behind them, "I'm sorry, I'm sorry."

"Don't be," he said, then leant forward in his chair. "Look, I know Fabia very well, she's an absolute gem. Why don't I go across the road and ask her if she can put you up for a couple of days? She lives just a few miles away in a market town called Pontygwyn. I've no doubt she'd be happy to have you. She knows the Mansells and, with your permission, I could tell her about your connection with them. I'm sure she'll keep it to herself if I explain that it's not public knowledge yet. And while you're with her I can contact the family, have a quiet word, and we can go from there."

"Do you really think she'd let me stay?"

"I'm sure she would. You stay here, I'll go across and speak to her. Make yourself comfortable." He indicated a soft leather settee below the window. "I'll get Stephen, he's my PA, to bring some more coffee and I'll be as quick as I can."

Anjali sank down into the cushions of the settee, leant back and closed her eyes.

* * *

Cath had gone off to do some shopping when John came into the gallery. He gave Fabia a brief explanation of Caradoc and Anjali's relationship. "It's one hell of a mess," he went on, "what with his will and everything. I'd give you all the details but, Rodric and Megan have no idea she exists yet. I'd best tell them about her first. I hope you don't mind."

"Of course not," Fabia said, but had to admit to herself that she was going to find it hard to keep her curiosity under control.

"The poor girl's pretty shaken up," John went on. "I really don't want to leave her on her own and, much as I'd like it if she did, I don't think it'd be appropriate for her to come and stay with me."

Fabia suppressed a smile. This was a side of John she'd not come across before.

"So, can you take her in?" John asked. "It won't be for long."

Fabia looked at his anxious face and wondered why he was so keen to help this unknown woman. And, she thought, having people to stay was all very well if they are friends, but a complete stranger? That's different. She valued her privacy and independence. On the other hand, she wanted to find out what exactly was going on.

"Well, if it's just for a couple of days…" She gave him a teasing smile. "And maybe she'll confide in me."

He grinned. "That's what you're hoping, isn't it?"

"You know me too well," Fabia said, the smile widening to a grin.

At that moment Paul Hewitt, the owner of the gallery, came into the room so quietly neither of them noticed until he was a few feet away. Fabia did her best to give him a welcoming smile. "Ah," she said, "just the person I need. I've got to rush off, Paul, could you look after things for the last hour?"

"I'm sure I can do that for you, Fabia," he said, making it sound as if he was doing her an enormous favour. "I've got some work to do on my laptop. I suppose I can sit out here just as easily as in my office. Is there a problem?" His eyes darted from John to Fabia, eager for confidences.

"Nothing I can't sort out. I'll see you tomorrow." At the door she turned back and said, "Oh, Paul, if Matt Lambert comes in, could you let me know? I need to speak to him."

"The gorgeous chief inspector," Paul said with a smirk, "will do."

As they crossed the road she muttered to John, "I wish I could like him, but he's so– so–"

"Smarmy?"

"Um, that's it. Never mind, it's probably just me."

"Lucky to have you, I'd say," John said.

48

Chapter 5

Soon after, Fabia set off with Anjali. For the last few minutes there'd been silence in the car. They'd talked a little as they drove through Newport and out onto the motorway. Fabia had told Anjali a little of the history of the area, Anjali had talked a bit about her work. Now they were on the short section of motorway that would take them to Pontygwyn, the market town that had been Fabia's home since she'd left the police force.

As often happened when she got to the outskirts of the town, she began to relax. It didn't matter how many times she drove along this road, in sun, rain or snow, she loved what she saw, although it had recently been a little overshadowed by events. As she slowed to a crawl in order to cross the ancient bridge over the river Gwyn, she looked to her left at the patchwork of fields, dotted with cream and, occasionally, black sheep. The grey and mauve hills of the Brecon Beacons rose up in the distance. To the right, the river meandered down across Gwiddon Park and widened into the pond where, hundreds of years ago, witches had been ducked – innocent if they drowned, condemned if they didn't. And yet those same poor women had given a name to park and pond – Gwiddon, Welsh for witch.

With a twisted smile Fabia wondered if she'd have fallen victim to that primitive misogyny. Probably, particularly if she'd been Superintendent Fabia Havard of the Gwent Force. She could think of quite a few of her male colleagues who would happily have watched her ducked in the murky depths, quite apart from the criminals she went after.

She told Anjali about the history of the park, explained the Welsh names, but she got the impression her companion wasn't really taking any of it in. She smiled occasionally but made no comment.

A moment later, they turned right into Parc Road, past the playing field where two schoolboy rugby teams, mud spattered and probably very cold, were traipsing off to the sports pavilion. Fifty yards on she turned into Morwydden Lane and, almost immediately, stopped outside her neat, double-fronted house.

"Here we are," she said as she switched off the engine.

"This is lovely," Anjali said, "you're lucky to live in such a beautiful place."

"I certainly enjoy it. A big enough town to have most of what I need, but not so big that you have the problems of city life."

As they got out of the car, Fabia noticed there was a large van outside the house next door. She looked at it with interest, and read the name on the side: Watkin's Removals, Bristol, Cardiff & Newport. Maybe, at long last, she would find out who her new neighbours were to be. It was about time. The house had been empty for months. It would be good to have neighbours again.

They walked up the short path to the front door. Fabia unlocked it and swung it wide, "Come on in, I'm sure you could do with a glass of wine."

"Oh yes," Anjali said. "That would be lovely. And Fabia, this is so kind of you, rescuing me."

"No problem at all. We're fellow artists, and I enjoy making new friends. Put your bag down there, we can take it up in a minute, I keep the spare room ready for visitors."

She didn't tell her she did so just in case Matt ever wanted to stay over, which occasionally he did. Maybe that would change one day and the spare room would no longer be needed. Fabia pushed the thought firmly from her mind.

She led Anjali through to the kitchen. "Red or white?" she asked.

"Red, please."

Fabia reached up and got some glasses from the cupboard, took a bottle of New Zealand Shiraz from the wine rack and twisted the top open. As she did so, the phone rang.

"Sorry," she said, "do you mind if I get this? Help yourself."

She grabbed the phone, "Hallo?"

"Fabia, it's me."

"Hi, Matt, I was just thinking about you. How's things?"

"Okay," he replied, but he didn't sound it – probably too much work as usual.

"Have you managed to pop into the exhibition yet?" she asked him, slightly nervous but desperate to hear his reaction.

"I have." His voice was cool. Her heart sank. What was the matter with him?

"When was that? I'm sorry I missed you." She smiled at Anjali who was now standing by the window looking out at the view, glass in hand. Fabia mouthed, "Be back in a minute," and wandered slowly down the corridor towards her dining room-cum-study.

"I went in this afternoon, the bloke there told me you'd just left with John Meredith."

"Yes, I'll tell you about that in a minute. So, what did you think? You did have a good look round, didn't you?"

"A quick look."

"And what did you think?" Fabia asked.

"It's good." His tone didn't match his words. She was beginning to be annoyed.

"You've obviously been busy," he said.

"Well, it is what I do now."

There was a tight little silence, each of them waiting for the other to go on. Fabia felt resentment mounting inside her and began to pace up and down. Why didn't he say something about the drawing? Maybe he'd missed it, or perhaps he hadn't recognised it as himself. Surely not. She'd thought it one of her best. It'd captured the angular body, the gloss of his dark hair, now showing flecks of grey, and the beauty of his long fingers. Come on, Matt, Fabia begged silently as she continued her pacing, tell me what you thought of it.

But he didn't, not directly, just asked, "Why didn't you tell me you'd done that one of me?" and he didn't sound very pleased about it either.

"The sketch?" Fabia hedged.

"Well, there was only the one, wasn't there? Or have you done a whole series without letting on?" he said.

"No, of course not, don't be silly." This conversation was not going well. "I just did the one. It was when you came around after the end of that rape case and you were completely knackered. You don't mind, do you?" Stupid question, because it was obvious that he did. "What did you think of it?"

"Well, it was a bit of a surprise, just coming across it like that. Why didn't you tell me?"

"I don't know," she said, knowing it was an inadequate response, "I just didn't think to."

"Come on, Fabia!" He sounded really exasperated now. "You do a – well – a pretty intimate drawing of me, asleep in your sitting room, get it framed, hang it in a public gallery for all to see, and you don't even bother to tell me? How do you think that makes me feel?"

Fabia could feel her heart beating faster. This was awful, not at all what she'd anticipated. But then, had she thought about how he'd feel? If the truth were known, she hadn't really allowed herself to speculate, just pushed it all to the back of her mind in the rush of preparations for the exhibition. Now she had to admit it had been niggling away just below the surface. She should have told him. He was such a private person. She should have asked his permission to hang the picture. That was obvious, but too late now, and here he was, fuming on the other end of the phone and she felt completely wrong footed.

"I'm sorry. I suppose I thought you'd be pleased, maybe flattered."

"How do you work that out?"

"Thanks, Matt!"

"No, what I mean is, well–" his exasperation was clear and stinging. "It took me completely by surprise. And that grinning idiot who owns the gallery, Paul whatever his name is, standing there looking coy and asking me if I'd found the damn thing. For Christ's sake, why didn't you tell me?"

"Maybe because this was the kind of reaction I thought I'd get," Fabia snapped, unwilling to back down. "Anyway, I've got a visitor, I'll have to go."

She didn't wait for him to respond, just cut off the call.

* * *

Curled up on the sofa in Fabia's comfortable sitting room, Anjali had gradually relaxed and opened up, probably helped by the red wine they had with their meal of omelettes and salad, and then the whisky afterwards.

"Whisky and soda is almost the national drink in Mauritius," she told Fabia, "after the local rum of course."

"That sounds like a place I'd like."

Anjali smiled. "You should visit. The taxi driver who drove me from the station told me he'd been on holiday to Mauritius."

"Lucky man."

There was silence for a moment, a companionable silence, then out of the blue Anjali asked, "How long have you known John Meredith?"

Fabia glanced at her, slightly taken aback. "Oh, for a while. I used to come into contact with him when I was in the police force, and I knew his wife as well, she died of cancer a few years ago."

"Poor man."

"Yes, a bad time for him. He's a good chap."

Anjali didn't ask any more and, in the end, Fabia decided to give in to her curiosity and ask the question that had been niggling away at the back of her mind. "How did your grandmother meet Caradoc?"

Anjali didn't seem to mind the direct approach. "My mother told me my great uncle was in the Mauritian police force and he met Caradoc when British soldiers arrived in 1965 – they were called in by the colonial government when a state of emergency was declared over some strikes or something. We learnt about it at school, but history wasn't my favourite subject and I'm afraid I didn't pay much attention. Anyway, my Uncle Nalen invited Caradoc to come to my grandmother's home, and he and Granmère fell for each other. The trouble was my grandmother's parents were in the middle of arranging a marriage for her, the man was a member of an important family and his father was a minister in the legislative council. Quite apart from that, I don't think there would have been any chance of them agreeing to a marriage outside their community, whoever she'd met."

"That must have been very difficult for her."

"You could say so," Anjali smiled, "but she must have been a feisty one, my grandmother. "Caradoc told me they made their own vows to each other and they thought of themselves as married."

"Good lord," Fabia exclaimed, "that was pretty brave for those days. It must have caused quite a stir."

"At first they managed to keep their relationship a secret, but then she got pregnant with my mum so, of course, it all came out. That was when he was sent home by the army, just marched off without any right to protest apparently, and they never saw each other again. Of course, Uncle Nalen was in disgrace as well, because he'd helped them. He was packed off to Canada by their parents. He joined the Mounties and married a Canadian woman, he and his family still live there. When my mum was born, they relented a little, let them live in the family home, but she says she doesn't think her mum ever got over it. She died when I was about nine. I remember her as a small, quiet woman who always seemed rather sad. Now I know why."

"And what about your parents?"

"Oh, they're quite different. I think Maman wanted to be free to make her own decisions after what her mother had been through. They were always very liberal, by Mauritian Hindu standards. Both of them are doctors. They trained at Kings in London and got married when they came back home. They run a private clinic, but they also do work in some of the poorer villages, mainly with mothers and babies. I think they'd have liked me to do medicine as well, but it was always art and design for me."

They talked long into the night, not just about Anjali's history but about Fabia's too. She told her about the awful events of six months before when her young friend, Amber, had been murdered. She spoke a little of Matt Lambert and their friendship, and how it had been blighted by her abrupt departure from the police force.

"I was investigating a fraud case and hadn't realised one of the high-ups in the Gwent police force was involved. I suppose you could say they set me up; that was what it amounted to. I was given to understand that if I went quietly, they'd not prosecute. You know the sort of thing?"

Anjali looked shocked. "How awful, but yes, I suppose these things happen at home as well."

"It was a good deal more complicated than I'm making it sound, but I won't bore you with the details. Anyway, the only good thing that came out of that dreadful time in April was that Matt managed to clear my name. I got my pension rights reinstated and a nice little bit of compensation."

"Did you not think of going back to the police force?" Anjali asked.

"Oh no. I love what I do now, but I do still have that urge to investigate." She grinned. "Hence my rather unsubtle interrogation of you."

"I don't mind. It's good to talk to someone about it." A look of sadness crossed her face. "And now Caradoc's in hospital and I don't know if I'll ever have the chance to get to know him."

"I'm sure he'll be fine," Fabia said, although she wasn't at all sure of it – Caradoc was eighty years old after all – but she added, "he's a tough old bird, you'll see."

* * *

Matt had not slept well. He felt a complete prat for making such a fuss over the sketch Fabia had done of him. He just couldn't work out what had got under his skin about it, and that conversation last night, it had just escalated. Why did they always seem to end up sniping at each other? He'd have to apologise, not a happy prospect.

He'd woken at an ungodly hour and realised he'd not be able to go back to sleep, so he decided to go into the station early and get on with work. Apart from several more local cases, the investigation into Mike Cotter's activities was beginning to get interesting. Although they hadn't got anything concrete yet, just a collection of rumour and coincidence added to a few definite pieces of evidence, his instincts told him there was something worth investigating. He'd spoken to a friend, Charlie Brewer in the Met, the day before.

"How come he's on your patch?" Charlie asked.

"His sister is married to a local landowner's son."

There was a low whistle from the other end of the line. "Is she indeed?"

"You mean your lot didn't know?"

"Not my department, but the border force chaps have probably got plenty of information. I wish you joy on this one. From what I've heard, he's a bit of a bad lot, but clever with it."

"Could you do some research for me? What they've got, how close they are to making an arrest, if at all?"

"Be delighted, it'll be a damn sight more interesting than the load of crap cluttering up my desk."

"Thanks," Matt had said.

He'd been surprised at how quickly his friend phoned back. "That didn't take long."

"It's called networking, mate," Charlie said.

This hit a nerve. Matt felt he'd never been good at networking – that had been Fabia's forte. God, how he missed her input, but then he could go and pick her brains, couldn't he? He pushed the thought away.

"So, what do you have on him?"

"They're busy giving him plenty of rope at the moment," his friend said, "keeping an eye on him but that's about it. They think he might have got on the wrong side of some of his local associates and could be keeping a low profile. They didn't sound particularly pleased that you're ferreting around, but I persuaded them you knew your stuff. Anyway, Cotter is on record as having links to a pan-European fascist organisation which has its headquarters, or what amounts to that, in Sofia in Bulgaria. They're dedicated to keeping immigrants out, particularly those from Africa, although they're pretty militant about Syrians and Iraqis as well, and they'd like to wipe out the Romanies, whichever country they come from."

"Okay, so anyone who isn't white European," Matt said. "The Hungarians seem to be going in the same direction."

"These people he's in with are a neo-Nazi group who're determined to turn the clock back to the glorious days of the Third Reich." The scorn in Charlie's voice was palpable. "They tell me he's probably in Wales trying to drum up funds from some local right-wing groups. His cover is legit, so far as it goes. They think he's importing artefacts, mainly East European, and wine from around that area, and he's buying antiques here to sell back to his pals in Europe. They suspect he's not too bothered about where they come from or how they're acquired."

"And they're finding it all hard to prove?" Matt asked.

There was a grunt of amusement from the other end. "Yup. They're still busy gathering evidence, but they are in contact with the guys in Sofia and various other East European capitals, which could be useful to you."

"The local family he's connected to, the Mansells," Matt told him, "are known to have some pretty valuable stuff, rare Welsh silver, some interesting paintings, jewellery, and the head of the family owns a very valuable stamp collection, but I gather he's not going to part with anything willingly. There was a theft of some silver at the house a while back, but they ended up spinning us some yarn of its being sent for restoration."

"Was Cotter staying there at the time?"

"I'm not sure. I must find out when he pitched up." Matt sat back in his chair. "Thanks for all that, Charlie, I owe you."

"A couple of rugby tickets will do it."

Matt laughed. "You should be so lucky. Anyway, must get back to the grind."

Chapter 6

Fabia was woken by her phone. Dragging herself out of sleep, she swung her legs out of bed, rubbed at her face and grabbed the handset, squinting at her bedside clock as she did so. Half past seven. Ugh! Who on earth was phoning so early?

"Hallo," she croaked.

"Fabia? It's Matt."

Immediately she was wide awake. "Matt! What sort of hour do you call this, for god's sake?"

"Sorry. I've been in work for over an hour now, feels like mid-morning." There was an awkward pause then he said, in a rush, "Look, I'm phoning to apologise for being such a prick about that sketch."

Fabia grinned, that must have cost him. "Don't worry about it, Matt," she said, "shit happens."

There was a slight pause. "Now," his tone had changed, "I wonder, can I pick your brains about something?"

"I thought there'd be an ulterior motive."

"Fabia!"

She grinned. "I'm not sure my brains will function that well at this ungodly hour, I'm a bit hungover, but pick away."

"When I was at your exhibition, I noticed a painting of White Monk Abbey; you know the family, don't you?"

Fabia frowned, that wasn't what she'd expected, and this was getting a bit spooky. Every which way she turned she came up against the Mansells, and now Matt was asking about them. What the hell was going on?

"Ye-es."

"You don't sound too sure."

"No, no, it's not that."

"I thought you were doing some work for the daughter."

"I am." Fabia ran a hand through her sleep-messed hair and took a deep breath. "It's all rather complicated, Matt, but why are you asking? What do you want to know about them?"

"Look, can I come and grab a coffee? I probably shouldn't be talking to you about it, but stuff that, I really need some background. I've got one of those feelings about this."

"What feelings, Matt? You always say police work is a matter of facts and evidence, hunches don't come into it."

"Maybe I'm learning the error of my ways."

"Matt." Fabia bit her lip, not quite sure what to say. "As I told you last night, I've got a visitor, someone connected to the Mansells."

"What?"

"She came down to meet up with Caradoc, you know, the father, and he's had a stroke, he's in hospital."

"Is he now? Who exactly is this visitor?"

"A – a relative of the Mansells. The situation was a tad awkward and she had nowhere to go, so John Meredith asked if I'd take her in."

"What's John got to do with it?" he asked sharply.

"It's all tied up with Caradoc's will and John's his solicitor."

"Couldn't she have stayed with them?"

"No, Matt, she couldn't. It's nice to have company, and I've got room, as you know. Anyway, come now. I doubt that Anjali will be up for a bit, we were very late going to bed last night." Fabia knew she was letting her curiosity get the better of her, but she couldn't resist. "See you in twenty minutes?"

He arrived fifteen minutes later. "Good lord, Matt," Fabia exclaimed as she led him through to the kitchen, "you must have been ignoring the speed limit all the way from Newport."

"Just kept my fingers crossed that Traffic were asleep on the job."

She grinned. "First it's hunches, then it's breaking the law, you're a changed man."

He returned her grin a little sheepishly. "Must be your bad influence," he said.

She made coffee and a pile of toast, knowing that he wouldn't have had breakfast, put butter and marmalade on the table and pushed a plate and knife towards him.

"Help yourself." She cupped her hands round her mug. "Now, what's all this about?"

"How well do you know the Mansell family?"

"I've known them all my life really, not intimately but they've always been around. Caradoc and my father were at school together and they remained friends, although they lost touch in later life. They both collected stamps and Dad used to say that Caradoc's collection was the best he'd ever come across."

"Who exactly is your visitor?"

Fabia bit her lip, not sure how much she could say. She wanted to help Matt and was deeply curious about his reasons for asking her about the family, but John had said to keep Anjali and Caradoc's relationship under wraps. Could she tell Matt about Anjali when Rodric and Megan, her aunt and uncle, didn't know of her existence yet? John had called it pretty awkward – Fabia felt that was one hell of an understatement.

"It's a bit awkward, Matt. I was asked to keep things to myself. Humour me, tell me what you want to know, and why, and then I'll see how much I can tell you."

He frowned, obviously not happy with this idea. "You seem to be pretty pally with John Meredith all of a sudden."

Fabia ignored this and there was a silent stand-off while he buttered and spread marmalade on his third piece of toast, but in the end he relented.

"Okay. Here's the thing. We're looking into Mike Cotter, Rodric Mansell's brother-in-law. He's a dodgy piece of work, in with some unpleasant European fascist groups, and he's been staying at the Abbey for a while. It's occurred to me that he might be considering relocating some of the family's valuables. We investigated a theft that turned out not to be one."

Matt told her about the silver.

"So, what exactly do you want from me?" Fabia asked, getting up to make more coffee.

"Just background, really. Have you met this Cotter guy? And, if so, what was your impression? Have any of them said anything about 'losing'" – he wiggled his fingers to indicate inverted commas – "any of their treasures, or selling them for that matter? Anything like that."

But before Fabia had the chance to respond, the phone rang. "Sorry, I'd better get this," she said as she searched around for the handset, which wasn't on its rest. She finally found it on the window sill.

"Hallo?"

"Fabia? It's John. I've just had a call from Rodric Mansell, and I thought you ought to know, Caradoc died an hour ago."

"Oh God, how awful. What was it, a stroke? His heart?"

"They're not saying, it's all a bit odd."

"What do you mean?"

"It seems there are some aspects to his collapse that aren't adding up. Apparently, the registrar at the hospital isn't happy, but Rodric was a bit cagey about it. There's going to be a post-mortem, which seems a bit heavy handed, so we'll know more after that."

"It could just mean the cause of death isn't obvious."

"I know, but it could mean a complete nightmare," he said, "given the changed will and Anjali's arrival."

"Changed will?"

"I can't go into details, sorry. I'll be round later to speak to Anjali. Look, I know it's a hell of an imposition, but could you tell her what's happened?"

Fabia felt a sinking feeling at the prospect but pulled herself together. "Yes, of course."

"Sorry to let you in for this," John said, "but she really needs someone to keep an eye out for her, fight her corner."

"What do you mean?"

"I've got to go, Fabia. I'll explain it all when I see you. Will you be in about half eleven?"

"I can make sure we are."

"Look, I'm sorry. It's not what I intended when I asked you to rescue her. Stupid, I should have realised something like this could happen."

Fabia replaced the handset and looked at Matt, a worried frown on her face. "That was John. Caradoc died early this morning, and there's going to be a PM."

"Did he say why?"

"Something about the doctor not being happy."

"Curiouser and curiouser," Matt said.

"The thing is, Matt, my visitor, Anjali, is a newly discovered granddaughter of Caradoc's, and now I've got to tell her that he's dead."

"Oh shit! How on earth did she end up staying with you?"

"It's a long story."

Matt waited, but Fabia didn't elaborate. When she said no more, he glanced at his watch. "Look, I'd better get back, and you need to concentrate on – what did you say her name is?"

"Anjali, Anjali Kishtoo, she's Mauritian."

"One of these days you're going to tell me the whole story, Fabia."

She laughed. "I'm sure I will."

* * *

As Matt drove back to the station, this time keeping to the speed limit, he went over and over what Fabia had – and had not – told him. How come this newly discovered granddaughter had appeared just at this moment? Could she have anything to do with Mike Cotter? He needed to meet her, and not knowing how long she'd be with Fabia, he'd need to make it soon. Maybe he'd drop in after work, whenever that may be – he never knew these days. Why had he decided to rush out to talk to Fabia? He was reluctant to admit to himself part of it had been because he just wanted to see her. He was quite relieved when his handsfree clamoured for attention.

"Dilys?"

"Where are you?"

"On my way back to the station."

"There's a message from a Dr Hari Patel at the Royal Gwent, he wants you to give him a ring. He says he's a bit concerned about Caradoc Mansell's death. He's asked for a PM."

"I know."

"How come?"

"Never mind. What exactly did he say?"

"Just that he wanted to talk to you, says there are aspects that he's concerned about – he didn't go into detail. Do you know him? Is he reliable?"

"Yes, he's a good chap. He's a member of the chamber choir and we often have a drink together after rehearsals, so I know him quite well."

"He said he'll be coming off duty in an hour and could you phone him then. Here's his mobile number."

"Don't worry, I've got it saved. But I'll be passing the hospital, so I'll pop in and see if I can speak to him now."

"Where exactly are you?"

"On my way back from Pontygwyn," Matt said without thinking.

"Been to consult with Superintendent Havard?"

He could hear the grin in her voice.

"Shut up Dilys. I'll see you later."

* * *

Matt managed to find a parking space at the hospital, relieved that they'd changed to free parking a few months ago. He went up to reception and asked for Dr Patel. Given that he'd expected to be told he'd have to wait, he was surprised at how quickly his friend strode towards him. He was a small but dapper man with a stethoscope dangling round his neck. The contrast between Matt's untidy six foot two and the doctor was marked.

"I got your message," Matt said, shaking the doctor by the hand. "I was passing and thought I'd drop in. How can I help?"

"Thank you for reacting so quickly. Come into my office."

Matt followed him down a short corridor and was ushered into a minute office crammed with a desk, filing cabinets, a couple of chairs, several photos of a smiling woman in a sari and children of various ages. Matt felt a stab of envy, wishing his office was crowded with photos of a family. But he dismissed such thoughts firmly and sat down in a chair opposite the desk.

"So, what can I do for you, Hari?"

His friend frowned and pursed his lips. "Look, Matt, I may be over-reacting, but I'm not entirely happy about the pathology results we got after tests done on Caradoc Mansell. There's nothing specific, it's as much a gut feeling as anything, but it's ringing alarm bells for me."

"In what way?"

"The thing is" – he leant forward, his arms crossed on his desk – "when he was brought in, we did all the usual tests, it wasn't a stroke, and his heart seemed strong enough, although the obvious conclusion was a heart attack, particularly in someone his age. But I phoned his GP, Dr Nash in Pontygwyn."

"I know him," said Matt, "he's Fabia Havard's doctor."

"Ah yes, the brave Miss Havard. Anyway, I just wanted to check up if there was anything on record. He says the old boy had an ECG and comprehensive blood tests, urine checked, etc, a couple of weeks ago, something to do with his health insurance, and Dr Nash said he was fit as a fiddle, eighty going on forty was his description. I've had every test in the book done, and I just can't explain exactly why he should have died."

"I gather you've asked for a post-mortem."

"I have." The doctor was frowning and fiddling with a couple of pens on his desk, straightening them this way and that.

Matt wondered what was coming. He didn't have long to wait.

"Recently we had a chap in from up the valleys, he'd had an accident on his farm. From what I can remember, the vet had been called in over a bull that had something or other wrong, don't know what, and they had to sedate the animal. When the vet had filled the syringe so that he could inject this prize bull, it got agitated, and somehow the farmer got the benefit of the sedation rather than the bull. The vet should have had the antidote with him, but he didn't."

"I should imagine he's in trouble!"

"Probably. Anyway, we managed to sort this chap out, with the help of a veterinary friend of mine, I have to admit. But the thing is, Mansell's symptoms were identical to that farmer."

Matt's eyes widened. "Were they now?"

"Yes, and that's what made me stop and think."

"But didn't it show up in the tests you did?"

"This damn stuff disperses very quickly, but the path lab said there were small traces."

"That's why you're asking for a PM."

"It is, and if I hadn't had that case recently, I don't think I'd have reacted like this, which is disturbing. But because of it, I checked his body for puncture marks."

"Hari!" Matt said, eyebrows raised. "You're turning into a detective here."

Hari gave him a slightly embarrassed smile. "Anyway, I did find a mark and bruising on the inside of his arm, just below the armpit, which I couldn't really explain, and I just wanted to give you the heads up in case something comes of it."

Matt was suddenly serious. "As it happens, we're investigating some of the extended family at the moment."

Hari's eyebrows shot up. "What for?"

"The daughter-in-law's brother is staying at the Abbey and he's got some rather dodgy friends; we're keeping an eye on him." He pushed himself up from his chair. "I'd be very interested in the results of the PM, but I won't keep you any longer."

"I'll give you a ring directly they come through."

"Thanks, Hari," Matt said, "Give my regards to Mina and the kids, I'll never forget that biryani she made for me, and I still haven't returned your hospitality."

"Don't worry. Maybe you could bring your girlfriend, Fabia, round next time. I'd like to meet her again." There was a teasing light in the doctor's eyes.

"She's not my girlfriend, Hari," Matt said, a warning note in his voice.

"No? Then you'd better get a move on before someone else snaps her up." But he was soon serious again. "She's a remarkable woman. I was very impressed with her strength after that attack. I hope she's fully recovered."

"I think she has."

"You don't sound too sure."

"She told me she had nightmares for a while afterwards. She hasn't mentioned them lately, but sometimes she seems a bit fragile in a way I'm not used to with Fabia."

"The physical scars fade quickly enough, Matt. It's the mental ones that linger."

"I know," Matt said.

His tone made Hari give him a sharp glance, but he didn't probe.

"With you to watch out for her, I'm sure she'll be fine; just keep a close eye," Hari advised, his eyes serious.

Matt realised now that he'd noticed a difference in Fabia since that dreadful time, but he had to admit he'd pushed it to the back of his mind. After all, until then they hadn't seen each other for over two years, the changes in her could be to do with so many different factors. Maybe he should keep a closer eye on her, if she'd let him; he must think about it.

"Give her my regards," Hari said, the twinkle back in his eye.

"I will," Matt replied and escaped before his friend could do any more probing about Fabia.

Chapter 7

In the shabby grandeur of the sitting room at White Monk Abbey, the family had gathered. They sat in stunned silence. Nonna, desperately pale, was on one of the sofas with her arm round Megan, whose eyes were swollen with crying. Rodric stood by the fireplace, his head bent and his hands thrust deep in his pockets. Delma was curled up in an armchair beside him, tense and anxious, her eyes darting between him and her brother, who stood on her other side. Mike's face was impassive and, for once, lacked that slight sneer. The silence was interrupted by the sound of footsteps hurrying across the stone floor of the hall. With an abrupt opening of the door, David Harris strode into the room, followed by Garan Price.

"I came as soon as I heard," David said. Megan jumped up and ran to him and he wrapped her in his arms, held her and stroked her hair, but his eyes were on Rodric.

"Is it true? Is he– is he dead?" Garan's voice shook as he spoke.

Mike frowned at Garan, obviously wondering why he was there. He opened his mouth to speak but, when he shot Delma a questioning glance, she shook her head.

Rodric took a deep, shuddering breath. "Yes, Garan, it's true. It seems it was a heart attack, at least that's what Dr Nash thinks, but there's going to be a post-mortem. We'll know more once that's done."

"But what I want to know is why they're doing it," Delma said, "he was old, it was bound to happen soon."

Nonna glared across at her, opened her mouth to speak, but Rodric forestalled her. "I'm not sure," he said wearily, "Dr Nash wasn't clear."

David led Megan back to the sofa and sat down beside her. "So, is there anything I can do to help?"

"Yes, and me," Garan said, "he was my father as well after all."

This was too much for Mike. "What do you mean, your father?"

Rodric gave him a look of acute dislike. "Garan is our half-brother. He has as much right to be here as Megan and me, a damn sight more of a right than you, that's for sure."

"Rodi," Delma protested weakly. Her husband didn't even look at her.

Mike held up his hands in mock surrender. "Sorry, I'm sure – your family's a mystery to me, mate." He walked over to the French windows and stood looking out. His sister watched him, chewing at her bottom lip and twisting her hands in her lap.

David looked up at Rodric. "Do we know when the post-mortem will be done?"

"No, we don't," Rodric said. "And no decisions can be made about anything until we know more. Could you contact your mother and tell her? She'd want to know."

"Yes, of course, I'll phone her directly I get home. She'll be devastated, they were great friends."

"I know," Rodric said, and a look was exchanged between the two men that spoke volumes. "Garan, you and Sheryl, we'll look after things, you're not to worry.

Until we have a better idea of what the old man's will says, nothing changes."

"Why are you talking about wills already?" Megan wailed. "Father's not even buried yet!"

"I know, I know, but he'd been hinting lately about changing it—"

Nonna straightened herself and got up from the sofa. "This is not a conversation to be had now. Have some respect, all of you. I'll go and make some sandwiches and coffee. We all need to eat something." There were murmurs of protest, but she ignored them. Megan was about to get up, but Nonna said, "No, no, you stay here with David. Delma, you can give me a hand."

For a moment it looked as if Delma would refuse, but one look at Nonna's face and the protest died on her lips. "If you insist," she said sulkily, and they left the room together.

Mike turned from the window. "I'll get out of your way," he said, as if he was doing them a favour, and followed the two women.

Garan muttered something in Welsh as he watched him go and Rodric gave a grim little smile.

"My sentiments entirely, Garan," he said, but the smile died a second later. "I've left a message for John Meredith to get back to me. I know it seems a bit early, but we do need to find out what the will says. It's possible it was just one of Father's wind-ups, and he's made no changes at all, but I've been thinking a lot about something he said before he went up to London. We'd been arguing about the finances, yet again, and he said everything would be changing soon. His exact words were 'There'll be someone else for me to think about, you'll see', but I couldn't get anything else out of him. It could just have been his usual— you know how he is... was."

Megan made a small sound of protest and Rodric turned to her, his tone harsh. "For goodness sake, Meggie, face facts, Father wasn't the easiest person in the world."

She looked at him and tears filled her eyes, then she turned her face into David's shoulder and began to sob.

* * *

"But I can't believe it, he was so vibrant, so alive." Anjali looked across the kitchen table at Fabia. There were no tears, but her eyes were bleak.

"I know, but he was eighty, a good age."

They sat in silence for a while then Anjali said, sadness in her voice, "I was looking forward so much to getting to know him, and the rest of his family, although they might not have been very pleased to meet me. Oh dear, I'll have to tell my mother, she'll be very sad about it." A moment later she added, "I suppose I might as well go back to London. I doubt they'll want me hanging around at a time like this. The trouble is, John Meredith told me he changed his will after he found out about me."

"So I gathered, although he didn't tell me exactly what changes Caradoc made." Fabia looked across the table at her, an enquiring eyebrow raised.

But Anjali said, "Nor me."

"I'm sure John will contact you soon," Fabia reassured her, then she went on, a little hesitantly, "I was wondering– look, tell me to shut up if you don't want to talk about it, but how did Caradoc find out about you after all these years?"

Anjali smiled a little. "That was down to the determination of two particular people. My grandfather's batman; that is the right word, isn't it?"

Fabia nodded.

"And his daughter. His name was Dewi – is that the right way to pronounce it?"

"It is."

"Dewi Jenkyns," Anjali went on. "He kept contact with my grandmother on behalf of my grandfather for a while after Caradoc was sent back to the UK in disgrace. As I told you last night, that happened when their relationship was discovered. It seems Caradoc–" She paused, mid-sentence. "I really feel I ought to call him Grandfather. Caradoc was what we decided on when we met, but now, oh dear, what should I do?"

"I think Grandfather would be fine, if it makes you feel more comfortable."

Anjali gave her a grateful smile, then went on with her story. "My grandfather told me when we met that he decided that he'd best stop trying to keep the contact going, he said he thought it would be better for my grandmother if he cut the ties. I find it hard to believe he could think that, but I hardly knew him so– anyway Dewi didn't agree, in fact they fell out because of it. Dewi continued to correspond with my grandmother and she sent him photos of my mother over the years."

"So, he got in touch with you."

"No, he died about 15 years ago. But when he died all his letters and photos were packed away by his daughter, Branwyn; then recently, because she was moving house I think, she decided to go through her father's papers. He kept diaries occasionally, not all the time, but enough for her to find quite a lot of information from them, and there were also letters from Grandfather to Dewi, and some letters he'd kept from my grandmother. It was Branwyn who did the research and finally got in touch with my mother. And since I was planning to come to London, I wrote to my grandfather. Maman wasn't so sure, but I was determined. He and I sent e-mails to each other for a few weeks, then he asked to meet me when I arrived."

"And have you met Branwyn?"

"No, but I've spoken to her on the phone, she sounds nice. She lives in Swansea. That's quite near here, isn't it?"

"Not that far, just down the end of the M4." Fabia smiled and sat forward, her arms folded on the table. "We could drive down there and meet up with her, if you like."

Anjali's face lit up. "I'd love that. Would you mind?"

"Absolutely not," Fabia grinned at her. "I am the nosiest person I know, I'd love to. We can do that before you go back to London."

* * *

Delma was desperate to be on her own, to escape, particularly from her brother. She just couldn't face him at the moment. No-one seemed to care about her, it was all so unfair. She hurried through the main hall towards the stairs but, just as she got to the first step, Mike strode in from the courtyard.

"Delma," he said, his voice low. "I need to talk to you."

"Not now, Mike, please."

"Now," he snapped. Grabbing her wrist, he dragged her after him round behind the staircase and into a small room at the back of the hall. This had been Elizabeth's private sanctuary and, since her death, was hardly used. It smelt musty and, with its mixture of old-fashioned furniture and patches on the wall where pictures had once hung, it had a gloomy, un-lived in atmosphere.

Mike went over to the window and pushed back the curtains, they billowed dust, but neither of them noticed. He turned to glare at his sister. "We've got to get our stories straight, make sure we're on the same page."

Delma was still standing by the door, rubbing at her bruised wrist. "What do you mean?" She knew, but she wasn't going to admit it.

"Don't act stupid." He strode towards her and she backed away until she could go no further, pressed against the panelling of the door. The handle dug into her back.

He lifted a hand, and she forced herself not to flinch, but he only leant it against the wall beside her. "How long do you think it'll be before they find out what you've been up to? People have inventories, you know, and they're inclined to see the light of day at times like this. They'll realise what's missing soon enough, bound to."

"No, no, I was really careful."

"What about that silver?"

"Rodi understood, I explained."

"Yea, yea, but there's the rest, won't be long before that's discovered."

"It was you that–"

"Keep your voice down." He slapped a hand across her mouth, and she made a tiny sound of protest, then was still. After a few seconds that felt like long, drawn-out minutes to Delma, he took his hand away. "You're going to have to put some story together, tell that bloody useless husband of yours that you suspect some kid from the village has been pilfering stuff, that you've seen them prowling around. I don't care what you say, just think of something."

"He won't believe me," she protested. "No petty thief is going to steal the stuff you've taken."

"I've taken? Don't you start that. Anyway, you'll just have to convince him. It was you who needed the dosh, so it's up to you to sort it."

"I know I couldn't have bought that colt without the extra, but we *both* needed the money," she hissed, "you know that."

He ignored this. "You seem to think those horses are the only thing that matters. What the hell would it matter if the old man had got rid of the stables? It wouldn't have affected us."

"But, Mike, it would. I've put everything into building them up. It's one of the only parts of the estate that's got the potential to make good money. But I desperately need more funds, especially now Ted Marsden's expanding."

"And that's why I helped you out."

"I know, but I need more." She flinched at the expression on his face, but went on, determined to convince him. "That's why I persuaded Rodi to agree to the filming. Think of it. We could afford to extend, buy in some really top-class stallions."

But all he did was sneer at her. "You just don't get it, do you? I couldn't care a sod about your bloody horses. I helped out because it worked for me. If anyone gets suspicious, I'll tell them you're as deep in this as me."

"Mike." It was a whisper of sound. "You can't, you wouldn't. It was you, I did it for you as well."

His hand came down on her shoulder, gripped it hard. She winced.

"Of course you did – I don't think." But suddenly his attitude changed. He stepped back and thrust his hands into his pockets. "That idiot sister-in-law of yours, dragging the police into this mess. What possessed her?"

"I don't know," Delma said, relieved that his attention was on someone else. "She panicked or something, typical of her." It felt better to be united in their contempt for Megan, but that unity didn't last.

"So, you get that story sorted. And if questions start being asked about why I'm here, you're to say it's brotherly love. Understand? I want to be with my little sister."

Delma said nothing.

"And if they start asking about my business interests," he went on, "you'll tell them I'm in import export, Bulgarian wines. I do have a scheme going with a friend out there, so if they investigate it'll come up kosher, but you tell them as little as possible, is that clear?"

Still she was silent. He obviously took it for agreement.

"Good girl." He smiled at her, just as if there'd been no confrontation, but she didn't smile back.

"You'd better get going," he said dismissively, "or that husband of yours will be wondering where you are."

Delma made good her escape. She left the room and hurried through the hall and up the stairs to her bedroom. Once inside, trembling and feeling sick, she flung herself on the bed and buried her face in a pillow.

* * *

Fabia was preparing a meal for herself and Anjali when the doorbell rang. She put down the knife with which she'd been chopping onions, ready to make shepherd's pie, wiped her hands on a cloth, and went to open the door to find John Meredith standing on the doorstep. "John, come in, have you any news for us?"

"I was going to phone," John said, "but then I thought I could pop in on my way home."

"Come through, Anjali's in the sitting room," Fabia said. She didn't remark on the fact that Pontygwyn could hardly be on his way home, since he lived on the other side of Newport.

Anjali had been curled up, dozing in front of the fire, which flickered comfortingly on the cold November night. She was worn out after the emotions of the day, but she rose as they came in, an enquiring look on her face.

"Sit down, John," Fabia said, "can I get you a drink, glass of wine, tea?"

"A cup of tea would be great," he said.

"And for you, Anjali?"

"Tea please."

He turned to Anjali, "I thought I'd come in and have a word about Caradoc's will and where we go from here."

"That's very kind of you," Anjali said, and Fabia was relieved to hear her add, "but can we wait till Fabia gets back before you start? I'd like her to know what's going on."

When Fabia returned with the tea, they were sitting side by side on the settee and Anjali was telling John about Mauritius and her family. Only when they were all holding warm mugs of tea, and Fabia was settled in an armchair by the fireplace, did John begin.

"When you met Caradoc in London, did he tell you what changes he was planning to make to his will since he'd found out about you?"

"No, not really." As she spoke, she twisted the silver bangles on her wrist round and round, but Fabia didn't think she was conscious of doing so. "He just said he'd be changing it." She frowned. "How did he put it? I think he said he'd make things right, and he said he'd be leaving something to Maman as well, but he didn't say what."

"That's easy to tell you. He's left her a Welsh gold locket. It belonged, originally, to one of his ancestors, Cornelia Mansell–"

Anjali smiled. "The woman who brought all the money into the family in the eighteenth century?"

John looked surprised. "The very same."

"Caradoc told me about her when we met. She sounded quite formidable."

"I think she probably was. The tradition, Caradoc told me, has always been that the locket is passed to the wife of the eldest male, which Caradoc was in his generation, but for some reason he never gave it to Elizabeth, and he was adamant that he didn't want it to go to Rodric's wife, Delma. In a way, I suppose he felt leaving it to your mother is an acknowledgement of his relationship with your grandmother."

Her eyes wide and glistening, Anjali pressed a hand to her lips, but said nothing.

After a moment, John went on. "I haven't brought the actual will with me. I thought I ought to show it to the family first, particularly Rodric, but I can tell you which parts affect you. I don't think they know that he made these changes, nor do I think they know about you."

"When we met in London," Anjali said, "Caradoc told me he hadn't told them about me. It worried me at the time, it does even more now. Maybe he said something when he got home, I don't know."

Fabia intervened. "But I'm sure they'll be pleased to meet you." She was sure of nothing of the sort, but she felt the need to say something comforting. "Don't you think so, John?"

He looked doubtful but didn't give her a direct answer, just turned back to Anjali. "What I thought I should tell you is that Caradoc e-mailed me from London on Sunday evening with the changes he wanted made, and he came into the office on his way home on Monday to sign the new will. I did suggest he should think about it for a few days. I'm sorry, but I thought he was being a little impulsive."

"I'm not surprised!" Anjali said with a worried frown. "I really didn't want him to do anything, well, not immediately."

"He was always one for quick decisions, Caradoc," John said with a slight smile. "Once he'd made up his mind to do something, there was no stopping him. The estate is entailed, so the realty, that's the land, the Abbey and other properties, goes to Rodric as the eldest, but Caradoc was free to leave all the contents to whomever he chose. Apart from some specific legacies, he's left all the personalty – that's his possessions, the horses, and the contents of a small savings account – to you."

It struck Fabia that, on hearing this sort of news, most people would at least be pleased and show some curiosity about the details, but all Anjali did was look absolutely aghast and say, "Oh no! The family is going to hate this. How could he do that to them?"

John seemed to be as taken aback as Fabia. "Well, it seems he wished to make up for what I think he saw as his desertion of your grandmother. He told me he'd never wanted to leave her, and it was only when he lost touch with her, some years later, that he married Elizabeth. He called it a marriage of convenience. I have no idea how she felt about it."

"The poor woman. Do you think she knew?"

"I never knew her. Did you, Fabia?"

"Yes, but not very well. She was very reserved, a quiet presence. My father once told me that she and her sister came from a very difficult background. Their parents were deeply religious, part of some extreme religious sect, and he thought she married Caradoc to escape from them. I don't think it was a particularly happy marriage."

"It's all so sad," Anjali said.

"Yes," John said, "but one thing I do know is that meeting you made Caradoc very happy indeed, in fact I'd never seen him in such a jubilant mood before."

"Thank you," she said quietly. "That makes me feel a little better."

"There will be some legal work to do in authenticating your claim. We have to prove" – there was an awkward little pause – "that you are who you say you are."

"I do have copies of my and Maman's birth certificates with me," Anjali told him. "And a letter that Caradoc wrote to my grandmother telling her that he was being sent home. It's very fragile now. I think she read it often. And I have his signet ring that he gave to Gran-mère. I showed it to him when we met."

Fabia could tell she was making an effort to keep her voice steady.

"Good," said John, giving her an understanding smile. "I think we must arrange to introduce you to Rodric – in my office perhaps? But I just thought you should be forewarned about the will before that meeting. I think the best thing to do is to ask Rodric to come in, say on Monday morning, and I'll bring him up to date on the situation. Then perhaps Fabia could bring you in and I can introduce you, before you meet the rest of the family. Would that be okay?"

Anjali nodded, but didn't say anything.

"I'll let you know if I manage to fix it up."

Fabia got up to see him out and, as she did so, her phone rang. "Hallo?" she said.

"It's me, Matt."

"Hi, Matt, look can I phone you back? I'm just saying goodbye to John."

"Oh? What – never mind. It doesn't matter." He cut off the call.

Fabia frowned and wondered what was up with him, then she followed John into the hall.

"I'm sorry, Fabia," he said. "I thought this would only be for two or three days, but it looks as if she's going to have to stay on until the weekend. I do hope that's okay with you?"

"It's not a problem, John, she's no trouble." Fabia's mind was half on him and half on Matt's strange call.

"So long as you're sure," he said.

She pushed Matt into the back of her mind and smiled at John. "Actually, I've rather taken to her, and it's good to have company."

He gave her a shrewd look. "Are you okay, in yourself? I know you've had a hard time these last few months."

"I'm fine," she assured him, wishing she felt as confident as she sounded.

When she came back into the room, Anjali was still sitting there staring into the flickering fire.

"I think," Fabia said, "that it's time for a drink, and I don't mean tea!"

Chapter 8

In his office, Matt sat looking at the mobile in his hand as if it had offended him. Why was John Meredith at Fabia's? Hari's words came into his mind, 'someone else will snap her up'. Nah, don't be stupid, he told himself, and was relieved when Dilys knocked on his office door and came in. They were both weary and ready for home, but there was one more thing they needed to talk about.

"This is going to be awkward," Matt said, looking across at Dilys as she sat down in a chair opposite his desk. "With the old man dead, and Hari Patel doubtful about the cause, barging in to question his daughter-in-law's brother is going to seem a tad intrusive."

"Intrusive!" exclaimed Dilys. She had no such sensitivities. "That's as may be, sir, but we really shouldn't wait now we've got this information."

"True. Okay, go over it again for me."

"Tom Watkins, you know, that young PC who's the size of a prop forward?"

"I remember him well from when we were making the arrest for the two murders in Pontygwyn, a useful lad to have around."

Dilys grinned. "He is, and he's bright as well. Anyway, as you know he was seconded to the Swansea force for an undercover job – they wanted someone from outside the area. He was doing a job with this nasty little fascist group, they call themselves *Milwyr Dragon Cymru* which translates as the Welsh Dragon Soldiers."

"I know that, Dilys! I'm not fluent like you, but I do have some Welsh."

"Sorry, sir," Dilys said, but the apology was perfunctory. "Anyway, a damn cheek, I call it, appropriating the Welsh dragon, that really winds me up, that does."

Matt grinned but didn't comment.

"They're based in Swansea," she went on, "and they have other branches, I suppose that's the right description, in other parts of Wales, but they're doing their best to spread their poisonous message further afield. They're known to have connections with other fascist groups in Germany, Hungary, Bulgaria and possibly further afield. Anyway, this Cotter bloke turned up at one of their meetings and PC Watkins was there."

Dilys pulled her laptop towards her and clicked away for a minute, then turned the screen round so that Matt could see what she'd brought up. "Tom had one of those mini cameras on him. The picture's not very clear but the conversation comes across well enough." She pointed at the screen. "That bloke there is one of the buggers we've got our eye on. He's a Swansea villain called Wayne Shuttleworth – good Welsh name that, I don't think! And this one here, just in the picture, is one Kevin Rees, been inside for petty thieving and a spot of GBH; and this one, with his back to us, is our London friend."

"Can you turn up the volume a bit?"

Dilys did so and they both leant forward to study the screen as they listened. After about five minutes she closed the laptop. "That's all Tom managed to get, but it's pretty useful, I'd say. Cocky bastard, isn't he? Comes over as if he thinks he's dealing with a bunch of idiot provincials that he can manipulate as he wishes."

"May not be far wrong with that lot."

"I s'pose."

"Um," Matt said as he leant back in this chair. "So, what it seems he's offering is some pretty substantial financial help based on these 'valuables' he says he's got hold of. He didn't mention the Mansells by name, but he did say he could – what was it – 'get access through my sister'. I don't suppose he's got another sister stashed away?"

"The Met info on him says there's just the two of them, their parents are dead."

"What are these valuables that he's talking about?" Matt wondered.

"We don't know yet, except for that business with the silver. I suppose his sister could have pinched the stuff and given it to her brother to fence – he's a dealer, he's probably got plenty of contacts, and then maybe when her husband found out, it was hushed up. And from what I've seen of that place, it's so full of treasures no-one's going to miss one or two, at least, not until it's too late to do anything about it."

"Lord, this makes the whole situation that much more complicated. Makes my brain hurt." Matt yawned and stretched. "Okay, Dilys, let's call it a day."

But Matt couldn't escape quite so easily. Just as he was putting on his coat, Tom Watkins poked his head round the door. "Can I have a word, chief?"

Matt sighed. "You still here Tom, haven't you got a home to go to?"

Tom grinned. "Won't take long, sir."

"Okay, what is it?"

"That Cotter bloke–"

"Dilys and I were just talking about him. We watched your recording, well done."

"Thank you, sir. I've just found out he's been down talking to his Nazi pals in Swansea again. One of my contacts came through earlier on. He used to be a member of this Welsh Dragon Soldiers outfit, then he got fed up with them, said they were getting too extreme, but he still has contact with one or two of them. Apparently, Cotter's been blowing his mouth off again about the Mansells."

"Did he mention them by name this time?"

"Yes, he did. He was going on about some 'good stuff' he's got hold of, said it'd make a packet for their campaign funds. He's also been talking about being owed money by Garan Price, the pub landlord. Didn't you say he's part of the family?"

"Yes, Caradoc's illegitimate son."

"You don't say! How'd you find that out?"

"Fabia Havard told me."

"Aah." He saw the look on Matt's face and thought it best not to remark on this further. "We should interview him about Caradoc, shouldn't we?"

"Yes," Matt said, slightly irritated. "Anyway, what else has Cotter been up to?"

"He's told a couple of them boyos down there that he might want them to have a go at this Garan, rough him up a bit to 'encourage him' to pay up."

"Has he now? Incitement to violence. I'll add that to the list we've got on him. I was talking to Dilys about bringing him in for questioning, Cotter that is." Matt sighed, thought for a moment, then made a decision. "In spite of the other situation, I think we'll have to go ahead. Let's get him in tomorrow morning, first thing. You can't go, he might recognise you, it'll have to be a couple of the others. Is Dave Parry here?"

"I think so, sir, shall I send him in?"

"Yup, and Tom…"

"Yes, sir."

"Good work."

"Thanks, sir. I'd be delighted to help put that load of shit away."

PC Dave Parry came in a few minutes later. Like Tom Watkins he was a big man, another rugby player, but older and more traditional in his attitudes.

Matt explained what he wanted. "Pick him up good and early tomorrow. Make it clear this is just an informal chat at this stage, and take that new PC with you, Gooding, she seems to be shaping up well."

"Shouldn't I take one of the men, sir, in case this Cotter gets nasty?"

"I don't think he'll risk that at the moment, and I'm sure she can handle herself perfectly well. Dilys tells me she's a black belt in some kind of martial art."

"If you say so, sir." Dave Parry obviously wasn't impressed, but Matt ignored his reservations.

As Matt drove home, he wondered if he should phone Fabia to bring her up to date. No, better not. John might be there.

* * *

At White Monk Abbey, the family was sitting round the kitchen table for the evening meal. It had been Nonna's suggestion they eat in the kitchen, something that had rarely been allowed when Caradoc was alive, but she'd said it would make things easier for her, and nobody had argued. Mike was absent. He'd announced he was going to get out of their way, as if he was doing them a favour. In truth he was. Not one of them wanted him around, particularly not his sister.

Rodric was the last to arrive, as he'd taken a call on his mobile just as Nonna had announced the meal was ready. He came in looking angry and haggard.

Nonna looked at him sharply. "What now?" she said.

He threw himself down in a chair, leant back and crossed his arms in a characteristic pose. "That was John

Meredith. It seems Father did make changes to his will, but John doesn't want to talk about the details on the phone."

"Why not?" Delma snapped.

"He was being all mysterious, bloody annoying in fact. He wants me to go into his office on Monday to go through it all."

"I'll come with you," said Delma.

"So will I," added Megan.

"No!" he barked, then took a deep breath and said, with barely controlled calm. "John says just me at the moment." But the calm didn't last. "It's preposterous. He says after he's spoken to me, he'll come and speak to all of us. That's when he'll bring everyone up to date on what's happening, all the interested parties, as he called it, like one of those ridiculous reading the will scenes. I don't know what the hell all the mystery is about. It's just not good enough."

With slow deliberation, Nonna ladled out bowls of spaghetti and passed them round. "Get the wine opened, Rodi," she said. "Delma, would you fetch some glasses? We don't want the food to get cold, and there's no point in going over it all this evening, so calm down and eat."

The habit of obedience to Nonna's wishes asserted itself. Rodric fetched a corkscrew and Megan picked up her spoon and fork and began to push her food back and forth in her bowl. With a resentful glare at Nonna, Delma flounced across the room and fetched four wine glasses. She slapped them down on the table but didn't hand them out. That was as far as she'd go when it came to taking orders from Nonna.

"Look, Rodi," Delma said, "I think, as your wife, I should be there. It's as much my business as anyone else's. I need to know what's going to happen to the stables, and what he's done about all the valuables. What's more, we must remember that the production company will be here in a matter of weeks. We've got to get all that sorted."

Rodric was incredulous. "Do you really think we're going ahead with that now?"

"We have to. You've signed the contract. And we have to have that money."

"Well, there's nothing we can do about it until I hear what John has to say."

"Rodi! You don't understand. All this uncertainty is killing me."

"It's not much fun for the rest of us," Rodi snapped. "Father died two days ago, for Christ's sake, so you'll just have to have a little patience. Is that too much to ask?"

Delma glared at him resentfully, then backed down. "Alright. But I still want to come with you tomorrow."

"But what about me?" Megan said, her voice full of tears. "He wasn't your father, Delma, and you didn't much like him anyway." Tears started to overflow and crawl down her cheeks.

"Megan, *bach*, stop crying and eat," Nonna said, handing her a tissue. "Delma, please let Rodi do things the way he thinks is best. Haven't we enough grief in this house without quarrelling?"

They all subsided, and the rest of the meal was eaten in heavy silence. Immediately it was over, the three younger family members left Nonna to clear away, unaware of the look on her face as she watched them go.

* * *

At the Mynach Arms, closing time had come and gone. Garan locked up and made his way upstairs, saying he was going to look at some accounts before going to bed. Sheryl wiped down the bar and all the tables, emptied the dishwasher and wrapped cutlery in napkins ready for tomorrow's lunch-time trade. With a quick glance round, she turned off all the lights and followed him slowly up the ancient stairs, avoiding the treads she knew would creak. Instead of making her way to their bedroom, she went into the tiny room above the front door that served as an office. There was barely enough space for more than a desk, a couple of chairs and a filing cabinet, and here she found Garan, sitting in front of his computer, his elbows on the desk and his chin resting on his hands.

Her heart sank as she came up quietly behind him and placed a hand on his shoulder. He jumped and grabbed the mouse, clicked the file closed, but not quickly enough.

"Oh, Garan, not again."

"What do you mean?"

"Don't treat me like an idiot. How much is it this time?"

"I don't know what—"

"Don't give me that! I thought we'd agreed," she sighed. "After that talk with your Mam you promised both of us you'd contact those Gamblers Anonymous people, and now I find you back on the net, gambling away another load."

He looked up at her, fear in his eyes. "You don't understand. He's been at me again. He says if I don't pay up soon, he's going to get some of his pals to 'come and visit' – that's how he put it, said they knew ways of disposing of bodies. I thought if I just had a go, like, I could make enough to pay him off."

"How's losing yet more money going to help?" Sheryl asked despairingly.

"No, Sheryl," he said, grabbing her by the wrist. "I could win big on this. I really feel lucky tonight."

"Crap!" she said, wrenching her wrist out of his grasp. "Don't give me that. You lose a pile to Mike Cotter in that poker game, then you think you're going to solve it by going online and losing another pile to those internet sharks? God give me strength."

Garan wouldn't meet her eyes. He looked like a small boy who'd been caught out stealing, but this was so much more serious than any kid's prank, this could threaten their whole livelihood and, if Mike carried out his threats,

Garan's life. Sheryl had no illusions about the man, he had some extremely unpleasant associates.

She crouched down by his chair. "Garan, listen to me, you know it doesn't work like that, you never win. We cannot afford for you to run up any more debts. And now Caradoc is gone, we've not even got him to watch our backs."

"But he said he'd make sure I was okay, he promised me and Mam. So maybe he's left me – us – enough to clear the debts."

"If you think that, why the hell are you back in front of the computer pouring more money down the drain?" She was shouting now.

He had no answer to that.

She got up, feeling an enormous weariness deep down in her body. "What's the use? I'm going to bed." But she turned at the door. "But I warn you, Garan, if you don't stop this, I'm leaving, do you understand? And then you won't have just lost a father, you'll have lost a wife as well."

Chapter 9

"Why did they come so early?" Delma wailed. "Why do they want to talk to Mike?"

Delma, Rodric and Nonna were in the kitchen at the Abbey. It was a quarter past seven in the morning and they were all still in dressing gowns and slippers, all bleary eyed.

"I don't know, they said it was just routine," Rodric told her, rubbing at his eyes. "But they were pretty firm about it. I think Mike did the right thing in agreeing to go with them."

"And they were clear they weren't arresting him for anything, Delma, just helping with their enquiries," Nonna said, sounding as if she rather relished the phrase.

"Helping with their enquiries! That's tantamount to being arrested."

"Try not to worry. I'll make some tea."

Delma ignored her as she gripped her husband's arm. "We must get hold of John Meredith, Rodi, get him to go and demand to be there when they question Mike."

"I'm sure that'd be premature. He'll probably be back in no time."

"How can you both be so calm?" Delma wailed.

"Delma, panicking isn't going to help. Haven't we enough to cope with without you losing it?" Rodric said, then he relented and put his arm round her shoulders. "Look, I'll mention it to John when I see him. Just drink your tea and try to calm down."

"Oh God, this is so awful." Delma sat down heavily on a kitchen chair and put her head in her hands. "I can't bear it."

"I think we all feel like that, Delma," Nonna said, with little sympathy. "Now, make yourself useful, take this mug of tea up to Megan."

"Where is Megan?" Rodric asked.

"Still in bed," said Nonna. "I made her take a sleeping tablet last night, that's probably why she didn't wake when the police came."

"I'll take her tea up," Rodric said, with a wary glance at his wife, "I've got to have a shower and get dressed, and I'd like to have a word with her before I get going."

He left the room and the two women sat on in silence, the atmosphere full of tension and resentment.

* * *

Dave Parry had put Mike Cotter in an interview room to cool his heels. He went up to Matt's office where his boss was drinking an extremely strong cup of coffee and chewing his way through a bacon sandwich.

"I could do with one of those," he said, "but my wife would kill me."

"If I had a wife, she'd probably say the same," Matt said as he looked up, then asked, "Where have you put Cotter?"

"I've stashed him in room two."

"And how did PC Gooding manage this morning? No unpleasantness?"

"It all went fine. Obviously, Cotter wasn't particularly pleased to see us at that time of the morning, nor was the rest of the family, but having a woman PC there, well, I have to admit it helped – sort of calmed things down."

"There you are then, Dave, you're learning," Matt said, with a grin. "Right, let's get going on this Cotter bloke."

Matt collected Dilys on the way downstairs. They'd talked about their tactics earlier, but they were so used to working together, little planning was needed.

Interview room two was on the ground floor. A window, blinds half drawn, looked out on to the station car park, and the walls, painted a dull blue, were bare except for a large map of the Newport area on the one facing the window. A table occupied the centre of the room, two plain office chairs faced one side, and on the opposite side Mike Cotter was slouched in another. His arms were folded across his powerful chest. He glared at them as they came in but said nothing.

"Good morning, Mr Cotter," Matt said.

Dilys put a file and a laptop down on the table then set up the recording of the interview. Once that was done, Matt went on. "Thank you for agreeing to come in and speak to us. I thought it would be best to ask you to the station, given the circumstances."

"What circumstances?" Cotter demanded.

Matt raised his eyebrows a little. "The death of your sister's father-in-law?"

"I see. Are you suggesting I had anything to do with that?"

Matt was surprised. Did this man know there were doubts about Mansell's death?

"What makes you think anyone did?"

"I don't, but I know what you lot are like. If you can pin something on a chap you will."

Matt ignored this jibe. "That isn't what we want to talk to you about," he said calmly. "It's something else entirely."

Cotter's expression didn't change. "Well, go ahead then."

Matt pulled the folder towards him. "I believe you're normally resident in South London." He opened the folder and glanced at the first sheet of paper. "In Stratford East, 21 Sandown Road; is that correct?"

All he got in response was a curt nod.

"And I have here information on your police record."

"My record? What the hell are you talking about?"

"Two cases of being caught speeding, one of driving without due care, one of threatening behaviour but that wasn't proved, and two of being suspected of handling stolen goods, but they weren't proved either. You've been very lucky."

"Lucky doesn't come into it. You lot just got it wrong."

Matt looked across at him and decided to change tack. "What's the purpose of your visit to South Wales?"

"I would have thought that was obvious? I'm visiting my sister, that's allowed, isn't it?"

"Of course. It's just that you've been doing quite a lot of travelling about since you got here, particularly to Swansea. Can you tell me what took you down there?"

Cotter uncrossed his arms and thrust his hands into his trouser pockets. There was a wariness in his eyes now, but he still sat back in his chair, apparently relaxed. "You've been following me around then?" he said with a sneer.

Matt didn't reply to this, just let the silence drag out.

After a moment, Cotter went on. "I have some contacts in Swansea and I thought, while I'm in the area, I'd do a little business. I'm not someone who can sit around doing nothing if a business opportunity presents itself."

"And what line of business is that?" Dilys asked.

So far Cotter hadn't acknowledged her presence, but at this he looked slowly round. A slight smirk on his lips, he looked her in the eye then, with great deliberation, his eyes went downwards and lingered. Dilys had an urge to cross her arms over her chest protectively, but forced herself not to, just waited for his answer.

"Import, export, I suppose you'd call it. I'm a dealer, antiques and valuables, and I also do a spot of wine importing, mainly from Bulgaria and other East European countries. Very popular, their wines are, and not too pricey."

"So, these contacts you have in Swansea," Matt said, "can you tell us who they are?"

"I'm not sure that's appropriate."

"Why?" Dilys's tone was sharp.

"Data protection, commercial confidentiality," he said, sounding very sure of himself.

Matt decided it was time to push a little harder. He turned to his file once again and said, "Perhaps we can help you out there." He turned over a few pieces of paper, taking his time about it, and finally selected a photo, swivelled it round and pushed it across the table. "Could you take a look at this?"

Cotter frowned and picked it up, looked at the photo and then slapped it back down on the table.

He looked up at Matt, his expression unreadable. "When was this taken?"

"I'm asking the questions," Matt said firmly. "Do you recognise the people in that photograph?"

"Not much point in my denying it since I'm in there too. How the hell did you get that?"

Matt ignored this question. "So, tell me who they are?"

"Some people I met recently. I had an introduction from a contact of mine in London. Can't say I know them that well, but since I was going to be visiting my sister, my mate suggested I should look them up."

Matt glanced at Dilys, she took the hint. "And who is this mate?" she asked.

"Just someone who's in the same line of business as me," he replied, but he watched with narrowed eyes as Matt opened up the laptop and clicked away at the keyboard.

"This one here," Dilys pointed at one of the men in the photograph, "is a petty criminal, a Swansea local, called Wayne Shuttleworth. The other is in the same line of business," she echoed his phrase deliberately, "one Nigel Rees, he's been inside for burglary, a spot of GBH, and what's more, both are members of an organisation we've got our eye on called *Milwyr Dragon Cymru*."

Cotter sneered, but he wasn't so sure of himself now. "I'm not a great one for your weird language. What does that translate as when it's at home?"

"Welsh Dragon Soldiers," Dilys told him calmly, "but soldiers they are not. They're a group of would-be Nazis with a very dubious record of fraud, extortion and incitement to violence. You name it, if it's against the law, they've probably tried it."

"We understand that you have sympathies with their political ambitions," said Matt, "that you offered to put money into their campaign funds?"

"You what? How'd you get that idea?" He sounded scornful, but it was obvious he was beginning to get rattled.

Matt turned the laptop round and increased the volume. The sound was a little muffled, but Cotter could clearly be heard talking about the access he might have to some valuables through his sister, telling them that he'd probably be able to make a few thousand, which he could donate to what he called their 'fighting fund'. Then there was mention of his Bulgarian contacts and how useful they could be, that they might be a source of funds as well, ending with something about bringing in some tasty toms, and a lot of lewd laughter.

"How did you get that?" He thrust himself forward in his chair. "This is fucking entrapment."

"Come off it, Cotter," Matt interrupted. "You know the score. If we suspect an organisation of planning criminal activity, we have every right to monitor that organisation, which we've done. Now, let's pick this apart. What are these valuables you're thinking of selling?"

At first Matt thought he wasn't going to answer, then Cotter waved a casual hand and said, "Some odds and ends of jewellery, bits my sister doesn't want."

"And she'd just give them to you? She'd not expect to be given the money if you sell them?" Dilys asked scornfully.

"She's very fond of me, my sister. It may be hard for someone like you to understand, but in the Cotter family we look after each other."

"There's looking after," Dilys said, "and there's demanding money with menaces. Is that what you did? Threaten her?"

A flash of pure anger lit his eyes and his hand jerked on the table, as if he'd only just stopped himself from lashing out.

"Why don't you ask her? She'll bear me out."

"I expect she will, but yes, we will be having a word with her," Matt said smoothly. "And what about these Bulgarian friends of yours? You were talking about wine earlier on. Are they wine merchants? Vintners?"

"They deal in wine, yes, amongst other things." He seemed more at ease now. "They're based on the Struma River, very good area for wine, as good as parts of Burgundy in my opinion, and there's also a Thracian Merlot I've brought in; well worth trying."

"And they have no connection with the Bulgarian National Front?" Matt asked.

Tom Watkins, who'd done his homework, had suggested this was a name that might get results. It was a shot in the dark, but the reaction was useful. Cotter didn't answer but he wouldn't look Matt in the eye and his jaw clenched. But a moment later he was defiant. "No idea. Never heard of them."

"You're sure about that?"

"Yes," he said, thrusting out his chin as he continued to glare defiantly at Matt.

They kept going for a while but couldn't get anything more out of him and, not long after, they wound up the interview. They warned Cotter not to leave the area and told him they'd probably want to speak to him again, then let him go.

Back in Matt's office, Dilys said, "There's one thing we didn't pick him up on, sir."

"I wonder if you're thinking of the same thing I am," Matt said.

"That bit about some 'tasty toms', looks as if people trafficking might be another of their activities."

"That's what I thought. I wouldn't put it past them," Matt said, sounding disgusted. "I'd love to bang him up, along with his grubby friends."

* * *

Mike got back to the Abbey in a towering rage and needed someone to take it out on. As usual, he went in search of his sister and ran her to ground in the stables where she was grooming her favourite horse, Moonlight.

"Leave that bloody nag alone, I need to talk," he said.

Delma's fingers tensed in the horse's mane and Moonlight turned his head, showing the whites of his eyes. He stamped and shifted in his stall.

"Mike, let me go," she protested, her voice quiet but urgent. "Ssh, boy, ssh," she said to Moonlight, stroking his neck to soothe him. She went on in the same deliberately quiet tone. "You'll have to wait until I've finished, or you'll have him lashing out at you."

Mike stepped back with a resentful look at the horse. "Be quick about it. I'm not going away, understand?"

He paced up and down the stable yard, his shoes echoing on the cobbles. A couple of the other horses poked their heads out over their stable doors as if wondering what the row was about. Mike ignored them.

After about ten minutes, Delma finally emerged from Moonlight's stall, her eyes wary and fearful.

"You took your time," he said, glowering at her.

"I was as quick as I could be. I had to calm him down. You just don't understand horses."

"Bugger the horses." He grabbed her wrist and, ignoring her protests, dragged her across the stable yard into the small room that served as an office. The walls were covered in photos of horses and rosettes from various events. Delma leant against the desk, as if she needed its support. Mike stood in the doorway, blocking her escape.

"What is wrong with you?" she demanded. "The police let you go, didn't they?"

"Oh yeah, they let me go, with a strong suggestion that I don't leave the area. They've been following me around, recording my business meetings, snooping bastards, and they're coming after you too."

"What do you mean?"

"They know you're planning to sell some of the family jewellery, they said it would be theft if you did it without getting your father-in-law's permission."

"No, it wouldn't! How did they know?" Delma's voice shook as she gazed up at him. "Did you tell them?"

He wouldn't meet her eye. "No, but I did mention it to some of my pals in Swansea; said that you could help with the funds and stuff. How was I to know the pigs had infiltrated the group with one of their undercover buggers? He took photos, recorded some of the conversation. I told that stuck up chief inspector it was entrapment, but he couldn't care a fuck. I'd like to smash his smug little face from here to kingdom come."

"How could you tell them that?" Delma demanded, her anger giving her courage. "You could ruin everything, and that would mean you'd lose out as well."

"Do you think I don't know that? But it's not my fault."

"No, nothing ever is," said his sister furiously. "That's one of your problems. Anything that goes wrong, it's always someone else's fault, not yours."

"Crap." He glared at her for a moment and Delma slipped around the desk and sat down. She felt safer having it between her and Mike.

"You were the one who came up with the idea of disposing of some of the valuables." She opened her mouth to protest, but he didn't give her the chance. "They don't appear to know about the other stuff yet, but it's only a matter of time. You said no-one would notice, and now look where that's got us."

"Mike!" It was a panic-stricken gasp.

"Don't worry. I'm on to it. I think I can sort it, damage limitations."

"What do you mean?"

He tapped the side of his nose. "I've been keeping my eyes and ears open. I've found out a thing or two about the people round here, stuff they'd much rather others didn't know. The old man's death is a mystery, is it? Well, I don't think so, and I could make a tidy little packet out of what I know."

"What do you know?" she exclaimed, her voice rising.

But before he could answer, they heard what sounded like footsteps on the cobbles outside.

"There's someone there," Delma whispered.

"Quiet," he hissed at her, and slipped out of the door, but he was back in no time at all.

"Who was it?"

"No-one. You're jumping at shadows again."

Delma wasn't so sure, but she didn't push it. "Mike," she said, keeping her voice to a whisper, "you have to tell me what you mean."

He gave a bark of laughter. "Not a chance. I'll deal with it in my own way. Just you keep shtum, understand?"

She nodded. What else could she do?

Chapter 10

At breakfast on Sunday morning, Fabia suggested to Anjali that they should get out of the house and do something to distract them from the events of the last few days. John had confirmed the meeting with Rodric would go ahead the following afternoon and Fabia felt it would be a good idea to take Anjali's mind off it. Dwelling on what might happen would do Anjali no good at all. What was more, much to Fabia's annoyance, Matt hadn't phoned to let them know what was going on; so the distraction would help them both.

Fabia had gone through all the places they could visit within easy driving distance. They decided against a trip to Cardiff, neither of them felt like wandering around the usual shops. They'd considered the Roman Baths at Caerleon and talked about Tintern Abbey, which was a bit further afield, but in the end they decided on Tredegar House just outside Newport.

"It's always been one of my favourite places," Fabia said. "The Morgan family, who built it in the seventeenth century, I think, used to own vast parts of South Wales. I suppose the Mansells could be thought of as similar, although on a much smaller scale."

"It sounds interesting, do the same family still live in it?"

"No, it's run by the National Trust now and the house and gardens are open to the public. The way they've set it up gives you a clear idea of what a stately home was like, in Edwardian times particularly. I think you'll love the fabrics."

Anjali's eyes lit up. "That sounds perfect, but what about you, Fabia? Haven't you got work to do?"

"Nothing I can't postpone," Fabia said, and grimaced ruefully. "To be honest I'm a bit stuck. The exhibition is nearly finished and, although I'll have to go and take it all down next week, Paul Hewitt says there's no hurry. As to the commissions I got, well, they'll just have to wait. And I really don't think I can talk to Megan about the book in the present circumstances. I should imagine it's the last thing on her mind."

"I see what you mean. Ah well, let's go, and, thank you."

They'd had a thoroughly enjoyable day. By mutual consent they'd decided not to talk about Caradoc's death and all the problems associated with it, and by the time they got back to Pontygwyn they were both much more relaxed. Having picked up fish and chips in the High Street, they sat in front of the television and ate their meal. But, by the time they'd finished, the shadows had returned.

Anjali straightened after loading their plates into the dishwasher. "I haven't told my mother about Caradoc. I think I should, don't you?"

Fabia didn't quite know what to say. "I don't know, only you can decide."

"I think I must," Anjali said, as if she'd come to a decision after much thought. She glanced at her watch. "It'll be quite late at home, but I don't think she'll mind. She was expecting me to skype her yesterday and she'll probably be wondering what's happening."

Fabia watched her as she left the room, a look of concern on her face. Poor girl, she really had been dumped into an awful situation and, so far, she was dealing with it very well.

* * *

Matt yawned, almost cracking his jaw. Mondays were never his favourite, particularly after having worked through the weekend. The phone on his desk rang and he picked it up. "Lambert," he growled.

"Well, if that's your attitude–"

"Sorry," he said, suddenly alert. Dr Pat Curtis, the pathologist, was a notoriously touchy individual and dealing with her was never easy, but he hoped she'd be answering a question that had been nagging at him since he'd spoken to Hari Patel.

"The preliminary report on the Caradoc Mansell post-mortem – I've just completed it. I've e-mailed it to you. I'm waiting for the results of a couple more tests, but I'm pretty sure of my findings."

"Which are?"

"I'm ninety percent sure he was poisoned but I can't pin-point exactly what was used, which means I've got to wait for those test results to come in."

"So, how long will these tests take?"

"I'm not sure. I've had to call in some expert advice."

"From whom?"

"From a vet."

Aha, thought Matt, that chimes with what Hari said. "So, you do have an idea of what was used?"

"An idea, but that's all so far." There was a strained little silence then she gave in. "I think he was injected with a hefty animal tranquiliser, but that's what I've got to get checked out. It surprises me that Dr Patel picked up on it."

"He's a bloody good doctor, sharp as they come," Matt said defensively.

"Did I say he wasn't? But, let's face it, he's no expert."

Matt decided to change tack. "And you don't think it was an accident?"

"I don't know yet, Chief Inspector." She snapped. "There was a puncture mark under the arm, just below the armpit, and if that was how a drug was administered, it makes an accident unlikely."

"Yes, Hari mentioned the underarm thing."

"Did he? Well, maybe he's sharper than I thought."

"Maybe he is," Matt said. "I'd be grateful if you could get the report to me as a matter of urgency. If it turns out to be murder, we need to start on this without delay."

"I realise that," she said, completely unsympathetic. "I'll do my best."

"You do that," Matt muttered and slammed the phone down.

He got up and opened his office door, looked across at Dilys who was sitting at her desk clicking away on her keyboard. "Dilys, got a moment?"

Dilys came in and settled herself in the chair opposite his desk.

"I've just had a call from the dreaded Curtis – God she irritates me – anyway, she says she thinks Caradoc could have been murdered."

"By what means?"

"Poison." He told her what Dr Curtis had said. "Interesting, isn't it?"

"I'll say," said Dilys.

"But she's not sure yet, there are more test results to come in."

"Right." Dilys sighed, then said, "But shall I brief the team anyway?"

"Yea, go ahead, that way we'll be able to hit the ground running."

"Will do."

"I'll have to apply for a search warrant. The chief isn't going to like that, but tough. And one of the first things on the list will be a thorough search of those stables – that'll mean a couple of officers who've got experience with horses, any ideas?"

"Well, there's Glyn Evans, he rides. He was brought up on a farm up the valleys, and I expect I can find someone else."

"Do that, would you?"

"Consider it done," Dilys said as she got up and left his office.

Matt sat for a moment, deep in thought, then grabbed his mobile from the desk muttering, "Sod it, why not?" and scrolled down to Fabia's number. She picked up almost immediately.

"Hallo, Matt, you just caught me." She sounded pleased to hear his voice. "We were about to go into Newport."

"Are you on your own?"

"Ye-es. Why?"

"You know you said your visitor has a connection with the Mansells."

"I did."

"Can you tell me how close a connection?"

There was a pause. "What's this about Matt?"

"Fabia! Just tell me. I need to know."

Fabia gave in to the urgency in his voice. "She's his granddaughter, from a relationship he had when he was in the army, in Mauritius."

"Is she now?"

"They'd only just discovered each other, so Caradoc's death has been a bit of a blow, to put it mildly. Come on Matt, what's up?"

"Pat Curtis thinks he was poisoned."

"Oh lord."

"She needs to get the results of a couple of tests before she'll confirm it, but it seems pretty certain. Of course, I can't move until I've got confirmation. As usual she sounded pleased about that."

"T'was ever thus with Pat." Fabia had worked with the pathologist in her days as a police officer.

She sounds as if she's still in the force, Matt thought, with a wave of regret that she wasn't.

"Things are going to kick off here if she's right. I'll have to interview the whole family, obviously, including your visitor. Remind me of her name?"

"Anjali Kishtoo. Look, Matt, we're about to go into Newport at John Meredith's request."

"Ah, John again," Matt muttered.

"What?"

"Nothing," Matt said.

"Anyway, he's seeing Rodric Mansell today, that's the eldest son, about Caradoc's will," Fabia went on. "Apparently, Caradoc made changes to it with Anjali in mind, and John wants us to stand by in case Rodric agrees to meet her. I really don't want to give her anything more to worry about, not yet, so I won't mention all this to her now."

"Changes to his will? That's interesting."

"It is, isn't it?" Fabia said, then added quickly, "but Anjali couldn't have had anything to do with his death, she was in London."

"You're very protective of her, given you've only just met her."

"I suppose I am, but I like her, she's a lovely girl, and anyway, she's a fellow artist."

"Of course, that explains everything," Matt said sardonically.

"Shut up, Matt. But do you agree I should keep this to myself for now?"

"Absolutely. As to the others, can you give me an idea of how many people might be involved, however tenuous?"

Fabia listed everyone who lived at White Monk Abbey. "And there's their neighbour, Ted Marsden. He's a right thorn in Caradoc's side apparently. Then there's Garan Price and his wife Sheryl, they run the Mynach Arms, which is part of the estate. Garan is Caradoc's illegitimate son and his mother, Bella, lived in the village until recently, but she's living in Bangor now. I know her quite well, since I nicked her for possession of cannabis when I was a lowly sergeant."

"What?"

Fabia grinned. "She's something of a gypsy, and a talented sculptor and potter. It was a very small amount of cannabis, for her own use, so I only cautioned her, but we ended up talking about art and that, although I wasn't painting professionally then. Anyway, we've stayed in touch and have been friends, off and on, ever since."

"You never fail to amaze me, Fabia," Matt said, but he soon got back to the matter in hand. "Mansell certainly spread it around a bit, are there any other children lurking in the woodwork?"

"Not that I know of," Fabia said.

"So, who else is there?"

"Well, there's David Harris, he's the estate manager; he and Megan are an item, but I don't think Caradoc knew."

"Would he have disapproved?"

"I'm not sure. He was something of a control freak, probably would have wanted a say on any man friend she may have."

"What a household, all a bit gothic, isn't it?"

Fabia laughed. "It is a bit."

Matt gave a gusty sigh. "I must get on." But he didn't want to end the call quite yet. "I– er– I missed having Sunday lunch with you. It's been a bit of a habit lately, hasn't it? Maybe next Sunday?"

"That'd be nice," was all she said, but he could tell she was smiling.

"Anyway, let me know how the meeting with John goes. I'll keep you posted on our progress."

"Thanks, I'll speak to you soon."

As he ended the call, he was feeling easier about his relationship with Fabia than he had in a while. He hoped she felt the same.

* * *

John Meredith was not looking forward to his meeting with Rodric. And, what was more, the damn man was late. They'd arranged it for half past ten and it was now nearly ten to eleven. At last he heard sounds of arrival in the outer office and a moment later his secretary, Stephen Powell, ushered Rodric in.

"I'll bring coffee," he said as he left the room.

"Thank you, Stephen," John said, and, coming forward to shake Rodric's hand he said, "Please, sit down."

"I'm sorry I'm late. Delma was nagging to come with me and it took me ages to persuade her not to. You seemed pretty definite you didn't want anyone else in on this meeting." Rodric, eyebrows raised, sounded a bit resentful.

"Best just you at the moment," John said, looking across at his visitor. What he saw was a pale replica of Caradoc, the chin weaker, the mouth not quite so firm. He wondered what on earth would happen to the estate now the old man was gone, but then remembered how reluctant he had been to take advantage of more modern methods and wondered if Rodric might actually succeed where his father had failed. He pulled himself together, speculation was pointless.

John pulled some papers towards him and took a deep breath. "Had your father mentioned that he was going to make some changes to his will?"

"He'd hinted at it a couple of times," Rodric said, frowning, "but it was a threat he often made when he thought he wasn't getting his own way."

"Well, this time he's actually gone ahead. There's no point in beating about the bush; the changes, I'm afraid, are substantial."

"What do you mean, substantial? What's he done now?"

The poor man has no idea, John thought, no idea at all. Before he could go on, the coffee arrived and John distributed cups, offered biscuits, glad of the opportunity to collect his thoughts. But there came a point when he could put it off no longer. He took a deep breath and launched into a slow but clear explanation, reading out the passages from the will that contained the major changes.

Fifteen minutes later Rodric was pacing about the room. "Christ Almighty. I cannot believe this. Are you sure? After all, this, this – what's her name again?"

"Anjali Kishtoo."

"This Anjali woman could be an impostor. I bet she is. You say she's got proof, birth certificates and photos and stuff, but they can be forged. How do we know they aren't?" He threw himself back into the chair opposite John's desk.

"Your father was positive she is his granddaughter. She brought photos of her grandmother, Prabha, as a young girl, at the age she was when they first met, and a letter your grandfather wrote to Prabha. As I told you, Dewi Jenkyns kept in contact with her for years; long after your father lost contact. There were photographs of them together that Jenkyns' daughter, Branwyn, found, and other letters as well."

"But all of that could have been fabricated," Rodric insisted stubbornly.

"There's also this," John said, and passed a small black and white photo across the desk to Rodric, who snatched it from his hand. It was a photo of a soldier, unmistakably Caradoc as a young man, looking down at the woman beside him. They were standing on a beach, tall casuarina trees to one side, black rocks to the other. She was looking up into his face, one hand on his arm, the other holding her sari to her shoulder, her dark hair falling in a long plait to her waist.

Rodric threw it back on to the desk. "Okay, but that could have been any woman that he met when he was in Mauritius."

At least, thought John, he seemed to have accepted that Caradoc had been to the island. "Yes, but on the back, in your father's distinctive handwriting, it says 'With my beautiful Prabha, July 21st, 1965'. Turn it over and you'll see." He watched as Rodric grabbed the photo and did as he suggested. "Your father gave it to me when he came to see me, on his way back from his meeting with Anjali in London last week, and that was when he finalised the changes to his will. He said it was the only photo he'd kept of her."

"Why? He was married to my mother, for God's sake!" It was a cry from the heart.

"Not at the time, and don't we all keep photos of people from our past?" John said gently. "I certainly have a couple of photos of ex-girlfriends. As far as I know my wife didn't mind, and I'm sure I'm not unique." Rodric said nothing and John went on in that same measured tone. "He was absolutely convinced of their relationship, Rodric, and I have few doubts about it myself."

"That's as may be, but if she's going to inherit the valuables, his stamp collection, the paintings, the jewellery – *my* mother's jewellery–"

"No. I thought the will made it clear that he's left anything that was specifically your mother's to Megan or to you. The entail is unbroken, the land, the properties, all those are left to you. And he's left those annuities to Rhiannon Giordano, Garan Price and the money to Garan's mother, Bella."

"Not exactly generous ones."

"I wouldn't say that," John said, a little impatiently.

But Rodric hardly heard him. "And what about the horses? How the hell am I going to explain that to Delma?"

John felt for him. He knew how difficult that would be. "I'm sorry, but I'm afraid that's what he decided. You know your father was never keen on expanding the stables to the extent that Delma has done. I think he was always rather afraid of horses."

"He hated them," Rodric said bitterly.

"I think there's a strong possibility Anjali won't want to keep them, so you could come to some kind of arrangement." John got up from his desk and took a chair nearer to Rodric. He leant towards him, his elbows on his knees. "Look, Rodric, I realise how difficult this is for you. I did try to reason with him at the time, but he'd made up his mind and, as his solicitor, I had to follow his instructions."

"Can we contest the will?" Rodric said suddenly, his eyes full of hope.

"I wouldn't advise it. It would cost a lot of money, and you've no guarantee of success. Why don't you wait until you've met Anjali? You may feel differently then."

"What do you mean, met her?"

"She came down to Newport at your father's invitation. He was planning to introduce her to the family, but by the time she arrived, he had collapsed. It's a very awkward situation for her."

"Awkward for *her*!" Now he was shouting.

The door opened a crack and Stephen peered in, eyebrows raised in enquiry, but John waved him away. He didn't think Rodric even noticed.

"She's staying with Fabia Havard. You know her, don't you? At least, your sister does."

"Of course I know Fabia. But how the hell has this Anjali woman come to be staying with her?"

"It's a long story. But Fabia has an exhibition in the gallery opposite, you know, the old chapel? I asked Anjali to wait there in case you agreed to meet her. Now, you really don't have to, not right now, but I think it might be a good idea. I think, once you've actually met her, you might find it easier to understand what your father has done."

Rodric frowned at him, chewing at his lower lip as he did so. John waited. Then Rodric sat back in his chair. "All right. Go on, fetch her, but I'm making no promises."

Chapter 11

"How long do you think we'll have to wait?" Anjali asked Fabia as they walked from the multi-storey car park to the gallery.

"I don't really know. I suppose it depends on how long it takes John to persuade Rodric to meet you." She didn't add that it also depended on whether Rodric agreed to do so at all.

"I feel quite sick at the prospect of this meeting."

"That's hardly surprising."

"But," Anjali added, "it's what my grandfather wanted, for us all to meet, so in a way it feels as though I'm fulfilling his wishes. Does that sound stupid?"

"Not at all," Fabia assured her. She could quite understand Anjali's worries. She felt nervous enough about it all herself.

And so they waited, distracted occasionally by a visitor, or by someone collecting a painting they'd bought, but both of them were preoccupied. Anjali paced about, Fabia watched her in sympathy, and when, at last, John's secretary appeared at the door, Fabia gave a sigh of relief. She called out to Anjali who was at the other end of the long room.

"Rodric has agreed to meet you," she told her.

Anjali put her hands up to cover her mouth, her eyes enormous above her fingers. "Oh dear. Fabia, you'll come with me?"

"If you want me to."

"Oh yes, I do." Anjali took a deep breath, straightened her back. "*Allon zi,* as they'd say at home."

Fabia quickly arranged for Paul Hewitt to keep an eye on the exhibition and then the two women followed Stephen across the road. He ushered them into reception and asked them to wait.

It wasn't long before John came out to greet them. He gave Anjali a reassuring smile then led them into his office. Rodric was standing over by the window. He turned as they came in. Except for a slight twitch to the corner of his mouth, his face was closed, giving nothing away.

"This is Anjali Kishtoo," John said. Fabia noticed he made no reference to her relationship to Caradoc. "And I believe you know Fabia Havard? As I told you, she's been kind enough to take Anjali in for a few days. Anjali, this is Rodric Mansell, Caradoc's eldest son."

"I am pleased to meet you," Anjali said, and Fabia noticed that her accent sounded stronger, probably due to her nervousness. She held out her hand and, after a moment's hesitation, Rodric shook it, gave an awkward little nod, but said nothing.

"Why don't we all sit down?" John suggested, filling the awkward silence. They settled in the chairs that he pulled forward and Fabia gave Anjali a reassuring smile. Rodric sat stiffly upright with his arms crossed.

Anjali plunged on. "I was very sad to hear about your father. I had only met him recently; in fact, I didn't even know of his existence until a few months ago. I wish I could have got to know him better."

"I'm sure you would," Rodric said, his voice tinged with sarcasm.

Anjali didn't react to his tone. "I suppose," she added hesitantly, "that you are my uncle."

"If your relationship to my father is proved, then you could say so."

Anjali's chin came up and Fabia admired her apparent calm. She guessed that it was taking quite an effort to maintain.

"I can understand your doubts," Anjali said. "It's occurred to me that we could have a DNA test, if you would like further evidence."

At this, Rodric had the grace to look a little embarrassed, but he didn't respond, and John intervened.

"That would be a good idea, just to confirm what you already believe, Anjali. But I have shown Rodric the birth certificates and photos. Did you find them convincing, Rodric?"

Before he could reply, Anjali put her hand in the pocket of her coat and brought out the small velvet pouch, tipped the contents into her palm and held it out to Rodric. "And I have this ring your father gave to my grandmother. She wore it all her life."

Rodric's eyes widened. He took the ring from her and looked at it. "That's our family crest," he said.

"I know," said Anjali, "he told me."

That's put him on the spot, Fabia thought, then immediately wondered why she was so much on Anjali's side in this situation; after all, she'd known the Mansells a lot longer. But she was a good judge of character, Matt and Cath had always said so, and she had faith in her instincts, which were telling her that Anjali was genuine. There was a clear-eyed honesty about her which was hard to doubt. But still, Fabia told herself, she must try to keep an open mind, particularly as she had her suspicions John was rather smitten and might not be able to be quite as objective as he should be.

* * *

"I've just heard from Pat Curtis," Matt told Dilys a couple of hours after his first conversation with the pathologist.

"That was quick," Dilys said, surprised.

Matt grinned. "Maybe she's not as much of a pain as I thought. Anyway, she's identified the drug that killed Mansell. Her final report should be coming through any minute." He glanced at his computer screen. "Ah, here it is."

Dilys came to read over Matt's shoulder. For a few minutes there was silence in the room.

"Well, it seems he died of heart failure induced by being injected with this animal tranquiliser." He pointed at a word on the screen. "God knows how you pronounce it."

"Give me a minute," Dilys said, and went to fetch her laptop. She clicked away for a few moments then turned it towards Matt, pointing at the screen. "This stuff is only licensed for use by vets, and the law states they must have the antidote with them whenever they're using it in case of accidents, which means whoever acquired it did so illegally, or is a vet. None of the family is, so far as I know."

"But if you own large horses, you'd probably know how to get hold of it."

"I suppose. Do you want me to find out which veterinary practice they use?"

"Yes, put Chloe Daniels onto it," Matt said.

"I've also got Glyn Evans and Dave Parry standing by," Dilys said as she sat down. "How many people are involved here?"

Matt glanced down at a scrap of paper on his desk. On it was the list he'd made after speaking to Fabia. He told Dilys what she'd told him.

"Rhiannon Giordano, that's a strange mixture of names," Dilys said. "How come?"

"Apparently she married an Italian immigrant who'd settled in Swansea. Seems it didn't last long."

"And you say that Garan Price is an illegitimate son, together with this newly found granddaughter who's from another relationship he had in Mauritius in the 1960s. He certainly put it about a bit," Dilys said, slightly disapproving.

"Seems so," Matt said. "She's actually staying with Fabia Havard at the moment."

"The granddaughter? How on earth?" Dilys asked, eyebrows raised.

Matt explained about Anjali's visit and the changes to Caradoc's will.

"Do you think she might be implicated?" Dilys asked.

"Fabia says not, but we'll have to check her out, obviously."

"Is there anyone else?"

"There's the neighbour, Ted Marsden, he and old Mansell were at loggerheads apparently. Why does his name ring a bell?"

As usual Dilys knew, she had a memory that was second to none. "He contacted us a couple of months ago, said the Mansells were encroaching on his land and he wanted it stopped, something to do with grazing horses."

"Ah yes. Pretty forceful bloke, as I remember."

"You could say that."

"But a hitter or a shooter rather than a poisoner, wouldn't you say?"

"Probably," said Dilys, "but you never know. Maybe he thought it would be poetic justice, given the horses."

"So, how are we going to go about this, Dilys?" Matt leant back in his chair and looked at his sergeant. "Like I said, we'll need a comprehensive search of the Abbey and the stables."

"That'll take some personnel. It's no mean size, that place."

"Can't be helped. Someone accessed this drug and we need to know who that was. We'll have to do a trawl through their computers and laptops, phones, tablets, whatever."

"The chief isn't going to like it." Dilys gave a rueful smile. "You know how he feels about influential local families. Look at his reaction when you nailed his MP friend in Pontygwyn. What's more, we're short staffed and under-funded, that's a given, so he'll use that as a reason for us not to go mob-handed."

"Chief Superintendent Rees-Jones can like it or lump it," Matt said, his voice hardening. "Granted, he's a dreadful snob, so us trawling around in the Mansell's dirty linen won't go down well, but murder is murder. Anyway, he's still smarting over the cock-up he made of clearing Fabia's name, so I think I can persuade him."

Dilys made no comment, but there was a gleam of satisfaction in her eyes. She and Matt were as one when it came to their boss.

Matt pushed himself up from his chair. "Right, let's go and brief everyone."

* * *

Rodric could remember little of the drive home that afternoon. His mind was in turmoil. Was there anything else that would come out about his father's past? They'd never been close, but he'd respected the old man and thought he knew him. Even when his mother had died, he'd never thought to blame him. Barely six years old at the time, he'd been too young to understand exactly what was going on. It was only as he grew older that he realised she'd probably committed suicide, although that had never been put into words. He just remembered her as a quiet presence, often ill, often taking to her bed, particularly after Megan was born. Nonna had always been there to look after them; she'd told them Mama wasn't well and they must be quiet and not disturb her.

Later, as a teenager, he'd been fourteen at the time, he remembered a boy from the village telling him Garan, whose mother ran the village shop, was his brother. He'd said, "My Mam says your Da is a randy old bugger". When he got home, with a spectacular black eye from the fight that ensued, his father had demanded to know what happened. He'd burst into tears and sobbed out accusations. He remembered it now as one of the few times his father had sat him down and talked quietly, explained that Garan's mother, Bella, was dear to him, but that their relationship hadn't lasted, although they were still good friends. That it had been her decision to keep the baby, and he'd promised her he'd always support Garan. In the end Rodric had felt quite glad to have a brother close by.

But now he was wondering how many other half-sisters or brothers were out there waiting to be discovered? He felt anger rising and slammed his hand down on the steering wheel. A second later, he realised he was about to drive straight past the Castellgwyn exit. He swerved across, prompting furious hooting from a van that nearly ploughed into his ancient Land Rover. Heart thumping, he told himself it'd be best to concentrate on the driving for the rest of the way home, but his mind still picked away at the revelations.

He was relieved there was no-one around when he got back and headed straight for his father's study. Quiet was what he needed, time to think and consider what to do next. But what could he do? He had found the evidence compelling, particularly the ring and the photo, and he was very much afraid she was who she said she was. Sitting down at the desk, he turned on the computer. He'd do some research on Mauritius and the background to his father's presence in the island. Maybe he'd find some flaws in her story.

He'd been back about half an hour when the door opened, and Megan came bursting in.

"Rodi! I saw your car and I've been searching all over for you. Why didn't you tell me you were back? What happened? What did John say?"

"Why don't we wait till everyone's here, then I can–"

"No! It's not fair to keep me in the dark," she insisted, her voice trembling.

He'd hoped to be able to talk to the family together. He'd had some vague idea there'd be safety in numbers, but he could see from the expression on his sister's face that she wouldn't be fobbed off.

"Sit down, Meggie," he said, resigned.

Megan sat down heavily in a chair opposite the desk, but Rodric couldn't keep still. He got up and began pacing back and forth. Hesitantly at first, he began to tell her about the morning's revelations. She gasped as he told her of Anjali's existence, but said nothing else until he had finished.

"I've agreed to the DNA test," he said, "but I haven't got much doubt that she is Father's granddaughter, what with the signet ring and all."

"But I thought Father was in Singapore when he was in the army. Mauritius? That's not anywhere near Singapore, is it?"

"No. I've just been checking on it. It's in the Indian Ocean, about 900 miles from South Africa. It was a colony then, and they were sent there to quell some sort of uprising. That part's true enough, there was a state of emergency declared in 1965 and British troops were brought in."

"And that was when he met this woman and–" she paused, then whispered, "and married her?"

"Oh my God, I hadn't thought of that." He threw himself into a chair and put a hand up to his forehead.

"It would mean," Megan's voice shook as she spoke, "that his marriage to Mother was bigamous."

"But surely John would have said."

"Yes, yes, of course he would."

Sister and brother gazed at each other in silent consternation, but not for long. "The thing is, Meggie," Rodric said as he continued his pacing, "I was planning to persuade Father to sell some of the paintings, and maybe his stamp collection, and now I can't do any of that. We desperately need the funds. In spite of the television people and their money, and I don't even know if that'll happen now, I think it'll take more than that to put the estate to rights. And as to the stables, you can just imagine what Delma's reaction is going to be."

Her eyes enormous, Megan gazed up at her brother, but before she could say anything else, with shocking suddenness, the silence was interrupted by a hammering on the front door.

"What on earth?" Rodric exclaimed and strode across the room to pull open the door. His sister followed in his footsteps and they both rushed through the hall. Rodric got to the front door first.

On the doorstep stood two plain clothes police officers: a tall, dark-haired man and a short, stocky woman who Megan recognized. Behind them were gathered several uniformed officers and the police vehicles they had arrived in were parked in the courtyard.

"Rodric Mansell?" the tall man asked.

"Y-yes. What's all this about?"

"I'm Chief Inspector Lambert, Newport police, and this is Sergeant Dilys Bevan, I believe you've met before."

"She was one of the ones that came when Father collapsed," Megan, who was standing just by Rodric's shoulder, told him in a breathy whisper.

"Can we have a word?" the chief inspector asked.

"Can I stop you?" Rodric said, but instead of sounding defiant he only succeeded in sounding stroppy.

"Well, that wouldn't be a very good idea."

"Like I said, what's it about? And who are they?" He waved a hand at the other officers in the courtyard.

"It'd be much better if we explained why we're here in private, don't you think?"

For a moment there was a stand-off, then Rodric's shoulders sagged and he stood back and led them into the hall.

As the chief inspector and his sergeant entered, Nonna appeared from the corridor to the kitchen, and Delma came rushing downstairs from the gallery.

"Rodi! Who are these people?" Delma demanded.

"Police," he said shortly.

"Again? What the hell do they want this time?" There was fear in her voice. "Where's Mike?" No-one answered her question.

As was so often the case, Nonna took charge. After glancing out at the cars and officers gathered in the courtyard, she said, "I think you owe us an explanation for this invasion, officer." Her voice was cold and calm, and Rodric was grateful for her intervention. "I can't imagine what business you have with us, and in such numbers. Don't you realise this is a house of mourning?" From anyone else this would have sounded ridiculous but, somehow, she invested it with quiet dignity.

"My apologies, but I think you'll understand once we've told you why we're here," the chief inspector said. "Perhaps I could have a word with you first, Mr Mansell?"

Rodric hesitated, looked from Megan's anxious face to Delma's, from Nonna's defiant one and back to the man standing before him.

"I think it's best you come through to the study," he said, and, turning on his heel, led the way across the hall, followed by the two police officers, and the three women.

When he got to the door, he turned. "Nonna, please," he said.

She gave a curt nod. "Megan, Delma, come, let Rodric sort these people out." There was no mistaking what she meant. The last thing Rodric saw, before he closed the door, was his sister looking stricken, his wife looking back over her shoulder with panic in her eyes, and Nonna calmly ushering them away towards the kitchen corridor.

Chapter 12

Matt and Dilys followed Rodric into a large room. Every inch of three of the walls that weren't occupied by bookcases, contained portraits – many with a distinct resemblance to the present-day family members – most of them in need of straightening on their hooks. In a bay window stood a shabby leather-topped desk. The opposite wall was occupied, in large part, by a grey marble fireplace, where sluggish flames flickered round stacked logs, giving little heat to the chilly air. Threadbare rugs covered the wooden floor, and in front of the hearth was an assortment of armchairs and a leather Chesterfield sofa. The whole place smelt of a mixture of wood smoke, damp and furniture polish.

Without offering them a seat, Rodric turned to the two police officers. "So, what is all this about?" he demanded.

"I'm sorry to say that the post-mortem on your father has revealed that he was injected with a strong animal tranquiliser which induced heart failure," Matt said, watching the man's face closely as he spoke. "The drug is only licensed for use by vets, but there's no doubt in the pathologist's mind that this was the cause of his death and we are, therefore, treating it as murder."

The blood drained from Rodric's face. He said one word, "No," then was silent.

"Do you know if any drug of this sort could have been stored anywhere at the Abbey?" Matt asked.

"No, no, of course it hasn't."

"In the stables perhaps?"

"No! Why would we keep such stuff on the premises? None of us is a qualified vet." There was an almost imperceptible emphasis on the word 'qualified'.

Interesting, thought Matt. "We understand," he went on, "that by law a vet must always have the antidote to hand in case of accidents. The post-mortem has shown that this was almost certainly no accident and, since it was used to inject your father, we're assuming it was acquired illegally; it was obviously *used* illegally."

Rodric didn't say anything further, he just glared at the police officers from under his brows.

"We will need to make a thorough search of the stables."

"But my wife won't allow—"

"The officers we have chosen for the task are experienced with horses. We'll also be searching the house and we'll need to take all computers, laptops and mobile phones for examination, including the ones used by your father. I have a warrant." Matt held out a piece of paper, but Rodric ignored it.

"Why on earth do you have to do all this?" Rodric demanded.

"Standard procedure, sir, in a case like this," Dilys said.

"And we'll be interviewing everyone individually," Matt said, "including Garan Price, who, I believe, is related to the family."

"He's my half-brother," Rodric said shortly.

"I would be most grateful if you'd inform everyone in the household that we need to talk to them," Matt said, "and ask them to make themselves available tomorrow morning."

"If you insist."

"So, perhaps we could get going," Matt said firmly.

For a few moments there was a silent stand-off but, in the end, Rodric gave in. "Oh, very well," he said and led the way out of the room.

* * *

The three women waited. Megan sat and chewed at a nail, looking scared and saying nothing. Delma paced up and down, her hands thrust deep into her trouser pockets, occasionally asking, "How long is this going to take?" and "What's going on in there?". The other two had no answer for her. Nonna kept herself occupied, did some washing-up, made a shopping list. Her movements were calm and precise. Only someone who knew her well would have known how tense she was.

She'd left the door wide open and, after about a quarter of an hour, sounds of activity filtered through to them. Nonna's hand stilled, pen held above her notepad, Delma stopped her pacing and Megan looked up, fear increasing in her eyes. There was a murmur of voices, the deep one of the chief inspector, and Rodric's lighter tones.

All three women made for the corridor, rushing along it, but Delma pushed the others aside and arrived in the hall first.

Rodric was standing by the open front door looking out. She grabbed at his arm. "What's happened? What are they doing?" she demanded.

"Are they coming back in again?" Megan asked, her voice low and trembling; then she noticed Dilys standing to one side and flushed to the roots of her hair.

"Yes," Rodric said shortly. "They want to search the Abbey, that's why so many of them have come."

"Search?" Nonna said. "What on earth for?"

"He says they suspect that Father– that Father was murdered." His voice shook on the word.

For a moment there was a cacophony of voices, each of the women questioning, denying, saying how ridiculous that was. Who would do such a thing? There must be some mistake.

At last, Rodric held up his hands. "Please. All of you. Quiet!"

Gradually the hubbub subsided. But not for long when, with a glance at his wife, he said, "They're going to be searching the stables."

"No!" Delma gasped. "They can't." She swung round to glare at Dilys. "You can't."

"I'm afraid it's necessary, Mrs Mansell."

"But you'll disturb the horses. Rodi, you must stop them."

"Delma, I can't, the chief inspector showed me a warrant."

"I'm going out there. I've got to be there."

She turned but her husband grabbed her arm saying, "No. Let them go ahead. He said the ones doing the stables know how to deal with horses. The others are going to go through the house."

"All of it?" Nonna asked, her eyes wide. "What on earth are they looking for?"

At the same time Megan asked, "Everywhere? Even the bedrooms?"

"Yes, everywhere," Rodric said flatly. "What's more, they want all our mobile phones, iPads, laptops, the lot."

At that moment the chief inspector came back in through the front door, followed by several officers who'd put on white all-in-one suits. Megan gasped and stepped closer to Nonna, who put her arm round her.

"Thank you for your co-operation," he said, addressing this to all of them. "Perhaps you could start off by handing over all the devices?"

"Well, you can't have my brother's" Delma said defiantly, "He's not here and he's got his phone and his iPad with him."

"We'll just have to check his at another time. For now, just tell us whose room is whose upstairs and some of us will make a start there – we'll be as quick as we can."

"Nonna," Rodric said, "could you show them upstairs?"

Several officers trooped after her as far as the gallery. The others heard her cool voice telling them which room was which, then she came back down, her face expressionless. "When do we have to give them our phones and all that?" she asked.

Dilys, who had been standing quietly to one side taking it all in, came forward. "Now would be best."

Nonna glared at her. "Oh, very well," she said. She rummaged in her pocket and held out her mobile.

"Perhaps you could put them all on here," Dilys indicated a heavy oak table to the side of the hall.

Nonna placed it on the table and, with bad grace, Delma and Rodric did the same. Megan said she didn't know where hers was, and Nonna told her, "It's in the kitchen Megan, I'll get it."

* * *

After about fifteen minutes there was a small collection of phones, iPads and laptops gathered on the table. Various police personnel had been dispatched to collect them from all over the house, and finally everything was packaged up into sealed plastic bags and carried out to a police van.

"Thank you very much for your co-operation," the chief inspector said to them all, then turned and made his way outside.

They all glared at his back as he went, then Nonna said quietly, "Let's all go into the study, Rodi, until they want to invade that as well, of course."

Obediently they followed in her wake.

Rodric walked over to the fireplace and stood facing it. He put up his hands and rested them on the mantelpiece, his head bent. None of the women sat down, they just stood in a group behind him.

Delma was the first to speak. "For God's sake Rodi, tell us what went on!"

He turned and ran a hand across his mouth then spoke slowly, "He said– he said that Father was poisoned. The post-mortem results are clear."

Megan sat down suddenly on the leather sofa, her face sickly white. "That's not possible," she whispered.

"I'm afraid it is." Rodric's voice was dull and matter of fact. "The chief inspector says they're confident the results are correct."

"They could have made a mistake," Nonna said quietly. "Mistakes have been made before."

"But it's nonsense. It was probably an accident," Delma protested. "Or it could have been suicide."

"No!" Megan protested.

Rodric looked at his wife, his expression unreadable. "They don't think so. And they're a hundred percent sure that a strong animal tranquiliser was used, the sort that vets use to sedate large animals."

Delma stared at him, aghast. "Are you accusing me, Rodi?"

"No, no, of course not, but I do need to know if you had access to anything like that, Delma, have you–"

"I cannot believe that you'd suggest anything so horrible. How could you, Rodric? You know only a vet can use that stuff. How dare you?" She stood defiant, glaring at her husband.

"But you are a vet, Delma," Nonna said, the malice in her voice quietly obvious.

"Not qualified, though," Rodric said hastily.

Delma turned her glare on Nonna. "Oh, I know, you'd love to pin this on me, wouldn't you?"

"Don't be absurd, Delma," Nonna said coldly.

"Yes, you would. I know you've always hated me."

"I really don't think–"

"Stop it! Stop it!" Megan burst out and slumped down onto the settee, covering her face with her hands. "I can't bear it."

Nonna sat down beside her and put an arm around her shoulders. "Ssh, cariad, don't upset yourself so." After a warning glance at Delma, then at Rodric, Nonna added, "So what else are they going to do?"

"After this search they'll be coming back tomorrow morning," he said, "and they'll be interviewing all of us, including your brother, Delma, so you'd better make sure he's here. The chief inspector made it clear we must all be here for that. Where is Mike anyway?"

Delma didn't meet his eyes. "He went to meet a friend in Swansea, just overnight. He should be back later."

Nonna gave her a contemptuous look. "Does anybody know what he's up to? He's been here for three weeks now? Doesn't he have a job to go back to?"

"You know he's between jobs, I told you, that's why he came to see me – us – now. I'm allowed to have my family to visit, aren't I?"

"Yes, yes, of course," Rodric said hastily, "but he does need to be here when the police come. You must text him."

"I can't very well do that since those bastards have taken my mobile."

"You can phone him on the landline," Nonna suggested. "I'm sure you remember his number. Whether or not he takes any notice is another matter. I get the impression he's not too keen on them."

"On whom?" Delma said haughtily.

"The police. He was talking about how he got the better of them just a few days ago."

"What are you suggesting?" Delma snapped.

"Shut up!" Megan shouted, her hands over her ears. "Don't you realise you're just making things worse with all this arguing?"

"Megan's right," Rodric said firmly. "We must stick together, not quarrel amongst ourselves. And I must contact Garan, warn him they'll be wanting to see him as well."

"Why Garan?" Delma asked.

"Because he's a member of the family."

"Only your father's–" Delma began, then caught Nonna's eye and subsided into silence.

* * *

Mike Cotter had enjoyed meeting his contacts in Swansea. He drove along the motorway, music blaring from the radio, ignoring the speed limit and feeling empowered and pleased with himself. They were so easy to manipulate, these idiots, and the last three weeks had been very useful. Apart from keeping him out of the limelight in London, he'd managed to get rid of quite a few odds and ends that had been burning a hole in his pocket and he'd helped Delma make a bob or two as well. What was more, the contacts in Bulgaria were proving very grateful for his networking.

He tried his sister's mobile, keen to let her know that he was on his way back and keep her on her toes. He was irritated that Delma didn't pick up. It was a pity he hadn't got the Abbey's landline number, but never mind, he'd bring her to heel when he got back. She was proving to be a little more difficult to handle than he'd expected, but he was pretty sure that, in the end, he'd be able to keep her under control. He knew too much for her to go rogue on him. He saw himself as the pivot around which others revolved, the puppet master pulling several interconnecting strings. He smiled in satisfaction as he came off at the Castellgwyn slipway. And now his dear little sister was going to inherit a tidy packet. That could be very useful, one way and another. The old boy's death couldn't have come at a better time. And as for that other matter, that could be even more useful, particularly if it

131

was proved the old man had been helped out of this world as Mike suspected. Okay, a police investigation could be somewhat inconvenient, with the spotlight being turned on his sister's family, but he'd had to deal with worse in the past.

His smile became broader. Yes, all in all things were going well. Maybe he'd pop into the pub before going back to the Abbey, make sure that idiot, Garan, was aware he was back and hadn't forgotten about what was owed. That'd round the day off nicely.

* * *

Sheryl had been to visit her brother in Chester. She'd left early in the morning and it was late evening when she returned, just after closing time. She found Garan sitting on a stool in the darkened bar, which was lit only by the lights behind the optics. He sat with his elbows resting on the counter, a large glass of brandy clasped in both hands. As she walked in, he looked round at her but said nothing.

"Hallo love," she said, bending to kiss his cheek, "what's up?" Her heart sank at his defeated look. She hitched herself up on to a stool beside him.

"He came in this evening."

"Who?" she asked, but in truth she knew.

"That fucking brother of Delma's, sitting there grinning and telling everyone what great butties we are, then making threats about the money I owe him."

"Did anyone hear him threatening you?"

"No. He made sure of that, he only said anything when no-one else was near." He took another gulp at his brandy. "He was going on again about how he'd told his pals in Swansea all about me, that they know how to deal with what he called defaulters. But it gets worse, Sheryl. He said he knows where Mam lives."

"How the hell did he find that out?"

132

"I don't know, do I? He said he might go and visit her, tell her all about her dear son's debts, that he might have some fun while he was there."

"Christ, that man is such a shit. Have you warned Bella?"

"I can't. I'd have to tell her about the money." He gave a twisted grin. "But I'd not give much for his chances up against Mam. She'd eat him for breakfast. When I spoke to her on Saturday, she was talking about coming down; she said she wanted to be here for us. I'll have to put her off in case she bumps into him. And then he had the flaming cheek to get me to fill up his hip flask, and with Penderyn malt too. Then he refused to pay once I'd done it, told me it'd go towards what I owe him."

"Garan, you must speak to Rodric. Tell him what's going on."

"I can't, not now the police are involved."

"What do you mean?"

Garan looked at her in consternation. "God, of course, you don't know yet," he said.

"What? Tell me."

"Rodi phoned earlier, the post-mortem on Caradoc has shown that he was poisoned. The police believe it was murder."

"Oh my God," Sheryl whispered.

"They were up there in force today, searching the whole place, taking away all the laptops and phones. I can't believe it. It's like living in a nightmare. Who would do such a thing?"

"They could be wrong."

"I doubt it. I don't think they'd have pitched up in such numbers if they weren't sure of themselves. Rodi said there was about ten of them. Given all that, you can see why I can't tell him about his stinking brother-in-law."

"I suppose. But maybe he had something to do with it."

"That'd be good. Not the old man being done in, but Cotter being arrested for it – that'd be really good."

"But what reason could he have?"

"I don't know. I've been going over and over it and I can't think of any motive he may have, unless Caradoc found out about his activities in Swansea and all that, but I can't see that as a strong motive, can you?"

Sheryl shook her head and frowned across at him. "So, what happens next?"

"They, the police, are descending tomorrow to interview everyone at the Abbey. They'll want to speak to us as well, Rodi says."

"Old Caradoc could be a bit of a pain at times, but deep down he was a good man, and he was always such a good friend to your Mam. When he died, I thought, well, at his age it was to be expected. But murder? That's dreadful, Garan, dreadful."

"Cotter hinted that I might be responsible, suggested I'd inherit enough to pay off my debts. He said he might mention that to the police."

"The bastard!" Sheryl said.

"But people could think that, couldn't they? Particularly if he starts shooting his mouth off."

Sheryl went behind the bar and lifted down a glass, poured some brandy into it and took a slow sip. She leant on the counter opposite her husband and said, her voice calm and measured, "No-one's going to listen to the likes of him. Perhaps Caradoc challenged him in some way."

"But how?"

"I don't know, do I? But who else is there?"

"Ted Marsden?"

"Over a bit of grazing?"

"It was more than that, and he's pretty fiery, he hates – hated Caradoc. You never know." He rubbed at his face, looked at his empty glass, but Sheryl wasn't going to let him have another. She reached for the glass and put it into the dishwasher along with her own, then came around and put her arm round his waist. "Come on, love, there's no point in speculating. Let's go to bed."

They turned off the lights and trudged up the stairs, but neither of them expected to get much sleep. Tomorrow, Sheryl decided, she'd phone Bella.

* * *

That evening Anjali went upstairs quite early. Fabia got the impression she wanted time on her own after the events and emotions of the last couple of days.

Fabia glanced at her watch. It was ten o'clock but she felt wide awake, definitely not ready for bed. She decided to go through what she'd sold at the exhibition and the commissions she'd been given. She'd rather taken her eye off the ball since she'd been concentrating on her visitor. But as she made her way to the dining room, her mobile rang.

"Hallo?"

"Fabia, it's me." Matt sounded tired. "Are you still up?"

"I am."

"Can I pop in, I'm just up the road."

"How come?"

"Well, actually, I was on my way to see you, then realised what the time was, so I thought I'd better ring first."

She grinned, delighted at the idea of seeing him and hearing how things were going, but she wasn't going to tell him that. "Okay," she said, "come on round."

Five minutes later there was a soft knock at the door. When she opened it, Matt was leaning against the side of the porch, hands thrust into his trouser pockets, the picture of untidy exhaustion.

"Sorry it's so late," he said.

"No worries," Fabia told him, and opened the door wider.

He loped into the hall and followed her to the kitchen. "Where's your visitor?"

"She went upstairs a while ago. She had some work to do on her laptop. Have you eaten?" she asked.

"No, too busy, been at it since six this morning. I seem to remember having a slab of lardy cake for breakfast, but nothing since then."

"Not exactly a healthy diet. Sit!" Fabia said.

She got out eggs, bacon and tomatoes, cut some slices from a crusty granary loaf and put them in the toaster. "Do you want coffee or wine?"

"Better be coffee, if I drink any wine, I'll doze off driving home." He leant his folded arms on the table and watched her as she went about preparing the food. When she'd placed a heaped plate in front of him, she poured herself a glass of wine and sat down opposite him. "Now tell me," she said, "what's been happening?"

"Like I told you earlier today," Matt said, through a mouthful of egg and bacon, "it looks like Mansell was poisoned with this animal tranquiliser. I put Chloe Daniels on to it–"

"The black girl with the lovely plaits?"

"That's the one, she's an excellent officer."

"I liked her. Bright as a button, I thought."

"I asked her to find out which veterinary practice the Mansells use. She's a fast worker is Chloe, came back to me within an hour. It's that big practice between Castellgwyn and Brecon, Dysart & Jennings, and the chap that's been dealing with the White Monk Abbey animals is a relatively new arrival by the name of Stewart Parker."

"You don't think it was the vet that injected Caradoc?"

"Anything's possible at this stage, but what motive?"

Fabia shrugged. "No idea. So, what else have you been doing today?"

Matt didn't say anything more until he pushed his empty plate away. "That was great," he said and accepted more toast from Fabia. "Got any of that plum jam of yours?"

Fabia smiled as she went to the fridge. "You'd eat that stuff by the spoonful given half a chance."

"No, on toast will do." He spread the jam liberally, took an enormous bite, chewed for a bit then said, "Now, where was I?"

"What else you've been doing since we spoke earlier."

He pushed back his hair, which promptly fell back over his forehead. "Once Pat had confirmed he was poisoned, we got the team together and went up to the Abbey."

"I bet they welcomed you with open arms."

"Of course," he said, then added, "actually it wasn't as bad as I expected." Matt went through the family's contrasting reactions. He made Fabia smile at some of his vivid descriptions: Nonna's cool contempt, Megan's panic, Delma's fear and Rodric's unsuccessful efforts to keep control of the situation.

"The treasures in that place are incredible," he said.

"Tell me about it! Did you know they have a couple of paintings by Huw Wystan Jones?"

"Who's he?"

"Matt! He was a Welsh impressionist, as good as some of the French school. I love his work."

"That can only add to your friend's inheritance," Matt said, then added. "You'd have thought someone would go for the granddaughter rather than the old man."

"But none of them knew she existed until a couple of days ago."

"Are you sure about that?"

"Ye-es, as sure as I can be. Rodric certainly didn't know until John Meredith told him. I was there when they were introduced, I could tell. Why do you ask?" Fabia said.

"Well, that inheritance could present several people with a strong motive. Most of those we've talked about for a start."

"True. You're definitely not hard up for suspects." Fabia grinned at him and Matt scowled back.

"Thanks for stating the obvious. Of course, there could be someone we don't even know about yet; some old enemy who's crawled out of the woodwork. Apparently, he wasn't the easiest person to deal with."

Fabia got up to make him another coffee and replenish her glass of wine. "You'll need to get on to John Meredith, get a look at the details of that will."

Matt's scowl turned to a glare.

"Of course," Fabia added hastily, "I realise you would have thought of that."

"What I wanted to ask you is," Matt went on, "what's your impression of them all and their relationships? It'd be really useful to get some background before we do the detailed interviews with the family, and you've known them for some time, haven't you?" Matt said. "So, tell me about the present family tensions."

Fabia frowned, where should she start?

Matt noticed her hesitation. "Fabia, I need to get a feel for these people. Okay, I met them all this morning, but they were obviously on their guard. Other than John Meredith, who has an obligation to them as their solicitor, I don't know anyone else to ask."

"Okay, but these are just impressions, nothing concrete."

"Fine," Matt said, sounding impatient.

"Don't snap at me!"

"Sorry."

Slowly and rather hesitantly Fabia began to describe her impressions of the Mansells, her family's connections with them and her renewed contact since she and Megan had begun to work together. Amongst other things, she told him how Rodric had married Delma at university without even telling his family; that Megan and David Harris were an item but Caradoc didn't know; that the whole family disliked Delma's brother and resented his presence; and, finally, that Nonna, the ever-present mother figure, watched over them all with firm benevolence.

Matt surprised her by saying, "You know those fairy stories of Megan's? I think your style would suit that kind of thing."

"Do you think so?"

"Yes. Fine pen and ink stuff, you're good at that."

"Thank you," she said, pleased and slightly embarrassed by this praise. She quickly changed the subject back to the Mansell family. "And of course, there's Garan Price. His mother, Bella used to run the village shop. She and Caradoc remained good friends. In fact I believe Bella was one of the few true friends he had."

"We'll be interviewing Garan Price. Do you know when his mother moved?" Matt asked.

"Yes. When the powers that be took the post office away, the shop closed, and that's when Bella moved up to Bangor. She's living in an artists' commune up there, suits her down to the ground."

"Sounds like you got to know her well after that cannabis incident."

"I did," Fabia said, smiling. "Fellow artists and all that."

They sat in silence for a couple of minutes, each lost in their own thoughts, then Matt pushed himself up from the table. "Well, I must get going. Early start again tomorrow."

"No rest for the wicked," Fabia said. "And, Matt, I don't mind you coming to pick my brains. You know me, I'd much rather be involved than not."

"You, Fabia? Surely not!"

She gave him a soft punch on the arm and grinned, but she was serious a moment later. "I know the family are friends, but if a killer's to be caught, those personal considerations have to be put aside, don't they?"

As they walked down the hall, she was looking so anxious that Matt laughed. "Don't worry, I'll keep you in the loop."

When they got to the front door, he turned to face her. They were standing very close. Matt put up a hand and cupped her cheek and, for a long moment, neither of them moved or spoke, then Matt said, "Fabia, I–"

But the mood was broken by the sound of a door upstairs being closed.

Matt dropped his hand to his side. "And given who your house guest is, you're already rather involved, aren't you?"

Fabia took a deep breath, trying to steady her heartbeat. She said, "I suppose I am."

Having waved Matt off, she made her way back to the kitchen, wondering what would have happened if Anjali hadn't been there.

Chapter 13

At the end of a long day, Matt and Dilys sat in his office. He wanted her help to get things straight in his mind. The white board in the corner of the room bore witness to his deliberations, but he felt as if he was getting bogged down.

"Okay, let's start with Rodric Mansell," Matt suggested, "what did you think?"

"Not a particularly strong character," Dilys said.

"That's what Fabia thinks."

Dilys made no comment. "I think he was probably a bit in awe of his father, but I'd say he cared about him. He seems genuinely upset by his death."

"I thought so too, but murder *is* upsetting, whatever the circumstances. Was it the death or the means that affected him most?"

"I'd say both, and he seemed to know nothing about the changes in the will before his father died, which is what would present him with the strongest motive."

"Of course, he could be lying," Matt said, "but I get the feeling he wouldn't be a particularly good liar."

"I agree."

"Did you notice he said he leaves the stables entirely to his wife? He was very firm about that. Do you think he realised how that came across?"

"You mean when it comes to the tranquiliser?"

"Yes." Matt frowned. "I'm not sure. He doesn't seem to be a devious character and I wouldn't have thought he'd deliberately drop his wife in it, that'd be pushing it a bit, even if they aren't on good terms."

"I don't know so much," said Dilys, more of a cynic than Matt. "But still, he didn't strike me as the vindictive sort, and you'd have to be to do that, wouldn't you? On the other hand…"

"On the other hand, what?" asked Matt when she didn't go on.

"Well, when we were questioning her about the use of a tranquiliser and asked about the vet, she went bright red and lost it a bit."

"Yes, I noticed that."

"What if she's been having an affair with the vet and her husband found out?"

"That's something of a leap," Matt said, "but it's worth a bit more investigation. Has the vet– what's his name?"

"Stewart Parker from Dysart & Jennings," Dilys said.

"Has he been told we want to speak to him?"

"Not yet. Best just turn up, I think, don't want him forewarned."

"True," Matt agreed. "What did you think of her otherwise?"

"Delma?" Dilys said. "I think she's a much more complex character than her husband. Interesting that she was studying to be a vet."

"Yes, Mrs Giordano made sure we knew that, didn't she?"

"I don't think there's any love lost between her and Delma Mansell," Dilys said. "I wonder at what stage she dropped out of her degree. Do you want me to do a bit more probing on that?"

"Please," Matt said. "Another thing about her, I got the impression she's very worried about her brother's activities."

"She certainly didn't like us asking how long he'd been in Wales. But then, if she knows about what he's been up to, I suppose it follows that she'd be defensive."

"After all the work she seems to have put into those stables, you can hardly blame her for being angry about the terms of her father-in-law's will – it's a bit of a slap in the face."

"I know. Do you think her obsession with the horses provides her with a strong enough motive?"

"I don't know." Matt leant his elbows on the desk. "And why the old boy? Wouldn't you have expected her to go for Anjali Kishtoo rather than him?"

"But they didn't know about her."

"True."

For a few minutes they sat in silence, both preoccupied with their own thoughts. Matt got up and stood in front of the white board, studying it for a moment. "The sister," he said, "Megan. She seems very upset about her father's death – more so, I thought, than the rest of them. Fabia told me she was scared of him, but then, I think they all were in their own way."

"I wish I'd met him," Dilys said. "He wasn't there when we went up to see about that silver. It's so much easier to understand the motivations and all that if you know the victim."

"But we very rarely do."

"I suppose."

"And then there's Mrs Giordano, Nonna. Isn't that Italian for granny?"

"Yes."

"But isn't she their aunt?"

Dilys shrugged. "Maybe it's a diminutive of her name."

"What did you think of her?"

143

"She seems a very calm person, but it could be like a swan, lots of stuff going on under the surface."

"I found out that she came to live at the Abbey after her Italian husband deserted her. She's been like a surrogate mother to Rodric and Megan. I wonder if there was more to her relationship with her sister's husband than just helping out with the children."

"Hard to tell. Why don't you ask Fabia?" Dilys said with a little smile.

Matt glared at her. "Shut up, Dilys."

Her smile turned into a full-blown grin, which Matt chose to ignore. Once again, he glanced at the whiteboard.

"And then we come to our friend, Mike Cotter."

"Well now, there's someone I'd like to take down," Dilys said.

"You and me both."

"Did you see the way he looked at me while we were interviewing him on Saturday? Slime ball."

"I did. He's certainly a nasty piece of work, the stuff Tom Watkins has turned up on him proves that. But, in relation to this, what motive would he have for getting rid of Mansell senior?" Matt asked.

"Maybe the old man found out about his activities."

"Possible, but I'd expect him to lash out rather than use poison."

"Perhaps he wanted to make it look as if someone else had done it."

Matt's eyes widened. "Now that, Dilys, is a definite possibility."

"Have we got any more on what he's been up to?"

"No," Matt said. "And since he wasn't there today, I don't think we can do much else about him at the moment. Just get Tom to keep a weather eye and glean as much as he can from his Swansea contacts." Matt rubbed at his eyes then glanced at his watch. "Come on, Dilys, that'll do for today; let's shut up shop and start fresh tomorrow."

***

Fabia had found it very difficult to settle to anything all day. As a distraction they'd gone out to do some shopping earlier and she'd introduced Anjali to Reynold's cheese shop in the High Street. Then Anjali had made a bee line for a newly opened fabric shop and spent ages talking to the woman who ran it. Now Fabia was preparing supper, pottering around the kitchen, her mind miles away from what she was doing as she wondered how Matt was getting on. When the phone rang, her heart leapt, but it wasn't Matt.

"Fabia? Is that you?" The hesitant voice was instantly recognisable. Megan.

"Hallo, Megan. I'm so sorry to hear about your father, it must be dreadful for you all."

"Oh Fabia, it's all so *awful*." There was a sob in her voice. "The police were here for ages today, questioning everyone. They go on and on and it's so difficult to work out what they think."

"I'm afraid they have to do that, Megan."

"But it's ridiculous. No-one would want to harm Da, no-one."

"However," Fabia said as gently as she could, "it seems someone did."

Megan ignored this. "I know he could be a bit difficult at times, but deep down he was such a dear. It could have been an accident."

"Could it?"

"Well, I know that wasn't what the post-mortem said." She seemed to take it for granted that Fabia knew what the result was. "But they could have made a mistake. You know about these things from when you were in the police. Surely there've been times when they got it wrong, haven't there?"

"I suppose, but not often. I believe the results were pretty conclusive."

"Have they interviewed you too then?"

"No, Megan, but I have spoken to–" Fabia could have kicked herself, stupid to say such a thing.

"To someone who's part of the investigation? Who?"

Fabia ignored this question, tried to change the subject. "I'm sure you want whoever is responsible to be caught. I know how unpleasant an investigation like this can be, and I'll support you in any way I can, but it has to be got through, and the more information you give the police, the sooner it'll all be over."

"Can I come around to see you tomorrow? It'd be such a help."

It occurred to Fabia that it might be useful to Matt if she talked to Megan. Without thinking she said, "Of course you can." And then she wondered if it'd be awkward, given Anjali's presence in the house, but she could always keep out of the way while Megan was there.

"Getting away from here would help so much. Did you send the chapters to your agent – what's her name?"

"Sheena Matthews. Yes, I did, she's interested to meet you, but maybe this isn't the time."

"But Fabia, it would help so much. It'd take my mind off this horrible business."

Fabia felt a little taken aback by this but didn't comment directly. "Well, if you're sure it would help."

"Can I come before lunch tomorrow?" Megan interrupted.

"That'd be fine."

"I know it may seem strange that I want to talk to you about the book, but I want to talk about everything else as well," Megan assured her. Her voice dropped to a breathy whisper. "I'm so worried, Fabia. What if Rodi was involved, or Delma? She was always arguing with Da about the horses. And there's that brother of hers, I wouldn't put anything past him."

Fabia didn't know how to respond to this. But she didn't have to as a moment later Megan said, in a totally different tone of voice, "Yes, yes, that's very kind, thank you. Goodbye." And the call was abruptly ended.

She guessed that someone must have interrupted the call and wondered who it had been. But there was nothing she could do about it, so there was no point in worrying, she told herself firmly.

* * *

Yet again there was a ringing, but this time it was Fabia's mobile and one glance at the screen told her it wasn't Matt. But still, it was someone Fabia was delighted to hear from.

"Hallo, Bella," she said. "I was wondering whether or not to give you a ring. How are you?"

But there were no preliminaries with Bella. "Fabia, what the hell is going on? Garan told me about Caradoc's death. He can't be dead, Fabia, I only spoke to him a couple of weeks ago." It was obvious she assumed Fabia would have all the details.

"I'm really sorry, Bella, but it's true."

"Sheryl sent me a rather incoherent text this morning saying there was more to it and that she'd phone later, but she hasn't. I couldn't get hold of her until this evening, and now she tells me the police are involved and they think he was murdered."

"She's right. I'm afraid it's been confirmed by the post-mortem. He was poisoned."

She didn't question it, just asked, "What with?"

"A hefty dose of some animal tranquiliser."

"Oh my God!" There was silence on the other end of the line for a moment, then Bella asked, "The sort they use on horses?"

"And other large animals," Fabia said, judiciously.

"But which of– I mean who would do such a thing?"

"I've no idea, Bella. It's only the start of the investigation. My friend Matt Lambert is on the case. Do you remember him?"

"Of course I do. He's that gorgeous man you used to work with, isn't he?"

"Yes. He's good, and he's got a great team in Newport. I'm sure they'll find out who did it."

"Do you think it has anything to do with Caradoc's will?"

Fabia was surprised by this question. "What do you mean?"

Bella went on, her tone a little tentative. "Caradoc told me he was going to make changes, but he wasn't specific. I knew he was a bit of a tight wad, used to tell him he had a hedgehog in his pocket, so I asked him outright if my Garan would be okay and he assured me he would – he was adamant he wouldn't be changing that part of the will. I believed him because he always told me he'd look after my boy. The thing is, there was the other family – the one in Mauritius – he'd been thinking about them a lot lately."

Fabia's eyes widened in surprise. "How on earth did you know about them?"

"He told me about them ages ago, bless him. I think I was the only one he had told in fact. We used to talk a lot when he came around to see me, we'd play backgammon and just talk, oh, about everything." Her voice broke slightly, and Fabia could hear her take a deep breath before she went on. "I think he found it a release, to be able to talk freely without all of them watching his every move and reacting to his every growl. And he knew I wouldn't repeat anything he said."

"You were a very good friend to him, Bella."

"I suppose." There was still a catch in her voice. "Garan was a mistake, a glorious one so far as I'm concerned, I love my boy to bits, but if the truth were known, Caradoc and I were never really suited. After those first few encounters, we decided just to be good friends. I was very fond of him and enjoyed his company and I think, in a way, we stopped each other being lonely. Can you understand that?"

Fabia smiled. "Of course I can."

"I can't believe he's gone. He was such a– a force of nature. I wonder if his daughter in Mauritius should be informed? What was her name? Something like Serena or Sabita."

Without thinking, Fabia said, "Sabita; she's been told."

"How come? Rodric and Megan don't know she exists, at least, that's what Caradoc told me."

"There've been a few developments, love," Fabia said. She took a deep breath and told her quickly about Branwyn Pierce's researches and the final result. "Did you know about Anjali?"

"No. Just about his first wife, as he called her, though I don't think they were actually married, and he told me about their daughter. But when he mentioned changing the will, I knew there was more to it. He did hint that he might have some interesting news for me soon, but he wouldn't tell me any more than that. I had no idea all this had been going on. I've been away for the last week, on a yoga retreat, but that's no excuse. I feel really bad now. Oh, Fabia, what a mess."

"It is a bit," Fabia said sympathetically. "So, you obviously weren't aware that he and Anjali had met up in London about ten days ago?"

"No, no idea at all."

"And no idea he'd changed parts of his will in her favour?"

There was a gasp from the other end of the line. "Oh lord, that's what he meant. Garan didn't tell me anything about that."

"Maybe he doesn't know yet," Fabia suggested.

"Maybe. What on earth has Caradoc done?" Fabia could visualise Bella running a hand through her mass of dark hair. "He was always impulsive, just like me. Garan wouldn't be here if we weren't, but I always thought he was determined to keep the estate intact, to pass it on to his legitimate children."

"I don't think that's changed, anyway the estate is entailed. But he has left a large part of the contents of the Abbey, and the stables, to Anjali, in spite of the fact he and her grandmother weren't married."

"But that wouldn't have weighed with him," Bella said. "Look at how good he's been to Garan, in spite of the waves of disapproval from Elizabeth's sister."

"Rhiannon? Did she disapprove?"

"I'll say, bloody Nonna. She used to cut me dead if we met in the village. It didn't bother me, I'm too much of a gypsy to care what people think of me. I put it down to her religion. She's a devout Roman Catholic, Elizabeth escaped it, I think, but Rhiannon stuck with what their parents believed. She thought it was all very immoral, Caradoc and me, and then when Garan was born, oh lord what a fuss!"

Fabia smiled. "I know what you mean about her. I don't think she approves of me either. She said something about artists when I was staying at the Abbey, what was it? Oh yes, how nice it must be to be able to do a little bit of painting, how she wished she had the time. I got the message."

"That sounds just like her. But she's always been completely devoted to the family. She's run that place like clockwork for years. You can't fault her for her devotion to them. I think she might have been a bit in love with Caradoc, but he wasn't interested, and I don't think it lasted long with her. Given how hard she worked for them all, I used to tell Caradoc he was damn lucky to have her."

"Look, Bella, there's something else. Anjali came down to Newport to meet him but, by the time she arrived, it was too late."

"Oh, poor girl."

"Yes, and, well, she's still here. She's been staying with me since last Thursday."

Bella reacted in a way typical to her. "Thank goodness you were there to scoop her up," she said, and then asked, "Is she going to meet up with the rest of the family?"

"She met Rodric, through their solicitor. He wasn't particularly welcoming. They've got a DNA test planned, but I don't think he doubts that she's Caradoc's granddaughter."

"I'm going to come down, Fabia. I want to see my boy anyway, and Sheryl's a bit worried about him. One thing she did tell me, this was before I went away, is that Delma's brother has been staying at the Abbey; Mike something or other, she says he's an absolute shit."

"His name's Mike Cotter, and Sheryl's right."

"She thinks he's responsible for Garan going back to gambling," Bella said, "which is very worrying. Sheryl said she thinks he's been threatening Garan."

"That wouldn't surprise me. Would you like me to mention it to Matt Lambert?"

"Would you?"

"Of course."

"Thank you, Fabia."

Fabia heard her take a deep breath.

"Right," Bella said. "It's definitely time for me to come and check everything out. Can we meet up?"

"Of course, let me know when you get to Castellgwyn and we can organise something."

"Thank you, my friend. It'll be like old times. And I'll bring you one of my new pots, I think you'll like them."

They ended the call and Fabia tried Matt's mobile, but it just rang and rang, so she sent him a quick text. She sighed as she put the mobile back in her pocket. Bella was right, it was one hell of a mess.

Chapter 14

It was a bright morning and Mike was very pleased with himself. Things were going well, in spite of the police interfering with his business activities. No way was he going to let them get anywhere with that.

He grinned to himself, thinking back to his conversation the day before. He prided himself on being a good judge of character and he'd got it right this time. He'd laid down his conditions: regular but reasonable payments – it was never a good idea to push too hard – but he'd made sure his terms had been clearly understood. There was no doubt in his mind this target could wriggle out of paying up – there was too much at stake. And if there was any sign of it, he'd come down hard. He grinned again at the thought.

Carrying his golf clubs over his shoulder, and jingling the car keys in his hand, he made his way to the Porsche, and patted the bonnet. A round of golf at Celtic Manor was just what he needed; perhaps he could do some networking. It had been a good idea to take out that short term membership. He slung the clubs in the boot and set off. As he drove through the gateway, he gave the stone dragons the finger. Ostentatious crap. If this bloody family thought they were going to get the better of him, they had another think coming. First, another good strong cup of coffee at the pub, which he wouldn't be paying for – that weakling, Garan, always gave in to a bit of pressure – and then he'd be on his way. As usual he drove at speed, down the lane from the Abbey to Castellgwyn, and screeched to a halt in the pub car park.

It was just after he got onto the motorway, half an hour later, that he began to feel sleepy and wondered why. It hadn't been a heavy night and that poor sod hadn't retaliated when he hit him. Mike flexed his fingers and grinned; that had been a good punch, it would teach the bugger a lesson. Then he frowned, shook his head. He was finding it hard to concentrate. What the hell? The car in front seemed to be accelerating then slowing, accelerating then slowing. God, the driver had to be some kind of dickhead. A moment later his vision became blurred and he shook his head again, trying to clear the fog, but it was no good. The Porsche seemed to be swerving to the left of its own accord. He heard a clamour of hooting and came to just long enough to see the tailgate of the juggernaut in front bearing down on him.

* * *

Anjali and Fabia were both working in the dining room, Anjali on her laptop, Fabia on a drawing pad. A companionable silence had reigned for some time, but it was interrupted by the ringing of the doorbell.

"That'll probably be Megan," Fabia said.

Anjali looked up. "I think I'll keep out of the way, if that's okay with you."

"Of course," Fabia said, and went into the hall to open the door.

Megan was standing there looking around her nervously, as if she thought she was being followed.

"Come in, come in," Fabia said, at which she scuttled in and Fabia closed the door.

"Should I take my shoes off?" Megan asked as she unwrapped two scarves from round her neck and brushed herself down.

"No need," Fabia said.

"I told the others I had some shopping to do in Newport," she said, running her hands through her untidy hair. "I didn't want them to know where I was going." She took a deep breath and, lowering her voice, asked, "Is she here?"

"Who?" Fabia asked, knowing she had to tread carefully.

"Father's– our – his granddaughter? John Meredith told Rodi she was staying with you."

"She is. Come through to the kitchen, I'll make us some coffee."

Obediently Megan followed her along the corridor, looking around as she did so, as if Anjali would spring out from some corner or other. Fabia was glad she'd stayed in the dining room. While she switched on the kettle and got mugs out, she said to Megan, "How are things at home? It must be very difficult for you all."

"Oh Fabia, it's so awful. The police questioned us all yesterday, asking so many questions. It was so confusing, my head was buzzing, and when they'd gone, I tried to remember what I'd said and couldn't remember a thing. Nonna said it wasn't the same officers that came and took Mike in for questioning on Saturday."

"Mike? Delma's brother?"

"Yes, they came really early. I was still asleep. I don't know why they came at that sort of hour."

Fabia found this very interesting, but all she said was, "Probably so they could be sure to catch him, before he went to work or out or something."

"I suppose so. But he doesn't work, he's on holiday; at least, that's what Delma calls it. She says he's between jobs, but I suspect he's not desperately keen on proper work. He came back mid-morning and wouldn't tell us anything

154

about it, just demanded to know where Delma was and went out to the stables to find her. When they got back into the house, she looked dreadful – poor girl. I actually feel a bit sorry for Delma, having such a – well – such an awful brother."

That was pretty critical for Megan, Fabia thought as she put a mug of coffee down in front of her visitor and pushed the sugar bowl across the table towards her.

"I really don't like him. I always like to find something positive about a person, but I've completely failed with him," Megan said.

"I've only met him the once, when I spent the weekend with you, but I have to say I'm inclined to agree with you."

"He's a bit scary, isn't he? Do you think he had anything to do with Da dying?"

"I've no idea, Megan," Fabia said firmly.

Megan gulped down some coffee then looked at Fabia, looked away again, then back. Fabia expected her to say more about the police and their questions, but she didn't.

"Rodi told me that Da changed his will, that he's left lots of things to– to Anjali. I don't really mind, I'm not that bothered about possessions."

Fabia thought this was probably true.

"But Rodi does mind. He says he was going to try to persuade Da to sell some of the paintings and stuff, and now we can't sell any of it because soon it won't belong to us anymore," Megan continued.

"It's very difficult for you both," was all Fabia could find to say.

"But still, I'm sure we'll find a way through. And part of me is so pleased to find Anjali. I know that may seem strange to you, but I don't think Rodi and Delma are intending to have children, and I just feel that finding her, our niece, has to be, well, positive."

"It's good of you to look at it that way."

"The thing is, Fabia," Megan went on in a rush, "I really think it'd be only fair if you could introduce me to her."

Fabia couldn't think how to respond to this, so she said nothing and waited for Megan to go on.

"I know Rodi has met her, when he was in John Meredith's office, but I got the impression from what he said that he wasn't very welcoming, and I thought, well, we should welcome her, shouldn't we? Because she's family, isn't she? And she came all this way to see Da and then he was in hospital, and then he died, and, well, it must be awful for her."

Fabia had known Megan for a long time and never found her devious, but this surprised her, and she wondered how honest she was being; maybe even deceiving herself. Was it curiosity that was prompting her? Or self-interest? It was hard to tell.

"All of this must have been a terrible shock for the whole family," Fabia said, feeling that she was stating the obvious.

"It has been. Everything's been turned upside down. I expect the police will come back again and again. I wish they'd just leave us alone."

"But, as I said yesterday, Megan, they do need to find out what happened."

"I realise that, but I think they've got it all wrong." She leant forward across the table. "They've taken all our laptops and computers. How am I going to go on with the book if I haven't got my laptop? It's really not fair."

"I don't think fairness comes into it," Fabia said quietly. "It's all part of the investigation into your father's death. They must find out who killed him, and why."

Megan winced and Fabia decided it was time to be firm. "Megan, love," she said gently, "a post-mortem has been done which proved that your father didn't die of natural causes, he was poisoned. I really think you need to accept that."

Megan gazed across at Fabia. "I know, I know," she said, her pale blue eyes anguished. Then she seemed to perk up a little. "But that's partly why I want the distraction of getting on with the book. Have you managed to get a meeting with the agent?"

Fabia was getting used to Megan's birdlike habit of flitting from one thing to another, one moment talking about the will, then anxious to meet Anjali, then the next moment eyes full of pain over her father's death, and now back to her book. She had a habit of almost childlike changes of mood from dark to light.

"Sheena's away for the rest of this week, she'll be back on Saturday. I could arrange a meeting for next week, say Tuesday afternoon."

"Oh, please do that. It'd help so much to have that to concentrate on."

"Fine. I'll get on to her and let you know."

"I hope you don't feel I'm being unfeeling, Fabia."

"No, of course not." But before she could say anything more, there was an interruption.

"I– I'm sorry to but in." Anjali was standing in the doorway with Fabia's mobile in her hand. "It's just that your phone, Fabia, it's rung three times and I thought it might be important."

Megan jumped up and said, "Oh!" then put a hand to her mouth.

Fabia took her phone and glanced quickly at the screen. The missed calls were all from someone who'd commissioned her to do a painting of her house, a rather pushy woman Fabia hadn't taken to. She put her mobile down on the kitchen table. "I'll deal with those later." She took a deep breath, "Anjali, this is Megan Mansell, Caradoc's daughter."

"And," said Megan quickly, "I think I can call myself your– your aunt, can't I?"

"I suppose you can," Anjali gave her a cautious smile, "if you believe your father was right about our relationship."

Anjali held out her hand and Megan took it between both hers. "Rodi told me that you've agreed to a DNA test, but he said he didn't have much doubt that you're our niece. He told me about the signet ring. I don't really think a test is necessary. Can we talk a little?"

"Of course," Anjali sat down.

"I'll leave you two alone," Fabia suggested, getting up.

"No, no," Megan said as she sat down again, "please stay, Fabia. After all, this is your house."

Fabia noticed that Anjali looked relieved at this.

"I'll make some more coffee."

As she switched the kettle on again and took down another mug, Fabia studied the two women sitting opposite each other. They couldn't have been more different, the one darkly elegant – her eyes wary but her hands still and calm on the table before her – the other untidy, with wild hair and clothes in a mess, her anxious eyes flicking from Anjali to Fabia.

Megan was the first to break the awkward silence. "I'm so glad to meet you," she said in a rush. "I was hoping I would if I came to see Fabia. Sorry Fabia," she added with a sideways glance.

Fabia just smiled as she handed over mugs and pushed a packet of biscuits into the middle of the table, then she sat down and prepared to take it all in.

* * *

On Wednesday morning Matt had, as usual, got into his office before dawn and now, in the early afternoon, he was feeling the effects. He was going through several transcripts of the interviews with the Mansells, when the phone on his desk rang. Without taking his eyes off the papers he was studying, he reached out his hand and picked it up. "Lambert."

"Matt, it's Alun Richards, have you got a moment?"

"Alun," Matt exclaimed, pleased to hear the voice of his friend who was an inspector in the traffic division. "Absolutely. I'd be delighted to take ten minutes off from this case I'm on."

"What case is that?"

"An old chap called Caradoc Mansell from White Monk Abbey, you know, up Castellgwyn way. Someone decided to pump him full of animal tranquiliser. Nasty."

"Ah," said Alun, "interesting."

"In what way?"

"Look, give me five minutes, I'll come to your office."

A few minutes later a thickset man with closely cropped grey hair appeared at the door of Matt's office. He grinned. "So, this is what you get when you make Chief Inspector, your own office. Tidy."

"Well, naturally we senior members of staff have to be treated with due respect."

"Bollocks."

Matt returned his grin. "So, what can I do for you?"

Alun sat down, serious now. "There was a nasty RTA on the M4 yesterday morning, just past junction 24. Initially we thought it was a case of speeding and losing control, but now we're not so sure. One of the witnesses we interviewed saw a very distinctive Porsche, turquoise with a black line down the side and a black roof..."

Matt gave Alun a sharp look but didn't comment.

"The witness says it was all over the place, going at a hell of a lick down the fast lane then veering across to the middle lane, then back again. This went on for a minute or two, then the Porsche simply ploughed into the back of a lorry. The driver didn't have a chance."

"Killed?"

"Outright."

"Any idea who he was?" Matt thought he knew.

"Yes, confirmation has just come through. He had several credit and debit cards in the name of Michael Cotter."

"I thought so."

"How come?"

"The car, I recognised your description. That explains why he wasn't at the Abbey when we wanted to interview him."

"I'm not with you," Alun said.

"We're interested in his activities." Matt gave Alun a quick run-down of their surveillance of Cotter and the interview a few days before, and about his connection to the Mansells.

"What you say fits with what we found on an iPad in the car. We got Aidan Rogers on to it. He's that new whizz-kid who can open up any device; it's like he's got some kind of can opener no-one else has access to."

"You're showing your age, my friend."

"Piss off," Alun said good naturedly.

Quickly Alun went through the information they'd gleaned from Cotter's iPad and mobile phone and Matt went through all the different personalities, ticking them off on his fingers as he did so.

"Good lord. Sounds a bit like something out of some TV drama," Alun said, shaking his head.

"Tell me about it. What's more, the Mansells are friends of Fabia's."

Alun gave a bark of laughter. "Trust Fabia to be involved, bless her."

Matt grinned ruefully, "You don't know the half of it. But what made you come to see me?"

"For a start, one of the e-mails on his iPad referred to you, and not in complimentary terms, but that's explained by you hauling him in for questioning. And it's obvious this Garan Price is a gambler and he owes Cotter a pretty packet. There are texts on Cotter's phone threatening to get some of his pals to sort Price out if the money isn't forthcoming – threats to Garan's wife and mother as well. And now you've told me about the case you're on, and the old man being poisoned, there's something else you'd be interested in."

"What's that?"

"We had a blood test done. We wanted to check if he'd been drinking or was on drugs. The pathologist says he had alcohol in his bloodstream, which fits with a hip flask we found in the car; we're getting the flask done for prints, but the interesting thing was the test also showed up a hefty amount of nitrazepam."

"Sleeping tablets?"

"That's it. The pathologist said there was enough to knock out a bull."

"So, you think someone drugged him with a view to causing an accident?"

"That about sums it up."

Matt looked across at his friend and frowned. "I was about to arrange another interview with his sister. She's got some more explaining to do when it comes to the animal tranquiliser."

"You said that was what was used on her father-in-law. Could she have any reason to get rid of her brother as well?"

"I don't know. He was a thoroughly unpleasant character, and it's always possible he had some hold over her," Matt said.

"And over this Garan Price bloke, it looks like, from what we found on his phone."

"Yes, those debts give him good reason to want Cotter dead."

"True."

"I'll have to do some pushing with Delma Mansell, but maybe not immediately," Matt said. "I think perhaps Garan Price comes first. But how the hell would he have got the stuff into Cotter's system at that time of day?"

"No idea. That's your department," Alun said.

"Thanks, mate."

Alun grinned at him but was soon serious again. "I'll have to inform the family this afternoon. I can't put it off any longer."

Matt pushed his hair back from his forehead and sighed. "Maybe I should do that. It might give me the chance to put his sister on the spot."

"Are you sure? What reason can you give?"

"I don't think I have to. They probably won't know it's anything unusual," Matt pointed out.

"Okay, you go ahead. It's not a job I relish, whatever the circumstances."

"Not one I particularly enjoy either," Matt said, "but studying the family's reactions to the news could turn something up in relation to both deaths, don't you think?"

"Possibly. Before you get going, I'd better copy you in on the accident report, and the pathologist's?"

"Thanks, Alun. And could you get me copies of the fingerprints on the flask?"

"Will do," Alun said as he left.

* * *

When the reports and other information came through from Alun half an hour later, Matt called Dilys in and brought her up to date with what he'd been told. They read through the reports and compared the fingerprints with those they'd taken from the family.

"These on the flask are interesting," Dilys said.

"They are?"

"Do you want me to come with you when you go to the Abbey?"

"Yes, it'd be good to have a female officer on hand, better you than Chloe, I think. The sooner we get it over, the better."

But Dilys didn't get up immediately. "Before we do that," she said, "there's something else that fits in with all this. Chloe and I went to interview the vet, Stewart Parker,

162

this morning; we drove up through Castellgwyn. As we were going past the Mynach Arms, she remarked on a car parked just outside, it was a blue Porsche with black trim."

"Was it now?" Matt said, eyebrows raised. "What time was this?"

"About half nine."

"But the pub wouldn't have been open then."

"Doesn't stop him knocking up Garan Price for a chat, does it?"

"It doesn't. It's not looking good for Price, is it?"

"You could say that. Or for Delma Mansell for that matter," Dilys added. "I must tell you about the vet. It was an interesting conversation, and not just what *he* said, his receptionist was quite forthcoming as well."

"How come?"

"Well, when we arrived, I asked her if I was right in thinking that Mr Parker looked after the horses at the Abbey, and her reaction was pretty revealing. She said, 'well, you could say that' with such a look on her face – sour as a bag of lemons – that I couldn't resist probing a little."

"What was her problem?"

"She said that she thought it wasn't just the horses he looks after at the Abbey."

"What do you think she meant by that?" asked Matt.

"We had to do a bit of a pincer movement with our questions, but in the end, she admitted she thought he'd got the hots for – her words, not mine – Delma Mansell. By the end of our conversation both Chloe and I got the strong impression she, her name's Helly or Hetty, something like that, tried it on with Stewart Parker and got the brush off. She's definitely smarting and doesn't seem to mind who knows."

"So, did you pursue it with Parker?"

"I did indeed. I started off by asking him about the tranquiliser and he told us what we know already, that it's licensed for use by vets and they must carry the antidote.

He categorically denied that he would ever let anyone unqualified handle it. When I suggested that he might have allowed Delma Mansell access to it because she trained as a vet, he blustered around, said he had no idea that she'd done so, and then contradicted himself and pointed out she'd never qualified. This backwards and forwards went on for a while and, in the end, I'm afraid I ran out of patience."

Matt's eyes widened. "What did you do?"

"I asked him outright if he was having an affair with her."

"You don't hold back, do you Dilys?" Matt said, grinning appreciatively.

She shrugged. "No point, don't you think? I thought he was going to burst a blood vessel, but Chloe intervened, did the softly, softly business – she's bloody good at that. Apologised for our having to ask personal questions but said that we were dealing with murder here and asked him if he didn't agree that it was important to find Caradoc Mansell's killer."

"Nice."

"Anyway, the outcome is he admitted that he and Delma had had a relationship, but he told us it ended months ago and there is no way she could have got the tranquiliser from him. We couldn't budge him on that. But at least we can use this when we go back to interview Delma Mansell."

"Absolutely, but I don't think we can challenge her on that today, not at the same time as giving her the news about her brother."

"Maybe not," said Dilys, sounding disappointed.

"Dilys!"

"Okay, okay, sir, I'll behave."

Chapter 15

Once again, Matt and Dilys drove along the gloomy road that dipped steeply down between high banks of greenery, dark beneath the reaching branches of the trees. Matt had to slow down as they came up behind a pheasant strutting along the middle of the road. It seemed unaware that it was in danger and continued to trot along until Matt sounded his horn.

They arrived at the gateway with the looming dragons. There was no escape now from the task ahead. Matt drove up the driveway and parked beside the two cars he'd seen there before: the ancient Range Rover and the equally decrepit Volvo estate.

"At least the cars mean they might be at home." He got out and took a deep breath. "Right. Here we go."

She glanced up at him. Sometimes she thought he was just too sensitive.

It was Mrs Giordano that opened the door. "Oh, it's you again," she said. "Who do you want this time?" With a bad grace, she stepped aside and let them into the hall.

"We'd like to speak to Mrs Mansell, please," Matt said, "and if Mr Mansell is here, perhaps we could see them both."

"What's it about?"

"I think it's best we speak directly to them," he insisted.

For a moment he thought she was going to argue, but a moment later she said, "Wait here, I'll fetch them." She disappeared behind the sweep of stairs and towards the back of the house.

Matt wandered about the hall while they waited, his hands clasped behind his back as he looked up at the dark paintings hanging on the walls. Dilys stood by the fireplace and waited in silence. After about ten minutes, they heard footsteps approaching and turned to see both the Mansells come into the hall, followed by Mrs Giordano.

"Good morning, again, Chief Inspector," Rodric Mansell said coolly. "How can we help you?" The words were courteous, but the tone wasn't. His wife just glared at them.

"I'm afraid I have some bad news."

They all reacted in slightly different ways.

Delma Mansell looked frightened and said, "Oh no. What is it now?"

Her husband frowned and muttered, "When is this going to end?"

And Mrs Giordano took charge, as was her wont. "Why don't you take them through to the sitting room, Rodi, rather than standing around in the hall," she said.

He glanced at her then nodded. "This way," he said to Matt and Dilys and then marched off. They were followed swiftly by the two women.

The large room was cold and little warmth came from the sluggish fire in the enormous grate. Matt wondered why they bothered to light it.

Matt cleared his throat and looked at Delma Mansell. "Mrs Mansell, I'm afraid your brother was involved in a road traffic accident this morning."

"Where? What happened? Is he alright?"

"No, I'm very sorry to say that he is not. He died at the scene."

For a moment there was silence in the room, only broken by a gasp from Mrs Giordano and the sound of a log settling in the fireplace. The silence dragged out until suddenly Delma whispered, "I don't believe you."

"Delma," Rodric said, and put his arm round his wife. "I'm sure the chief inspector has no reason to make this up. Come, sit down."

But she shook him off. "How did it happen?"

"A witness has told us that his car was being driven erratically, then it veered across from the fast lane to the middle one just behind a lorry. We'll be going over the wreckage carefully in case there was something wrong with the vehicle," Matt said.

Delma said no more but stood staring at them, her eyes wide in her pale face, almost as if she was in a trance. There was no sign of tears.

"There will obviously be a post-mortem," Matt went on, watching them carefully as he spoke. "We took some blood tests and they show he'd taken a large dose of sleeping pills which, together with alcohol, could have had a profound effect on his driving."

"But that's ridiculous, Mike never would have taken something like that," she protested. "It must have been his car. He took it to the garage only last week."

For the first time since they'd arrived, Rhiannon Giordano intervened. "That's true. I remember him saying he thought there was a problem with the brakes."

"I'm sure our accident investigation team will be able to check on that. In the meantime, could we have a look at his room? Perhaps he did have some sleeping tablets in his possession."

"Is that really necessary?" Rodric Mansell asked, glancing anxiously at his wife.

"I'm afraid so, sir."

"Oh, very well, Nonna, would you—?"

"Of course." She went to the door and stood waiting for Matt and Dilys to follow her, then preceded them up the stairs. As she went, she said quietly, "This is yet another tragedy for us to cope with, but I'm afraid it doesn't surprise me – Mike was a very reckless driver. I'm sure you'll find that was the cause of the accident."

"But that doesn't explain the drug, does it?" Matt said.

"I suppose not, but it wouldn't entirely surprise me if he was taking drugs. He had some very dubious associates." She said no more, simply opened the door of a room on the landing and closed it behind them.

Matt and Dilys found nothing different to what had been found in the search made of the room a few days before, until they opened a drawer in the bedside table. Here they found a packet marked Alodorm; there was one tablet left in the blister pack.

"Were these missed in the first search or have they been put there since?" Matt asked.

"I don't know," Dilys said. "I'll check."

Matt put the packet into an evidence bag and fifteen minutes later they decided to call it a day and went back downstairs, to be greeted in the hall by Rodric Mansell.

"It will be necessary for a member of the family to identify the body," Matt told him. "It's a formality but it has to be done. Would your wife–?"

"No, no," Mansell said. "I'll do that."

"Thank you. I'll let you know when, sir. We'll send a car for you."

Mansell nodded and said, "If you wouldn't mind, I think you should leave us now."

"Very well, but I'm afraid this cannot influence our investigation into your father's death. We will have to continue with the interviews and searches we still have to do. Perhaps you could both make yourself available tomorrow?"

There was a blaze of anger in Mansell's eyes, but he masked it quickly. "I'm sure we all understand that you have to continue with your investigations. Obviously, we won't stand in your way. I'll see you out."

* * *

Early on Thursday morning, Chloe Daniels knocked on the door of Matt's office.

"Sir? Have you got a minute?"

"Sure, how're the team getting on with the inventory?"

"That's what I wanted to talk to you about. I think we've got a pretty good idea of what's missing now, although this one doesn't include any jewellery. We haven't found one for that yet."

"We'll have to ask Rodric Mansell. Is this one dated? Sod it, I should have checked that, but I didn't."

Chloe glanced at him. "Yes, it is," she said, "it was updated at the end of last year, probably something to do with a change to the insurance premiums."

"I expect you're right. So, what's missing?"

She handed over a piece of paper containing a neatly typed list. "I thought I'd print it out in hard copy, Dilys says you prefer that."

"She's right, I do. Must be something to do with my age."

"I doubt it," Chloe blurted out. Matt raised an eyebrow at her, and a blush rose under her dark skin. "And this one," she said hastily, "is a copy of the insurance company's inventory."

He pulled the two lists towards him and ran a finger down one and then the other. "All of this is easily disposed of, small pieces, nothing overly valuable, although it looks as if these two silver bowls could fetch a pretty penny at auction, I think they're under-valued by the insurance company. My father used to collect silver, so I know a bit about it. Have you checked their present value online?"

"I had a look on a couple of auction house websites and on e-bay," Chloe said. "I think they could fetch about a thousand each, but probably not that much if they were being sold to a fence."

"Yes, I think you're right."

There was silence for a moment while Matt went on studying the lists, then he looked up, his finger resting on one point. "This painting, it says it's a Huw Wystan Jones; that's a whole different ball game. Fabia Havard mentioned him the other day and I did a bit of research. You see here, on their inventory they've got one marked as being in the study, and they also have one of his listed for what's called the small sitting room. But that's not on our inventory. All we've got for that room at the back is a couple of paintings of bowls of fruit and dead pheasants – ghastly things. I suppose whoever took it away thought the family wouldn't notice since it was stashed away in a room that's hardly used."

"Could be."

"Well, that's very useful, Chloe, thank you. Could you ask Dilys to come in?"

"Will do, sir."

Dilys appeared five minutes later. "You know we found those sleeping tablets in Mike Cotter's room yesterday?" she asked before Matt could say anything.

"Yes."

"Well, there's no record of them being there in the first search; interesting, don't you think?"

"It could mean nothing, maybe someone just put them back there having borrowed them or something."

"I don't know, sir, seems odd to me."

"I see what you mean. Anyway, have a look at this list of stuff missing from the Abbey. Chloe and her team have done a damn good job. We definitely need to go through this with the Mansells, particularly Delma, but before that I want to follow up on this phone call from the neighbour, Marsden. What exactly did he say?"

"Dave took the call, let me give him a shout." She left his office but came back a moment later, followed by Dave Parry.

"Ted Marsden, Dave, what was he after?" Matt asked.

"He'd heard that foul play, as he put it, was involved in Caradoc Mansell's death and believes he has some information that might help our enquiries. When I asked what that information was, he said he wasn't about to give any details over the phone. He asked for you by name. I think he's one of those that prefers to talk to the organ grinder and not the monkey."

"I don't know, you don't look much like a monkey to me."

"Thank you, sir," Dave said with a grin. "Anyway, he wants you to go and see him at Manor Farm. An authoritative bloke, he sounded like. I got the impression he's used to having his commands obeyed without question."

"I think he's ex-army, that's probably why," said Dilys, "I checked on his regiment. It was the Royal Corps of Transport, at least, that's what it was called back in the day. They were in charge of getting people and materials from place to place, supplies and all that – not what one would call glamorous."

"Ah, not exactly the Welsh Guards," Matt said, grinning. "That was probably another source of friction between him and Caradoc Mansell, I bet there was a bit of snobbery involved. Thanks, Dave."

Matt turned back to Dilys. "Ready?"

"Yes, but before we get going," Dilys said, "I thought you ought to know the tech blokes have turned up some interesting points already."

"Have they now? What, specifically?"

"Let me go and get my laptop."

She was back within seconds. Not one to waste time, our Dilys, Matt thought.

Pulling up a chair beside Matt, Dilys put the laptop on the desk. "Right," she said, "this bit here, not specifically technical information, but relevant. The keyboard from the computer in Caradoc Mansell's study, it's been wiped clean, not a trace of a fingerprint anywhere; same with the screen and the computer case itself."

"Could that just be someone being conscientious about the dusting?"

"I wouldn't have thought so. All the others have plenty of evidence of who's been using them, and when I was in that study, I noticed how dusty the room was."

Matt smiled – cleanliness was something Dilys was always aware of.

Dilys glanced at him, gave a rueful smile, "I hate dust and dirt, that's all. It looked as if the place hadn't been cleaned for days. It was only the computer that'd been given the treatment, which I find odd."

"So do I. Anything else?"

"Yes," said Dilys. "There are several e-mails back and forth between Caradoc Mansell and Anjali Kishtoo, they go back quite a few months. Aidan Rogers says Mansell didn't use a password. It was just a case of turn it on and straight in, so anyone could have accessed his e-mails. What's more, the pin number for his iPad and mobile are about as obvious as they could be: just his date of birth in digits."

"So, anyone the least bit computer literate could work it out."

"Exactly."

"Anything else from the other devices, laptops, phones?" Matt asked.

"They're still working on them, although they do have some stuff on this one here," she scrolled to a particular section. "Whoever uses this laptop is pretty savvy when it comes to the net, some complex searches here, which is interesting."

"Whose is it?"

She told him.

Matt frowned. "Not what I would have expected. Ask them to go into more detail on that one, and on the mobile phone that goes with it."

"Will do." She closed the laptop and got up. "Ready, sir?"

"Yup. Let's get going."

* * *

Manor Farm was a neat building, much more recent and a good deal tidier than White Monk Abbey. The house, whitewashed and square, had a front door flanked by two windows either side on the ground floor and five lined up above. It stood at right angles to other farm buildings, which were all in good repair. Immediately in front of the house neat flower beds contained rose bushes, still with the occasional bloom struggling against the approach of winter.

Dilys parked the car and she and Matt approached the glossy green front door and rang the bell. It was answered almost immediately by a short, well-built man in his late sixties. His greying hair was neatly cropped, and he was wearing a checked shirt, blazer, corduroy trousers and a cravat at his neck. At his side stood a black Labrador with a greying muzzle. His voice, when he spoke, was that of a lifelong smoker, deep and gravelly, and showed no trace of a Welsh accent.

"Chief Inspector Lambert? Thank you for responding to my request for a meeting. Please come in."

"Thank you. This is Detective Sergeant Bevan," Matt said, indicating Dilys as they followed him into the hall. Marsden gave Dilys a curt nod, but then turned back to Matt.

"A sad business, old Caradoc dying like that. Anything I can do to help, I will."

He strode ahead of them, followed by the dog, its claws clicking on the tiled floor, and they went into a room at the back of the house. It looked comfortable enough, although rather sparsely furnished, with dark panelling and leather armchairs. French windows looked out on to a formal lawn with neat flower beds and, beyond that, the hills rose into the distance. The room smelt of furniture polish and tobacco smoke.

"Have a seat," Marsden said, waving a hand at two armchairs.

He sat down opposite them, and the dog settled itself at his feet. Leaning forward, he put his hands on his knees. There was a sense of suppressed energy about the man and Matt got the impression that, any moment now, he'd leap up and start to pace about the room.

"When you phoned, sir, you told one of my team that you'd heard Caradoc Mansell's death was down to, er, foul play, have I got that right?"

"You have."

"Who did you hear it from?"

"My gamekeeper. He was in the Mynach Arms and heard some talk, came and told me."

"I see. Well, he was right. We've now confirmed that we're dealing with murder," Matt said. "The pathologist's report was very clear. Mansell was injected with a strong animal tranquiliser."

"Ah," Marsden said, and nodded.

Matt was curious. "That doesn't surprise you, sir?"

"No. It matches up with what I wanted to speak to you about." He didn't go on immediately and Matt wondered what was coming next, but he didn't say anything, just waited.

Finally, Marsden went on. "Perhaps it would be a good idea if I filled in some of the background. As you obviously know, our two estates run alongside each other. As far as I'm concerned, the border between the two is clear enough, but Caradoc Mansell did not agree. He searched out some ancient deeds, in Welsh, that placed the border in a different place to the deeds I have, which are in English."

The slight contempt in his voice when he mentioned the older deeds wasn't lost on Matt. He got the distinct impression Marsden thought the English ones would be more reliable. He let it pass, although he noticed Dilys stiffen slightly.

"We've been in discussion – I suppose you could call it that – for some time trying to sort out which one is correct. I offered to pay a nominal sum for the disputed land, but the Mansells, well Mansell senior, would have none of it. The son's a more reasonable fellow, but his wife definitely isn't. She persists in allowing her horses to graze that land and even lets them encroach on parts of my estate, and no protest from me has made any difference."

Matt began to wonder when he would get to the point, but he didn't have long to wait.

"A couple of weeks ago, actually more like three weeks I think, she'd allowed that stallion of hers, inappropriately called Moonlight – Devil would be a more suitable name for him – the run of my top field. I wasn't about to try to catch the damned horse, it's a vicious beast, so I walked down to their stables to have it out with her. Anyway, there was a car parked in the yard and I recognised it; it belongs to Stewart Parker, one of the vets from Dysart & Jennings. I've used him myself for this old girl" – he patted the Labrador's head – "and for some of my milkers."

Dilys glanced at Matt and quickly away again as Marsden went on.

"I could hear voices from the stables office, so I made my way across the yard." For a moment he looked a little embarrassed. "Now, I wouldn't like you to think I was eavesdropping deliberately, but when I got close enough to hear the conversation, I realised it was rather – er – rather intimate."

He glanced at Dilys, but she continued to sit there, impassive.

"Then I heard Delma Mansell say something about needing some, what were her words? 'Some of that tranquiliser you used on him before'. She said sometimes Moonlight got out of hand, which didn't surprise me one bit, and that she needed help to control him, particularly as her husband wouldn't always allow her to call out the vet because of the expense. The vet agreed to let her have some, but he told her she mustn't, on any account, let it be known that she had it; that his job would be on the line if she did. They then went back to their, um, previous activities and I made good my escape."

Matt was amused to see that Marsden's face had reddened a little.

"Nearly got caught by that aunt of theirs, Mrs Giordano, on my way out," Marsden went on, "but I managed to escape unnoticed."

"Would you be willing for us to take a statement from you about this?" Matt asked.

Marsden screwed up his face at this, but then relaxed. "Oh, very well, I suppose I must."

"I'll send one of our team along to record one then," Dilys said, speaking for the first time. "Would this afternoon be convenient, sir?"

He looked at her as if he was seeing her for the first time and Matt had the distinct impression that he wasn't used to dealing with women.

"Fine, fine, I'll be here," Marsden said, addressing Matt.

"Thank you, sir," Dilys said, giving him a dazzling smile. Marsden blinked and Matt only just stopped himself from laughing.

"Right, well, I'll see you out." He and the dog escorted them to the front door and stood watching as they got into the car.

As she started up the engine, Dilys said, "When we interviewed Stewart Parker, he was adamant his affair with Delma ended some months ago. What Marsden said indicates that wasn't true."

"It does. He seems to have hung around ear-wigging for some time, doesn't he?"

"Well," said Dilys, with a twisted little smile, "he's got to get his kicks somewhere hasn't he?"

"Dilys!"

She grinned. "I think we send a male PC to take his statement, don't you?"

Matt laughed. "Definitely. I wonder if there's a wife in the background."

"I believe there used to be, but she scarpered, which could explain his attitude."

"How the hell did you know that?"

"Glyn Evans told me. His wife knew Mrs Marsden years ago; same WI."

"Your fount of local knowledge never fails to amaze me. You and Fabia between you probably know everything there is to know about everyone within a hundred-mile radius."

Dilys grinned. "I don't think I can rival Fabia Havard, sir."

She was soon serious again. "So, do we go straight to talk to Delma Mansell? We did warn her we'd be back for a further interview. Do you think she could have been involved in both her father-in-law and her brother's deaths? By all accounts her brother was a bully. She may have been forced to give him stuff from the Abbey to sell and it seems to me she might have had good reason to want to get rid of him."

"I suppose you're right, but they're not exactly going to welcome us with open arms. Maybe I should have left it to Alun to tell them about Cotter's accident. Too late now. Okay, let's go and see if she's at home."

Chapter 16

Garan felt as if the day had gone on forever. He put up a hand to his face, his nose was swollen, and he had a spectacular black eye. He'd had to fend off questions several times during the morning. He'd told Sheryl, and anyone else who'd remarked on it, that he'd tripped when he'd been carrying a beer barrel and hit his head. No way was he going to tell her the truth. He didn't know if Sheryl had believed him, but she hadn't persisted with her questions. With that and everything else, he was feeling hounded.

The Mynach Arms was busy, a good deal more so than usual for a Thursday lunch-time; in fact it had been like this ever since the news of the murder enquiry had spread through the village. The locals, most of whom were aware of Garan's connection to the Mansell family, seemed to have decided that the pub was the place they needed to be. How else would they be first with the latest news? Both Garan and Sheryl tried to avoid being drawn into conversations about what was happening up at the Abbey, but this didn't stop the continual speculation. How was Caradoc killed? And for what reason? Who were the possible suspects? Was Rodric responsible? Never to God would they have thought that. Didn't they think it was more likely that Delma Mansell's brother had something to do with it?

On and on it went and it was very difficult to remain polite to their punters at the same time as stemming the flow. No-one had suggested, yet, that Garan could have had anything to do with Caradoc's death, but he was very much afraid someone would do so soon if he showed his anger and distaste at the bright curious eyes and the probing questions.

"Of course, that Ted Marsden, up to Manor Farm, he never got on with old Caradoc. I wouldn't put much past him."

"No, no, he's a good enough bloke for an Englishman. He gave me some work a while back and paid well, he did."

"What about that other Englishman, visitor at the Abbey, he was in the pub a couple of days ago. What's his name, Garan?"

Appealed to direct, Garan answered, "Mike Cotter."

"He's the brother of Rodric's wife, isn't he?"

"Yes," said Garan shortly.

"I didn't take to him one bit, and I'll tell you for why," said the mechanic from the garage up the road, "when he brought in that car of his…"

Garan took himself off to the other end of the bar to avoid any further questions and Sheryl came up behind him, put her hand on his back and spoke close to his ear, "Don't let them get to you, cariad. Hang on in there."

He turned and gave her a twisted smile, then winced as his bruises reacted to the movement. "I'm trying, but bloody hell, it's hard."

"I know. Just smile and plead ignorance."

This conversation was interrupted by a commotion at the door of the public bar. Two of the regulars, who'd been muttering away to each other at a table nearby, suddenly jumped up.

"Bella *bach*!" said one elderly but spry old man. "What a sight for sore eyes! Have you heard what's been going on round here?"

"You come to see your boy, have you?" asked his companion. "There's trouble up to the Abbey, you know. Hey! Garan! Your mam's here," he shouted.

Conversation stilled and every eye in the room turned towards the door. Bella, her grey flecked auburn hair flowing down her back, and her dark eyes searching, stood there in a bright patchwork jacket, enormous gold hoop earrings at her neck.

"Dai, Fergi," she smiled at the two old men and gave each of them a kiss on the cheek. "Behave," she advised them, and then began to thread her way through the crowd, pulling a small overnight bag behind her, and briefly greeting a couple of others as she went.

Garan came from behind the bar, his expression a mixture of pleasure and wariness. She wrapped him in a hug and said, "Hallo darling, it's so good to see you. Good lord, what have you been doing to yourself?"

"An argument with a table when I was shifting barrels," he said, getting used to the lie now. "But Mam, why are you here? You shouldn't have driven all that way."

Sheryl joined them. "Bella!" There was only pleasure in her face. She put an arm round her mother-in-law and pulled her close, said quietly, "Thank you so much for coming down, we really need you."

The buzz of conversation round them had resumed, but several people close by were straining to hear what was said.

"You knew she was coming?" Garan asked his wife. He didn't sound pleased.

"Yes. Look, let's go around the back," Sheryl said, taking charge. "One of the girls can look after things for a bit, and Mick will give her a hand." She turned to a young man who was leaning on the bar, nursing a pint. "Do us a favour, Mick, come this side for a few minutes and give Ellie a hand."

"Sure," he said, "no probs."

"Pour me a glass of red first, love," Bella said to Sheryl.

"Don't worry, we'll take a bottle with us into the back lounge," Sheryl said. She grabbed a tray, put a bottle of red wine and three glasses on it then ushered Garan and his mother through to the back of the pub, watched by several curious customers.

They sat down round a small table in an alcove and Sheryl poured wine into their glasses; then Bella looked at Garan, put a hand up to his cheek. "Bless you, darling, you look as if you haven't slept for a week."

"Not too far from the truth, that," Sheryl said.

"I wish you hadn't come," he told his mother, then turned an accusing look on his wife. "Why did you ask her?"

"Don't start blaming Sheryl. Yes, she texted me, but I also had a long conversation with Fabia Havard and she gave me all the details of what's been happening – that's what persuaded me to drive down."

"He's been wearing himself to the bone worrying," Sheryl told her.

"What about?"

"What about!" Garan echoed sharply. "Mam, my father has just been murdered! The place is crawling with police. They've been questioning everybody, taking fingerprints, the lot. They haven't come back again yet, but it won't be long before they do."

"Of course, I know you must be worried sick about it all, and grieving, as I am. He wasn't just your father, he was my very good friend and I loved him." Her voice cracked on the words and she drew a deep breath to steady herself.

"But no-one's going to think you had anything to do with it," she went on briskly. "That would be ridiculous."

Bella didn't miss a quick glance between Garan and Sheryl. "Okay," she said, "what are you not telling me?"

There was a loaded silence, then Bella gave Garan a direct look and asked, "Is it to do with money?"

"Oh, for God's sake, why should you immediately jump to that conclusion?" Garan said defensively, but he wouldn't meet his mother's eyes.

"Because I know you, my darling, and if you've been gambling and getting into debt again – on top of everything else –it's enough to give anyone sleepless nights."

"Tell her, Garan," Sheryl urged.

He leant back in his chair and rubbed a hand across his mouth, then looked from his wife to his mother, his eyes agonised. "Oh Mam!" he said, letting his breath out through trembling lips, "I've really screwed up this time."

Bella's heart sank and, in order to hide her fear, she lifted her glass to drink some wine. "Garan, love," she said, "it doesn't matter what you've done, we can sort it out. Now, tell me."

Slowly at first, he began to tell her about the online gambling, the poker games, the debt to Mike Cotter and his threats when Garan couldn't pay up immediately – Mike hinting that he'd suggest to the police that Garan could be responsible for Caradoc's death. Then he told them about the two men, tall, built like heavyweight boxers, who'd pitched up the day before. This was new to Sheryl.

"You didn't tell me about them. Who were they?"

"I didn't want to worry you."

"Garan! Did you get their names?"

"No. They laughed when I asked. They said they were friends of Mike Cotter and he'd sent them to get what was owed, with interest. I told them straight, I did, to get the hell out of my pub, but they just laughed again, said they'd teach me a lesson. They looked around the pub and said what a pity it would be if it burned down. I was effing lucky the brewery van arrived. I know the blokes and they could see I was having a spot of bother, so they sort of squared up to them. I don't think they liked being out-numbered, but before the bastards left, they promised they'd be back."

"You have to tell Rodric, Garan, you just have to," Sheryl said, sounding scared.

"And the police," insisted his mother.

Garan shook his head as both women listened to the rest of his story in silence: the amount of money he owed, which made Sheryl gasp, and the times that Mike had come in to threaten and wind him up. At last, he stopped talking and leant forward in his chair with his elbows on his knees, his head in his hands. "Now do you see what I mean," he said, his voice muffled, "when I say I've really screwed up?"

"Yes, I do," Bella said, then she gave him a very straight look. "And what happened this morning, with that black eye?" she asked.

Garan didn't reply.

"Come on, my darling, I know you too well. What happened?"

The seconds ticked by and at last he took a deep breath. "It was when you were at the gym, Sheryl. That bastard, Cotter, came sailing in the back door without so much as a by-your-leave, demanded that I make him a cup of coffee and fill up his bloody flask. It's not the first time he's done that, and he doesn't pay. I threw the damn thing back at him."

"You refused?" Sheryl asked, sounding more positive for a moment.

"I tried to, but he just told me I'd do as he asked if I knew what was good for me. I lost it a bit, tried to hit the fucker, but he swung at me first and this" – he pointed at his eye – "was the result. Then he marched behind the bar, filled the flask himself, with our best Penderyn malt, like he's done before."

"And what about the coffee?" Sheryl said wearily.

Garan gave her a sideways glance. "He said he'd give the coffee a miss, but he'd be back."

Bella leant forward and filled their glasses. "Okay, first things first, you're going to get on to the police and tell them everything."

Garan protested but she ignored him.

"No arguments. Sheryl and I are here to help, we'll back you up, won't we?"

Sheryl nodded. She didn't seem as sure as her mother-in-law, but she didn't contradict her.

"No arguments, darling," Bella said, "you're going to tell them all about those two shits from Swansea. Fabia told me her friend, DCI Lambert, is in charge of the investigation into Caradoc's death and he's a real tidy sort. Then you'll tell them, in detail, all about Mike Cotter and what he's been up to."

Garan's shoulders sagged. He seemed to have given up protesting. Bella was about to go on, but at that moment they were interrupted. David Harris and Megan came through into the lounge, each carrying a glass. They did not, at first, notice the three in the alcove, but sat down on a small sofa the other side of the room. David took Megan's hand and they heard him say, "Now, tell me exactly what happened."

Megan, her voice quiet but still audible to the three of them. "That policeman, Chief Inspector Lambert, and the woman, I can't remember her name, came to the Abbey and asked for Delma. Rodi thought it was yet more questioning, but it wasn't. They'd come to tell her Mike was killed in an accident on the motorway, he—"

On hearing this, Garan jumped up and Megan and David quickly turned to look in his direction.

"Garan?" Megan exclaimed. "Sorry, we didn't see you there."

He walked over to them. "Did you say he's dead?"

"Yes," Megan told him. "They said he'd taken some drug or other and they think that's why he crashed his car."

"Drug? What drug?" Sheryl asked.

"I don't know, but apparently it was much more than a person should take, normally. It's awful, isn't it?"

"Oh my God," Garan muttered, "I hated the bastard, but I didn't want him dead!"

Both Sheryl and Bella looked up at him, alarmed. "What do you mean?" Bella asked, her voice sharp.

Garan wouldn't look her in the eye. "Just what I said. There's no point in pretending I liked the bloke just because he's dead."

Bella continued to look up at her son as a dreadful thought began to push into her mind.

* * *

The day before, Matt had phoned to ask Fabia how she was getting on with the notes about the Mansells. Having agreed to do as he'd asked, she still felt a bit doubtful about it, as she'd explained to Cath.

"It's not that I don't want to help him," she'd told Cath earlier. "It's just that I feel sort of pulled both ways."

"That's hardly surprising, Fabia," Cath had said. "You've known the Mansells for a long time."

"And I rather resent him using me."

"I hope you don't mind my saying so, but that sounds a bit hypocritical."

"Cath!" Fabia had protested. "That's hardly fair."

"Think about it. You always say you'd much rather be involved than not. If he kept you at arms' length when it comes to his work, I'm sure you wouldn't like that one bit."

"You're probably right," Fabia had had the grace to admit.

"I think this is more to do with your personal relationship with Matt than anything else."

"What do you mean?"

"Well, it's only six short months since the two of you met up again and renewed your relationship."

"We're not in a relationship," Fabia insisted.

"Friendship then," said Cath. "Quite apart from anything else, you got so used to being angry and hurt by Matt's behaviour, and not trusting him, that it'll take a while to get out of that mindset."

"But I'm not angry with him anymore!" Fabia had exclaimed.

"I'm sure you're not, but you were for two years; it's like breaking a habit. And it's not been the easiest time for you. You went through the sort of experience that would traumatise even the strongest person. What's more, he may have cleared your name, but you told me there's been some pretty nasty stuff posted online, in spite of the fact everyone should know the truth by now. Matt's been supporting you through all that, hasn't he?"

"Oh yes, bless him. Did I tell you he actually managed to arrest one of the trolls?" Fabia said.

"Yes, and as I remember you said he was like a dog with a bone over that. You must accept that you can't run before you walk. Give it time."

Fabia could hear the smile in Cath's voice as she went on. "Anyway, you told me you only wanted a platonic relationship with Matt."

For a moment Fabia was silent then she said, "I lied."

"Well, I knew that."

"But I do value my independence," Fabia insisted.

"For goodness sake, Fabia, he doesn't have to move in. Just enjoy each other and see how things go. A bit of sex would do you both a world of good."

Fabia laughed. "Cath, you're a wicked woman." But she was soon serious again. "There's nothing I can do about me and Matt at the moment. It'd be impossible while Anjali is staying here."

"I suppose, but she won't be playing gooseberry forever, will she?"

"I suppose not, and she's a lovely girl, no trouble."

"But you haven't known her very long," Cath said. "It must be stressful looking after someone you hardly know who's going through what she is. Poor girl, she must feel very far from home."

"I'm sure she does. Megan keeps phoning to ask her to go to the Abbey."

"Well, why don't you encourage her to do so? Would the rest of the family welcome her?"

"I'm not sure. Rodric was certainly stand-offish when they met, but then, finding out about the will must have been a hell of a shock. As to Delma, I think she'd probably give her a hard time because of the stables. I don't really know what Rhiannon Giordano would feel about it, she's a devout Roman Catholic so she'd probably take a dim view of Caradoc having an affair with a Hindu woman."

"But she can hardly blame Anjali for that."

"Of course she can't."

"Until Anjali actually meets them all, neither of you is going to know how they'll react. It's such a complicated situation. I don't envy her."

"Well, if she does go to the Abbey it won't be until next week now," Fabia had told her. "She has to go up to London tomorrow for a meeting with someone interested in her designs, and she did suggest she should stay in London and wait until the rest of the family decide to meet her, but when she mentioned that to John Meredith, he said he thought it would be best if she was on the spot until the business with Caradoc's will is clarified."

"Is that absolutely necessary? You said he seemed quite smitten with her. Maybe he just wants to keep her close."

"That had occurred to me, but he's a pretty professional bloke, John. Anyway, London isn't that far away."

"I know, but still," Cath had added, and Fabia could hear the smile was back. "To go back to what we were talking about just now, if you're going to be on your own, why don't you invite Matt round?"

"Cath! That'd be a bit obvious, wouldn't it?"

"Yes, but who cares, go for it."

"For a vicar you're a very bad influence."

"Coward," Cath had said.

Now Fabia read through her notes again. She realised that, as she'd tapped away at her keyboard, certain things had begun to emerge as particularly relevant. She scored through them with a yellow highlighter. But soon Fabia felt as if she was getting bogged down in petty details and it was a relief when her phone rang. She stretched her arms above her head then answered it, pleased to see that it was Bella.

"Hallo, Bella, are you in Castellgwyn?"

"Yes, I am." Three short words, but Fabia could tell that something was wrong.

"What's up?"

"It's– oh God, Fabia, I need your help – advice. I don't know what to do." Bella's voice shook as she spoke.

"Just tell me what the problem is," Fabia said, her voice calm, "and I'll help as much as I can."

"I'll try to begin at the beginning. Did you know that Delma's brother, Mike Cotter, was killed in a car accident?"

"Oh lord, no I didn't."

"Megan and David came in while we were in the back lounge," Bella told her.

"Who was? In the back lounge, I mean."

"Sorry, Garan, me and Sheryl, I'd just arrived. And while we were sitting there, the two of them came in and we heard them talking about it."

"When did it happen?"

"Yesterday morning, but it looks as if it wasn't an accident, he was drugged."

"Drugged?" Fabia exclaimed. "Who by?"

"That's what I wanted to talk to you about. You see, he came to the pub yesterday, early." Fabia heard Bella take a deep, shuddering breath. Her heart sank. "Sheryl was out. He told Garan he wanted to talk about some money my boy owes him. He's been hounding him for days, even sent a couple of heavies who threatened to beat Garan up and torch the pub. Luckily the brewery van arrived and the men helped Garan see them off."

"Good for them."

"That's what I thought. Anyway, Mike Cotter demanded Garan make him a coffee and Garan says he refused, but they had this enormous row and the bastard hit him. Garan's got one hell of a black eye."

"Yes, and what else?" Fabia asked quietly.

"But, oh Fabia, I have this dreadful feeling he may have, you know, made the coffee and drugged it."

"Why on earth would you think that?"

"I don't know. It's just the way he reacted when he heard what Megan said. I'm sure there's something he's not telling us."

"You mean you and Sheryl."

"Yes."

"And what does Sheryl think? Does she agree with you?"

"I haven't mentioned it to her, I didn't want to upset her. All I could think of was to come outside and phone you. What should I do?"

Fabia thought for a moment. "You haven't asked Garan direct?"

"No, I daren't." Bella sounded anguished. "I'm so scared of what he might say."

"He'll probably say he didn't, and that could well be true. I wouldn't be at all surprised if he's pleased Mike Cotter is gone, given the crap he's put Garan through, but don't mistake that for guilt." She tried to sound as reassuring as she knew how. "Has he spoken to the police?"

"Sheryl and I were trying to persuade him to, or at least tell Rodric about what's been going on, and then Megan dropped this bombshell."

"Look, Bella, the best thing he can do is tell them all about it, as soon as possible," Fabia urged. "They need to know about those two thugs for a start. You never know, they might be able to identify them, and he's got witnesses, which is all to the good. Get through to Matt Lambert and ask him to talk to Garan."

"You think?" Bella sounded uncertain, but then went on, "I know you're right. Okay, I'll go and tell Garan now."

"Let me know what happens," Fabia said.

"I will."

* * *

It was only half an hour later when Fabia's mobile rang once more. "It's me again," Bella said, when Fabia picked up. "We rang them, they're coming now. Fabia, I know it's a hell of an imposition, but would you come?"

"What? Now?"

"Yes, it would help so much to have you here."

Fabia wasn't at all sure her presence would go down well with whoever arrived to interview Garan, but she couldn't resist the pleading in Bella's voice. "Okay, I'll be there as soon as I can."

"Oh, thank you, thank you."

Fabia ended the call and sat for a moment trying to assimilate what Bella had told her. If it was proved that the drugs had been the cause of the accident and that Garan was responsible, and found guilty, he was probably looking at a custodial sentence for manslaughter. What would that be? Eight, ten years? If he had drugged the coffee, he'd have to take responsibility for what he'd done. But it just seemed so out of character. Then another thought came to

190

her which made her feel cold to her bones. What if this wasn't the first death he was responsible for? Had he killed Caradoc? He may have thought his inheritance would enable him to clear his debts. But she found it hard to believe Garan would have gone to such elaborate lengths, it just didn't connect up in her mind.

Anyway, speculation was pointless. She must get going. Fabia called up the stairs to Anjali, who was working in her room, to say she'd be out for a couple of hours, then made her way quickly to her car.

Chapter 17

As Dilys drove slowly through the narrow lanes that ran between Manor Farm and White Monk Abbey, there was silence in the car until Matt's phone rang.

He answered it. "Yes, Chloe? Hold on, give me that again, Dilys needs to hear this as well." He switched to speakerphone.

"We've just had a call from someone called Bella Price at the Mynach Arms, she's the publican's mother." Chloe's voice echoed clearly in the car. "She asked for you specifically, said Fabia Havard told her to do so."

Dilys glanced at Matt, eyebrows raised, but he didn't comment.

"Mrs Price wants you to talk to her son. She says he has some important information about Mike Cotter."

"Okay. Sounds interesting. Dilys and I are on our way to White Monk Abbey, but we can make a detour and pop into the pub first. Did she give any other information?"

"No. Just that."

"Thanks, Chloe, we're on our way." He ended the call and looked at Dilys. "I wonder what all that's about. And how come Fabia's involved?"

"She seems to know everyone round here."

"Never mind seems. She does."

Dilys couldn't quite work out whether he thought this a good thing or not. "Ah well, we'll find out soon enough," she said as she turned down Cwmbach Road and away from the lane that would take them to the Abbey. Not long afterwards they turned into the pub car park and, as they did so, a bright red Skoda pulled in next to them.

"That's Fabia's car," Matt said as Dilys switched off the engine.

"So it is," Dilys said, suppressing a grin at his tone.

Matt noticed that Fabia was looking worried as she got out of her car. "Hallo," he said, "what brings you here?"

"Bella asked me to come."

"And I gather you advised her to get hold of me, us."

"I did. Let's get inside, Matt. Best they tell you what it's all about." She strode towards the back door of the pub and, as they got to it, a woman with flowing dark hair came to meet them.

"Fabia," she said, and Matt watched as the two women hugged, then Fabia turned to him and Dilys. "This is Bella Price, Garan's mother." She introduced Matt and Dilys. "Shall we go in?"

Matt felt a little irritated. It was as if Fabia was in charge. She glanced at him and noticed the tightening of his lips. "Sorry," she said, holding her hands up in surrender.

Matt nodded acknowledgement of the gesture. "Mrs Price," he said to Bella, "we got your message."

"Come in," she said, "we're upstairs."

They followed her and Fabia up the creaking stairs to a room on the first floor of the pub. It was a messy, comfortable living room. Garan and Sheryl Price were sitting close together on the sofa, hands clasped. They looked up, concern tinged with fear in their eyes, as the four of them trooped in. Matt noticed the bruising and the black eye immediately – they were hard to miss. He took charge.

"Your mother tells us you have some information about Mr Cotter."

No-one spoke for a moment and the silence was heavy in the room, until his mother said, "Do you want me to tell them, Garan?"

Matt noticed Fabia glance at the other woman and shake her head very slightly. Maybe having her here wasn't such a bad idea after all, she might help to keep things under control.

"No, Mam, I will," Garan said, and slowly the story emerged, ending with the confrontation that morning.

"I refused to make him a cup of coffee. I was damned if I was going to take orders from that– from him, so he hit me then helped himself to some of my best malt," Garan said. "I swear I didn't drug him. I swear it."

"I'd like to get a full statement from you, and I think it's best if we do that at the station."

"Why?" Sheryl protested.

"Because that's where we have all the appropriate recording equipment, Mrs Price," Dilys told her calmly.

Fabia was standing by the door, looking worried. Matt walked over to her and spoke quietly, "I'm going to contact the station, get them to send a car to pick Garan up. Can you stay until they arrive?"

"Of course."

He and Dilys went out into the passageway and, without thinking, Fabia followed them.

"Could you phone and get Dave and Chloe to come and collect him?" Matt said to Dilys. "We really can't put off that interview with Delma."

"Will do," Dilys said. With a quick glance at Fabia, she stood aside and took out her mobile.

"Matt, I– I feel as if I'm in the way. Sorry." She wasn't used to apologising and it came out sounding resentful. She was relieved when Matt gave her a rueful smile.

"Having asked for your help when I came round, I can hardly complain about you being here now, can I? Particularly as these people are friends of yours too."

Fabia was delighted with this endorsement but tried her best to hide it. They went back into the sitting room leaving Dilys muttering into her mobile.

"We're contacting the station, they'll send a car for you, Mr Price. We're grateful for your cooperation and helping us with our enquiries."

"Doesn't that mean you're going to arrest him?" Sheryl protested.

"No," Matt said, "it means just what it says, he's helping us."

Sheryl bit at her lip as if she was trying to stop herself saying anything more. Bella said nothing, but Fabia's heart was wrung by the fear in her eyes.

Garan, looking utterly defeated, said, "I understand."

"I want to go with him," Sheryl burst out.

"I really don't think that's necessary," Matt said firmly.

"But it would save you having to bring him home after."

Bella intervened. "You've got the pub to see to, Sheryl. Best to keep busy."

Sheryl, in tears now, flung her arms round her husband and Bella put her arms round them both as Fabia stood on the sidelines, feeling helpless. It seemed from their reactions that they both expected Garan to be arrested, and she found that disturbing.

* * *

Half an hour later, Matt and Dilys left the pub and made their way to White Monk Abbey. At first neither spoke, then Dilys glanced at Matt and said, "Do you think he drugged the coffee he denies having made?"

"I don't know, but I'm pretty sure there's more to it than he's telling us."

"Maybe he's protecting someone else?"

"I hadn't thought of that." Matt frowned. "And we still don't know how much the drugs had to do with it. By all reports, Cotter was a lousy driver. We'll just have to wait for the result of the PM and the witness statements."

"What was that Fabia said about an analysis of the Mansell family?" Dilys asked a moment later.

Matt glanced across at her, but she had her eyes firmly on the road ahead.

"I– er– I asked her to make some notes about them." He felt slightly embarrassed at having to admit this to Dilys. "Just to help me get an idea of the personalities, you know, background and all that, and anything she might have noticed when she was at the Abbey."

"She's been there a lot?"

"She and Megan Mansell are working on a project together. She spent a weekend there recently."

"Good idea to co-opt her then," Dilys said.

"You think?"

"Definitely. She's a great asset is Fabia."

"I know, but I have to be careful, it can be a bit awkward at times."

"In what way?"

"Well, I know that, since we met up again, I've been inclined to take advantage of her experience, and the fact she knows people in this area, but she's no longer my boss, and that can be hard to forget; and she does interfere, at times, in ways she shouldn't now she isn't a police officer."

"But I don't think we would have solved those two murders in Pontygwyn nearly as easily, or as quickly, if she hadn't been on the spot – it was her local knowledge that did the trick."

"We could have sorted it ourselves," Matt protested. "And she nearly got herself killed in the process."

"I know, and that was awful, but she's fully recovered now, isn't she?"

"I'm not sure. She talked about having frequent nightmares soon after, but she hasn't mentioned them recently, and I think she's been easier in her mind since we dealt with that bastard who was trolling her, but then I catch an expression on her face, a sort of haunted look, and I wonder. I must ask Hari Patel about it. I wouldn't like to think she was suffering from some form of PTSD and I hadn't picked up on it."

"You could Google it."

"I know, but I'd rather talk to someone face to face. I must remember to give him a ring."

"You worry too much."

"Maybe." Matt sat in brooding silence for the rest of the journey.

* * *

Rodric was determined to keep busy, it was the only way he could keep his mind off the disasters that seemed to be accumulating around them. For want of anything better to do, he decided to drive up to the farm suppliers in Raglan. He'd wandered around the place, with its familiar smell of animal feed and fertiliser, bought a new wax jacket he didn't really need, a chew for Mabel who was sitting patiently waiting in the car, and loaded the back of the Land Rover with bags of winter feed for the sheep. It was always a good idea to be prepared, he told himself, knowing perfectly well that they'd have to get a load more delivered soon enough.

He told himself that when he got back, he was going to have things out with Delma. There was so much she wasn't telling him, he knew that, but part of him was too afraid to push her for answers. He swept through the gateway, up the drive and into the courtyard, then let Mabel out of the car and strode up the steps. As he did so he called for Delma, but there was no reply. He took the stairs two at a time to their bedroom, but she wasn't there, so he went back downstairs and checked the other rooms, with no result. Finally, he went along the corridor to the kitchen, where he found Nonna busy making pastry.

"Where's Delma?"

"I don't know, Rodi, probably in the stables as usual." She glanced at him, then went back to rolling out the dough on a marble slab. "The police were here earlier," she said.

"Not again! What did they want this time?"

"They came to see Delma. I don't know what about, exactly. They were very polite, but they made it clear they wanted to speak to her alone."

"This is harassment," he muttered. "Don't they realise what we're going through?"

"They have little respect for grieving, those people."

He sighed. "I suppose they're just doing their job, given what's happened."

"But what if the post-mortem result was wrong, Rodi? I've heard of that happening, particularly now the funding for such things has been cut. What if your father's death is down to something else entirely?"

"I don't think that's likely, Nonna," he said, frowning at her. "I wouldn't have thought it was the kind of mistake a pathologist would make. That's just wishful thinking."

"I suppose." She gave him a straight look. "I tell you something, though, I wouldn't put it past that brother-in-law of yours."

"What? You mean he was responsible for Father's death?"

She nodded. "Think about it. Your father might have found out about that business with the silver and challenged him."

"But I didn't tell you–"

"I know, but Rodi, I'm not stupid. And had you noticed there's other stuff missing? It's possible Caradoc noticed too."

"Nonna! Like, what?"

She stopped rolling, laid a cloth over the pastry and wiped her hands. "Come with me," she said.

Nonna led him through the hall and round the back of the staircase to his mother's deserted sitting room. Once there, she pointed to a patch on the wall where a picture had hung. "You see that space?" she asked him.

Rodric glanced at the rectangle of darker wallpaper, surrounded by a faint line of dust. There was even a triangular mark where the string had rested against the wall, hanging from the dado rail above.

He looked at Nonna. "But that was the sheep in sunset picture, I remember it now. You used to tell us it was Mother's favourite."

"Yes, and it was very valuable – a Wystan Jones. Someone had replaced it with that," she pointed to a rather ugly still life propped against the wall.

"Where has it gone?"

"I don't know, Rodi, I've looked for it everywhere. If your father sent it to be cleaned, he never told me, and I don't think he would have done so anyway, he very rarely came in here. And it's not the only thing that's missing. The police making that inventory made me wonder," she went on, "so I thought I'd do some checking. There are several small pieces missing from the china cabinet in the sitting room. It's so crammed with bits and pieces that I didn't notice until I had a really good look. So far, I've discovered that your Mother's Fabergé egg has gone, as have the two Roman coins from Caerleon; they were in a leather case, do you remember them?"

He nodded wordlessly.

"They've gone, and that set of eighteenth-century Limoges trinket boxes – they were rare and worth quite a bit – they've gone as well. I haven't finished checking everything yet, so I don't know if anything else is missing."

Taking a deep breath, he asked, "And what are you suggesting, Nonna?"

The look she gave him was full of compassion. She put a hand on his arm. "In spite of the silver, Rodi, it may be that Delma knew nothing about these– these other bits and pieces. Perhaps it was Mike. I wouldn't put it past him to have simply helped himself, but unfortunately now we can't ask him. But I think you must tackle Delma. She won't tell me anything, I'm sure of that, but she might talk to you. Maybe he forced her in some way. I think she was afraid of him, so perhaps she had no choice, and now he's gone she might be more willing to talk, since he's no longer here to bully her."

"You're not suggesting she might have–" Rodric couldn't bring himself to finish the sentence.

"What?"

"No, that's absurd." He shook his head, rubbed his hands down his face. "Okay, leave it with me, I'll try and talk to her."

"I think it would be best, Rodi love, I really do."

Nonna went back to the kitchen and her pastry and Rodric followed her. Mabel, who had settled herself comfortably in front of the Aga, got up and trotted after him as he made his way out of the kitchen door and through the grounds to the stables. It was the only place he hadn't looked for Delma so far.

He called for her and, a moment later, she came out of Moonlight's stall, a currycomb in her hand. "Oh, you're back," she said, without meeting his eye.

"I am. I gather the police came while I was out."

She gave a gusty sigh. "They did."

"What did they want?"

"Oh, yet more questions."

"Obviously, Delma," Rodric said, sounding exasperated, "but what about, exactly?"

She shrugged and turned back to Moonlight's stall. "Just more of the same."

"Delma!" His voice echoed around the courtyard. "Don't give me that. I've had enough! Do you hear?"

She turned slowly to look at him, contempt in her eyes. "And what about me, Rodi? My brother has just died, been killed for Christ's sake, probably by your half-brother if what I heard Megan say was right, and all you can do is shout at me?"

Normally he would have backed down for the sake of peace, but it had gone beyond that. "Only when you drive me to it," he said, "and what do you mean about Garan?"

"Ask Megan," she snapped.

"I'm asking you."

"She said he reacted as if he'd had something to do with it."

"She told you that?" Rodric was incredulous.

"No, not me, I heard her talking to Nonna."

He sighed. "I'll ask her about it."

"Go ahead if you don't believe me."

Rodric ignored this and said, "Put that damn comb down and come inside. I've got to talk to you, and I'm not taking no for an answer."

"I'm busy," she said, but she wasn't so sure of herself now.

Teeth gritted, he said, "Delma. Come inside, now."

Her eyes widened in surprise tinged with shock. This wasn't what she was used to from him and she wasn't sure how to deal with him in this mood. For a moment there was a stand-off, then she went back into Moonlight's stall. Rodric heard her talking quietly to the horse and, a minute later, she came back out and, glaring at him, said defiantly, "Okay, but I will not be shouted at, do you understand?" Her defiance didn't quite mask the fear in her eyes.

He followed her into the house and when they got to the kitchen, Nonna was no longer there. Rodric ordered Mabel to stay and said to Delma, "There's something I want to show you in Mother's sitting room."

When they got there, he pointed to the wall. "The picture hanging there was very valuable, and someone had replaced it with that." He pointed to the still life. "Do you know where it is?"

"How should I know?"

"Nonna says it's nowhere to be found."

"So? Maybe your father got rid of it."

"He wouldn't do that. You know how he felt about family heirlooms. And it's not the only thing missing. Come on." Grabbing her by the wrist, he marched out of the room and Delma was forced to follow him. She did so without a word.

Standing in front of the glass fronted marquetry cabinet, Rodric turned to his wife. "There are several pieces missing from this, some Limoges, a couple of Roman coins, Mother's Fabergé egg, and Nonna says there could be other bits missing; she's not checked against the inventory yet." He turned and studied her expression, his eyes hard. "So, do you know what's happened to it all?"

"Why should I?" She sounded defiant, but her voice shook.

"Delma! After you took that silver you promised me it wouldn't happen again, you said it was a one-off. Now we find piles of other valuables are missing. Did Mike steal them?"

"Steal? He wasn't–"

"Don't give me that! If he didn't, who did?"

"Okay, yes, it must have been him." She sounded relieved, as if she'd found a solution that would take the spotlight off her. "He must have taken them."

"You knew about it, didn't you?"

"No, I swear I didn't."

"Don't give me that," Rodric said with weary scorn. He knew her too well. "And now we have no way of checking. That must be a relief for you."

"How dare you say that?" Delma demanded, trying to retrieve some dignity from the situation.

"Oh, for Christ's sake, woman, give me a break. I've done with playing these ridiculous games." He pulled her over to a chair and forced her into it, then pulled another up and sat down in front of her, barring her escape. His behaviour was so out of character that she succumbed without a murmur.

"Now," he said, "you're going to tell me exactly what's missing. If Mike took the stuff, tell me. I'm willing to grant that he may have forced you to cooperate, but I'm absolutely sure you knew about it. How did he persuade you, Delma?"

Head bent, she stayed stubbornly silent.

"You told me that's what happened over the silver and, more fool me, at the time I agreed not to tackle him about it. God knows why, now I look back on it. I suppose I didn't want Da to be upset. But this is different, this isn't a couple of thousand, this is much more, and precious family pieces at that. How could you?" he asked, sounding anguished.

Slowly she raised her head. Her eyes were swimming with tears, but unusually, they had no effect on Rodric.

"He forced me, Rodi."

"At last we're getting to it."

She stretched out a hand to him, but he sat back and crossed his arms. "Go on."

It all came tumbling out. Mike had threatened her, he wouldn't leave it alone, and when he was like that, he scared her so much, she'd had no choice.

"Why? What did he threaten you with?" Rodric asked.

"He said he'd tell you things."

"What things, Delma?"

She started crying in earnest now, sobbing into her hands. "Oh Rodi, I never wanted to hurt you."

"Look, things couldn't get much worse than they are. You'd better tell me everything."

"It was just a fling. I was bored. It didn't mean anything."

What she was trying to say gradually dawned on him, but his feelings were dulled now, he was hardly surprised. "You've had an affair?"

"Yes, but I tell you, it didn't mean anything," she said again, her tone pleading for understanding.

"Who was it?"

"I don't want to say."

"Who was it?" he shouted and grabbed at her shoulders, his fingers digging into her flesh.

"Rodi, let me go! Alright, alright, I'll tell you. It was Stewart Parker, the vet, but Rodi, it ended ages ago."

Abruptly Rodric let her go and she slumped back in her chair. He stared across at his wife, his voice quiet now, and asked, "Wasn't he the one who came and treated Moonlight? He had to sedate him." There was real fear in his eyes now. Slowly he went on. "He was here only last week. And you want me to believe it's all over?"

They sat silently gazing at each other, neither saying a word, then Rodric pushed his chair back, got up and stalked from the room, slamming the door behind him.

* * *

"You look exhausted," Anjali said when Fabia finally got home at about five o'clock. "What's happened?"

Fabia told her all about it, ending with the fact that Garan was being interviewed by the police.

"That's not good. Why did they take him to the police station?"

"That sort of interview has to be recorded," Fabia told her. "I think he's telling the truth. I don't think he would have drugged Mike, but if he didn't, who did?"

"From what you've told me, Mike doesn't sound like a very nice person. He's what my gran-mère would have called a *mauvais garçon*, a bad boy."

"That's putting it mildly," Fabia commented.

"All this trouble," Anjali said, frowning. "It seems, since I arrived, that everything is going prune shaped."

Fabia smiled briefly. "I think that's pear shaped, actually."

"Sorry, sometimes my English fails me."

"And suggesting you're in any way responsible for what has happened is nonsense," Fabia said firmly, although it flitted across her mind that it probably wouldn't be what the Mansell family would think. That was one of the reasons she was wary of Anjali going to stay at the Abbey, but she wasn't going to think about that now.

Anjali gave her a hesitant smile in response, then straightened her shoulders. "You know what the Mauritian medicine would be? A large glass of whisky and a good curry. What do you think?"

"You're a woman after my own heart. Come on, let's go for it. I've got some takeaway menus."

"No, no," Anjali said, smiling. "I've got it all planned. I am going to make you a Mauritian *curri poulez* for supper."

"Does that translate as chicken curry?"

"Yes, but this is the best ever, you will love it." A look of uncertainty came into her face. "Sorry, I'm being a pushy. Maman tells me this is one of my worst faults. I went to the High Street, to that delicatessen we passed when we went to buy the cheese? I found all the spices that I needed. Shall I get started?"

"You go ahead," Fabia said, "I'll get the drinks."

Once they both had a glass in hand, Fabia subsided on to a chair. Normally she might have found it difficult to have a guest taking over as Anjali was doing, but she felt so miserable that it was actually quite a relief. She sat at the kitchen table, her fingers round her glass, and watched as Anjali cooked and talked about the dish she was putting together. The scent of garlic, onions and spices began to permeate the kitchen and, as she sipped at her drink, Fabia was grateful for Anjali's presence, and her tact. Firmly she pushed aside a wish that Matt was there too.

Chapter 18

Fabia's eyes snapped open. Scrabbling for the light switch, she flung the covers back and swung her legs out of bed. She could feel the sweat on her body chilling as it came into contact with the night air. She shivered, but not only because of the cold. Come on, breathe deeply, she told herself. As she waited for her heart to stop thumping, she squinted at her bedside clock. It was ten past two.

She hadn't had the nightmare for weeks. Why now?

She stumbled to the bathroom and splashed her face with water, gasping at the cold. She was glad that it woke her completely, but the lingering visions still retained their terror. She knew from experience they'd hang around, haunting her, for hours. As she curled up under the duvet, once more her mind picked at the wound, unable to leave it alone.

There had been a balcony of polished wood, or something like it, and a woman running. Dark haired, in some sort of long, full-skirted garment, the material swinging about her legs, heels clicking. There'd been stone steps and enclosing, claustrophobic walls. The dread that she had become used to had pervaded the dream, but this time something else was added, some knowledge she had that threatened her, or was it someone else that was threatened? Someone she cared about? She couldn't work it out.

In her dream she'd found herself on the balcony and, leaning over, she'd seen a body far below, splayed out on the flagstone floor, the colourful garment spread around it like untidy wings. She'd known someone was behind her, that she might be the next one to be pushed down on to the floor below. Terror had spread. Should she run or turn and face whatever or whoever it was? But she couldn't move. She'd felt a blow to her back, and then she was falling... in that instant she knew who it was behind her.

That was the moment she woke up.

A shaft of moonlight cut through a gap in the curtains. Fabia had never liked moonlight, it always felt threatening to her. She'd have to get up and close the curtains, shut it out, but it took her some time to pluck up the courage to extricate herself from her safe cocoon. Don't be stupid, she told herself. You're not a child, you're a grown woman. Quickly she padded across the room and, a moment later, was back in bed, the duvet drawn up tight. It was only then that she realised what it was that had been different about this dream. Pushing herself upright, she switched on the light once again, grabbed the notebook she always kept by her bed, and began to scribble. Tomorrow she must phone Matt.

It was a long time before she managed to sleep again.

* * *

In the morning, the nightmare lingered in Fabia's mind, she couldn't shake it off. The first thing she did was to read through the notes she'd made in the middle of the night. She wasn't as sure of her suspicions now as she had been, but she still wanted to speak to Matt as soon as possible. She tried his mobile but got no response – he had probably let the battery run down again – so she plucked up her courage and phoned police headquarters. Usually she avoided doing so if she possibly could, there were still people who thought of her as someone who'd left the force under a cloud and that made her angry. Resentment at the injustice of it all still lingered.

There was no need to look up the number, she knew it by heart. She tapped it out and listened to the messages that told her all calls would be recorded, etc. Finally, she got through to a human being. Taking a deep breath, she said firmly, "Could you put me through to Chief Inspector Lambert please?"

"Can I say who's calling?"

"Fabia Havard."

There was a small pause, then the voice said, "Of course, Superintendent Havard, I'll find out if he's available."

Fabia was taken aback. That was not the reaction she'd expected. "Not superintendent anymore, I'm afraid. Who am I speaking to?"

"Oh, we've not met, I've just read– sorry, ma'am. I'll put you through."

For some reason Fabia felt cheered by this interchange, until she heard the curt, "Chief Inspector Lambert," when Matt picked up.

Oh dear, she thought, he sounds stressed. She hoped he wasn't going to be difficult. She reminded herself that she was the one doing him a favour.

"Matt, it's Fabia."

"Hallo." At least he sounded pleased to hear her voice. "How are you this morning?"

"I'm okay, worried about the Prices, obviously," she rushed on, "but anyway, I wouldn't normally phone you on the landline, but I had no luck with your mobile."

"Oh lord. I should have put it on charge first thing. I'll do it now."

A moment later he was back with her. "Have you had time to do those notes?"

"I have, they're on my laptop." She desperately wanted to ask him about Garan but was afraid she'd be snubbed if she did. "The thing is, Anjali's going up to London. I'm taking her to the station to catch the 10.30. What I thought was, I could bring my laptop with me and pop into your office – if you think that would be a good idea." She was annoyed with herself for sounding hesitant.

"Let me just check what Dilys has got lined up."

Fabia could hear a muttered conversation in the background. He was back within a couple of minutes.

"That'll be fine. Why don't you come into the office immediately after you've dropped her off and we can go through your notes?"

"Okay, I'll– I'll see you in about an hour."

Fabia ended the call and sat for a minute, her teeth gripping her lower lip. This would be the first time she'd been back to the building that had once been such a large part of her life. It was hard to believe that, in spite of being so closely involved in Matt's work six months ago and, once again, in the last couple of weeks, she hadn't set foot in the place for nearly three years. She took a deep breath. Onward and upward, she told herself, a phrase her father had used whenever life presented him with obstacles.

* * *

Having dropped Anjali off, Fabia made her way along the familiar route to police headquarters. She had to make herself relax her hands on the steering wheel. "Stop being such a coward," she muttered, "pull yourself together." She made her way into the building and gave her name. There was no reaction from the officer on the desk and she was shocked by the wave of relief she felt about this.

Matt came down to greet her in reception and led her upstairs. As they made their way through the main office, Fabia was conscious of curious glances from people craning round their computer screens to have a look. Some she recognised, but many she didn't. Dilys got up from her desk to greet her. "Hallo," she said, sounding slightly awkward and Fabia wondered if Dilys disapproved of her presence.

"Do you want me to get some coffee for you, sir?" Dilys asked Matt.

"Ask Simon to get it," he said, referring to one of the clerical assistants.

"No worries, he's busy, I'll do it," said Dilys.

"Thanks, that'd be good."

"How do you like yours, Fabia?"

"White, no sugar please."

Matt ushered Fabia to a chair and, as she sat down, Fabia said, "I don't think Dilys approves of me coming to see you here."

"Why would you think that?" Matt asked, frowning.

"I don't know. I just got the impression she's not happy about it."

"I think you're being oversensitive. It's more likely that she's worried for you. She knows it's the first time you've been here since you left."

"Oh, maybe that's it," Fabia said, feeling a bit of a fool.

"For goodness sake, Fabia, stop worrying. She's a great fan of yours, you know?" He sounded irritated.

She wanted to ask him how he knew that, but she didn't pursue it. It would seem so self-obsessed.

"Anyway," Matt said, sitting forward in his chair, business-like now, "what have you got for me?"

Fabia placed her laptop on the desk, while Matt pulled his chair round to sit beside her.

"I've done what amounts to a biography and personality analysis of each member of the family," she told him, "as much as I know, that is. Then I've made some notes of times I've met up with them, mainly to do with Megan and the book. I've also made a diary of the weekend I was there in as much detail as I could remember, you know, how they interact, and stuff like that. Now, this is a conversation I had with Delma about the horses, I don't think it's an exaggeration to say she's obsessed with them. I managed to ask if she had private money that she could use to maintain the stables."

"Fabia!" Matt exclaimed, impressed. "How'd you manage to do that?"

"Well, I said it must be very difficult for her needing money for the horses and running the stables when the rest of the estate was so expensive to run, but then I added that perhaps she had her own money and that would help."

"And what was her reaction?"

"She went very pink and said, rather bitterly, that she had no money of her own and she had to rely entirely on what Caradoc and Rodric would let her have, other than the money she gets from giving riding lessons. Then she added, well, sort of muttered, 'but that's going to change soon'. I asked her how come, but she clammed up."

"You know I told you about the silver that disappeared?" Matt said.

"I do."

"Well, when we did the full search, we made an inventory of the contents of the house which we matched up with the one they had done for insurance purposes. It shows several things missing, mostly small artefacts, but also a painting by your favourite Welsh impressionist."

"Wystan Jones?"

"The very same. It's a large landscape and it was marked down as being in 'the small sitting room'. Dilys said it looked as if the room isn't much used, very dusty and a bit damp, she notices that sort of thing, does Dilys. So, they possibly hadn't realised it was gone. One of the team's been checking the net to see if it's turned up."

"On the National Mobile Property Register?" Fabia asked, just to make sure he knew she was still on the ball.

Matt grinned. "Yes Fabia, on the NMPR, well remembered."

Fabia said crossly, "Don't be patronising."

"Sorry." But he was still grinning. "Ah, here's Dilys. Thanks," he added as she put three lidded cups down on the desk.

"I went over the road to the coffee shop. I know you can't stand the stuff the machine produces. That one's yours, Fabia."

"You're a star," Matt said. "Have they found anything more on the Register?"

But Dilys had no news on that front. "We're still searching, though. But I do have more from Aidan Rogers, he's one of our techies," she said. "They've been working hard on all the devices and they've turned up a few interesting bits and pieces. The records on the computer in the stables' office are clear as day. Delma Mansell seems to have been researching auction websites on that. And her phone produced a few odds and ends, including some texts back and forth with Stewart Parker, the vet." She turned to Fabia. "The tone and the content bear out the fact they were having an affair."

"Oh dear. Poor Rodric."

"As to him," Dilys went on, "his laptop turned up some recent research into animal tranquilisers, but that was after his father died, so he could simply have been checking up on it after we told him. We also found similar research done by whoever used the computer in Caradoc Mansell's study, that goes back a couple of weeks, so it seems more than one person was interested in the drug."

"That could have been any of them," Matt pointed out.

"True."

"Incidentally, Fabia," Matt said, "the keyboard to that computer, its screen and case had been wiped clean as a whistle, which we found interesting, as the rest of that room was pretty dusty, and all the other keyboards were full of dust and had all the appropriate fingerprints still intact."

"That's interesting, why just that one?"

"You may well ask," said Matt. "Maybe whoever murdered the old man was using it rather than their own."

"But wouldn't that indicate the person was aware how difficult it is to get rid of information on a computer?" asked Fabia.

"Not necessarily, but it's worth thinking about. What do you think, Dilys?"

"It's a good point. I'll go and have a word with Aidan," Dilys said.

"Thanks for all that," Matt said as she left the room.

Fabia sat back, wondering whether to ask the question that had been nagging at the back of her mind. She decided to take the plunge. "What's happening about Garan?"

Matt frowned across at her. "We've not charged him with anything. There is no evidence he had anything to do with drugging coffee, which he firmly denies having made. We might have to do a search of the pub, but if he did have any of those sleeping tablets hanging around, I'm pretty sure he'd have got rid of them by now."

"Do you think he's lying?"

"I'm not sure. They couldn't shake him, but we'll be keeping an eye."

"What a mess."

"It is rather."

"Did you get any more out of Delma?"

"Ah yes, I haven't told you about that, have I? Luckily, when we got there yesterday, she was on her own. She categorically denied giving her brother anything to sell, said he was probably just boasting to his friends. We couldn't shift her on that. Dilys got the impression there was no love lost between brother and sister, and so did I."

"Do you think she might be responsible for drugging him?"

"I wouldn't put it past her," Matt said, "but obviously she denied it. She told us he drank quite heavily, and she said he used to take drugs when he was younger, but he'd given that up when he took up bodybuilding. The alcohol I can believe, there's evidence of that, what with the flask and all, but I'm not sure about the drugs. I wouldn't put it past him to deal in them, that'd go hand in hand with people trafficking?"

"What?" Fabia exclaimed.

"Oh yes. One of our chaps went undercover with this fascist group Cotter had contacts with in Swansea, that's how we found out he'd been getting valuables to sell from his sister, and they were talking about bringing in some 'tasty toms'."

"It gets worse and worse with that ghastly man, doesn't it?" Fabia said, looking disgusted. "Once you find out who drugged him you should give them a ruddy medal!"

"I wish," said Matt. "Anyway, I don't think he'd be into taking drugs, except perhaps steroids, given the bodybuilding, but nothing else."

"Did Delma say anything about the vet?"

"Oh, she admitted to having a fling, but insisted that it was over at the end of the summer, but that's not what Marsden told us."

Eyebrows raised, Fabia asked, "Ted Marsden? What's it got to do with him?"

"He told us he overheard her and Stewart Parker, as he put it, being 'intimate' together when he went to the stables to complain about her horses encroaching on his land." Matt grinned. "He got quite embarrassed having to tell us about their activities, I think Dilys cramped his style. And he also said something about hearing her ask Parker for more tranquiliser."

Fabia's eyes widened. "That's pretty incriminating."

"You could say so, but it doesn't mean she was the one to use it on her father-in-law," Matt said, playing devil's advocate, "it just means that it would have been available to whoever did."

"I suppose."

"Anyway, Delma said she'd told her husband about the affair and he'd forgiven her."

Fabia frowned. "I don't believe that."

"She was adamant."

Fabia still looked doubtful.

"What about," Matt suggested, "say, Megan, found out and threatened to tell him?"

"I hadn't thought of that, there's no love lost between Megan and Delma, but Megan isn't malicious," Fabia said, frowning. "And what about the tranquiliser, did Delma admit to having any of it in the stables?"

"No way. She insisted she wasn't qualified to use it and would never dream of doing so. She admitted that it had been used on one of her horses and that it had been Stewart Parker who'd administered it, but that it had been completely above board. We also asked about her veterinary science degree and she said she'd given up on it three years into the course, when she and Rodric got married. She seemed to think that proved she couldn't have used the tranquiliser, which, of course, it doesn't."

"What other interviews have you got lined up?"

"We've got to speak to Rodric Mansell again, and Mrs Giordano, although she's a bit of a clam," Matt said.

"She's such a mother hen that I don't think she'd ever tell you anything that would damage the family. They're all far too important to her, particularly Megan and Rodric."

"Talking of your friend, Megan, we need to speak to her again, particularly as she was there when the Prices found out about Cotter's accident. And I need to have a word with Anjali Kishtoo."

"What for?" asked Fabia, then thought what a silly question that was.

"That should be obvious, Fabia."

She didn't say anything else but felt the colour rising in her cheeks.

"We want to find out if Caradoc Mansell told her anything when they met that could help us untangle this mess."

"She should be coming back Monday morning – give her a ring then." Fabia changed the subject. "If you've got a memory stick, I can copy these notes on to it."

"That'd be a good idea." Matt too seemed relieved to get on to more practical matters. He went around his desk and rummaged in a drawer. "I know it's here somewhere," he muttered.

Fabia's smile was a little malicious. Matt had never been the tidiest of people. "Looks like it's still a case of chaos reigns," she said.

"It may look a mess, but I know where everything is," Matt insisted.

"No, you don't, you wouldn't be rummaging in that drawer if you did."

"Shut up, Fabia." And a moment later he handed the memory stick across the desk. "There, see?"

She grinned at him and slotted it into her laptop.

"Thanks for doing that, Fabia," Matt said, serious now.

"No problem." After copying the files, she said, "I'll get going then." But she didn't move immediately. "I had another of those nightmares last night," she told him.

"You poor thing, I thought they'd stopped," Matt said, looking worried.

"So did I." She frowned. "There was something about it that I thought was, well, relevant. I wrote it down, and you're not to laugh at me."

Fabia rummaged in her handbag for her notebook. She described the dream to Matt. "It was more specific this time. Before there was just a threatening atmosphere, just me, on my own, trying to escape something terrifying but imprecise. This time it was, sort of, peopled."

The dream, still vivid in her mind, was easy to describe to Matt.

"Maybe your subconscious is going back to the second murder six months ago," he said, "what with balconies and all that."

"Perhaps. But one thing really worried me, the body on the floor was wearing a coat very like one of Anjali's creations."

"That's an easy connection for your subconscious to make," Matt said.

"I suppose. But the person I felt was behind me, I think I identified who it was."

"In your dream?"

"Yes," Fabia said, exasperated as she glanced at Matt and saw he was trying not to smile.

"Take that smirk off your face," she told him. "I know you don't believe in premonitions or any of that, but still–"

"So, who was it?"

Fabia told him.

His smile grew. "Fabia, I don't think that's very likely."

"You're probably right, it's just that I have this sort of hunch."

"That's par for the course with you." He was no longer trying to hide his amusement.

"Sometimes I don't like you at all," Fabia said, glaring at him.

"Ah, but you know you love me really," Matt said, then the smile disappeared, and an arrested look came into his eyes. For a moment they stood facing each other, neither spoke, but there was tension in the air that hadn't been there before.

Fabia took a deep breath and made herself smile. "Okay, well, I hope those notes prove useful."

"I'm sure they will." Matt sounded brisk now, and he wouldn't meet her eyes. "I'll see you out."

"No need, I know my way."

"I'd better come down with you, security and all that."

"Of course," Fabia said, kicking herself for being such an idiot. She should have realised that.

The atmosphere between them as they made their way back downstairs was full of things unsaid. As Fabia started up her car, she felt a wave of regret that she was no longer an integral part of the life the building contained and deep frustration that her relationship with Matt seemed to be so difficult to navigate.

Chapter 19

Matt stood watching as Fabia drew out into the traffic. It had been going so well, he thought, and then the mood suddenly seemed to change. He shouldn't have been so dismissive about that dream. And then following that up with talking about love, of all things; what had possessed him? Back at his desk he picked up the memory stick, but all he did was twist it over and over in his long fingers. He was still sitting there, staring into space, when Dilys came in a few minutes later.

"We've got some more from that computer in Mansell's study." She stood waiting for his response. "Sir?"

"Sorry, Dilys, I was miles away. Okay, what have you got for me?"

"The computer in the study," she said again, settling herself in a chair. In her hand were several sheets of paper clipped together. "There are reams of e-mails back and forth between Mansell and his granddaughter. They go back to the end of August when she first got in touch with him. She told him she'd been contacted by someone called Branwyn Pierce, whose father," she checked the notes, "was Mansell's batman when he was in the Welsh Guards."

"So, how did this daughter find out about the connection?"

"I'm coming to that. Anjali told her grandfather it was only recently that Branwyn Pierce had gone through her father's papers, when she moved house. She lives in Swansea now. Anyway, that's when she discovered loads of his letters and photos, which made it obvious her father had kept contact with Anjali Kishtoo's grandmother for years after he and Caradoc Mansell were sent home from Mauritius. It seems Mansell was pretty dubious at first, but you can tell from the way the tone of the e-mails changes that he came around quite quickly. And then there's this."

Dilys undid the bulldog clip keeping the papers together, selected one and handed it over to Matt, who glanced at the heading.

"But this is to John Meredith."

"Yes, read it," she said, "and look at the date."

"Twentieth of November," Matt muttered, then read slowly down the transcript of the e-mail. "So, he told John he'd decided to change his will. What's this? 'In line with what we discussed' and he asked him to draw it up ready for signature on the twenty-ninth." Matt frowned. "But that doesn't fit. He was dead by the twenty-ninth."

"Exactly," said Dilys, excitement in her voice.

Matt grabbed his mobile and scrolled down. "I'm going to check with John."

He was lucky, he didn't have long to wait.

"Granger, Meredith and Llewellyn." It was John's PA, Stephen Powell.

"Chief Inspector Lambert here, could I have a word with John Meredith please?"

"I'll just check if he's in, Chief Inspector. Hold on please."

A moment later John was on the line. "Hallo, Chief Inspector. What can I do for you?"

"It's about Caradoc Mansell's will. We've been going through the e-mails on his computer and it seems he made a date to come in and sign the new one on the twenty-ninth, is that right?"

"Yes, but he changed his mind after meeting Anjali in London."

"Ah, then when did he actually sign it?"

"He came into my office on his way back from London on the twenty-third. He was like a different man. I'd never seen him so – I don't know – so delighted with life is about the only way I can describe it." John paused, then added, "Poor old chap."

Matt said nothing, but it dawned on him that John was speaking of a friend, and that friend had been murdered. Ripples in a pool, he thought.

"Anyway," John said, "what difference does it make?"

"I'm not sure yet, but thanks for that, John. I'll come back to you."

Matt ended the call, looked across at Dilys and sighed. "Sometimes I forget these puzzles we unravel are – oh, I don't know."

"I know what you mean," Dilys said, her tone sympathetic. "It's not always your ordinary villain we're dealing with."

"Yes, that's just it." He leant his crossed arms on his desk. "So, for a start that computer was available to anyone in the house, and since the keyboard was wiped clean, we can't check who did and didn't use it, and all these e-mails were on there for anyone to access."

"That's about it."

"That means anyone in and out of the Abbey could have accessed them. And anyone who thought they were going to lose out to Anjali would want to prevent him from signing the new will and, if they saw this e-mail to John, they'd think they had until the twenty-ninth to do something about it."

"And," added Dilys, looking slightly smug, "there's this, dated a couple of weeks earlier." She selected another piece of paper and handed it over to Matt.

He read through it slowly then looked up at her, his eyes wide. "Well, well, so not only had he discussed the changes, he'd e-mailed a list of them to John, and in detail too. This is beginning to make sense."

"There's one more thing that Aidan found that's interesting." For the third time she passed him a piece of paper. This time it wasn't an e-mail, it was a simple list, the first item on it was 'Elizabeth's Fabergé egg'. "Now, we've compared the two inventories, the one we made and the Mansells' insurance one, and nearly everything on that list we found on his computer corresponds with what's missing off the Mansells' list, although some of the descriptions are slightly different. So, if Caradoc Mansell made that list, not only did he know that stuff was going missing, but he actually knew what specific pieces."

"And if he tackled whoever he thought was responsible?"

"Yet another motive," said Dilys with a satisfied nod. "All of this widens the field, doesn't it?"

"It does, Dilys, it does." Matt pushed a hand through his hair. "But none of it gets us much further. Maybe I should just resign myself to taking Fabia's hunches more seriously."

"She's pretty perceptive, is Fabia."

"I know, but this time I think she's gone out on a limb."

"Why? What's she got a hunch about?"

But Matt didn't want to tell Dilys about Fabia's dream and the suggestion she'd made. He was quite willing to tease Fabia himself, and laugh at her premonitions, but he didn't want anyone else doing so.

"Nothing specific, but she did bring in some notes I asked her to make, I've got them on this," he picked up the memory stick. "Anyway, I need to stretch my legs, I'm going to go and get a sandwich, do you want anything?"

"No thanks," she said with a smile, and Matt guessed she knew he wasn't telling her everything. It wasn't just Fabia who was perceptive.

* * *

After the row with Delma and her revelation about her affair, Rodric had de-camped to one of the spare rooms, unable to contemplate sharing a bed with his wife, but he'd hardly slept at all and, in the end, he got up at half past five. It was still dark outside as he made his way downstairs in the quiet house. He wanted to look for an article he'd seen in the local newspaper.

Mabel looked up from her basket as he came into the kitchen, then put her head down and went back to sleep, this was far too early for her. He made his way to the old larder off the kitchen where Nonna stored the recycling. Pulling up a chair, he leafed through the pile of papers, and finally found the one he wanted. Yes, here it was, an interview with the vet, Stewart Parker, about his plans to start up a business travelling round local sheep farmers with a mobile sheep dip.

In the middle of the night he'd decided he must tackle Stewart Parker, so this would be a good excuse. He phoned as soon as he thought they'd be open to make an appointment.

"Yes, Mr Mansell," the receptionist said, "he's got a cancellation at half past eleven so he could see you then."

"Thank you," Rodric said, and ended the call.

* * *

Some time later, as he drove along the road towards Brecon Rodric thought back on all those years being in the shadow of his father, who'd once told him, in the middle of a blazing row, that he was weak and gutless. The old man would never believe that he was on his way to tackle his wife's lover and tell him to keep away from her. He felt quite proud of himself but, by the time he'd parked outside the surgery, he was regretting his decision to come. No, he told himself firmly, he had to go ahead. Weak and gutless? He'd show the old man yet.

Rodric was not kept waiting long. Stewart Parker came out and greeted him with a handshake.

"Good morning, Rodric, good to see you." Parker, normally a confident, assertive man, looked unsure of himself for once.

All to the good, Rodric thought.

"Come along to my room," Parker said, and the two men went down a short corridor to a room at the back. There was the usual stainless-steel covered table, a glass-fronted cabinet full of drugs of different kinds, and charts on the wall outlining various problems that small animals may have. To the side was a desk and two chairs in front of it. Parker indicated Rodric should take one, then sat down in the other.

"So, my receptionist tells me you wanted to ask about the mobile sheep dip I've invested in."

"That was what I told her," said Rodric, "I thought it best not to tell her my real reason."

"Oh? And what is your real reason?" Parker didn't sound so friendly now.

"First of all, did you know that my father was killed by an injection of a tranquiliser normally used on large animals?"

"I should have said – um – please accept my condolences on your loss."

"Never mind about that," Rodric snapped, "did you know?"

"I did not. The police were here a couple of days ago." He didn't look Rodric in the eye. "But they didn't say anything about that."

Rodric didn't believe him, but he didn't say so. "Okay, so there's one thing I want to tell you and one thing I want to ask you." The atmosphere in the room had chilled considerably.

"Go ahead." Parker folded his arms across his chest. Rodric had an urge to smash his fist into the man's smug face.

"I want to tell you that I know about your affair with my wife."

Parker opened his mouth to speak, but Rodric didn't give him the chance. "Don't bother to deny it," he snapped. "Delma has told me all about it. She also told me it ended some time ago, but I don't believe her. I know you visited the stables recently."

"Yes, to see to her stallion, Moonlight, a very valuable horse."

"And were you seeing to my wife at the same time?"

"I resent–"

"Resent away," Rodric said, his voice full of scorn. He leant his elbows on his knees and stared across at the man opposite him. "But there's a far more serious matter, and I would like an honest answer to this question. You could say your career depends on it." He noticed the blood drain from Parker's face. "Did you allow Delma to have access to the tranquiliser? Did you give her some to keep in the stables in case Moonlight became uncontrollable?"

"Absolutely not. How dare you suggest such a thing?"

"I dare," Rodric replied, "because my father has been murdered, pumped full of that drug you used on Moonlight, and it seems logical to me that Delma got it from you?"

"But– but– has she been arrested?" There was real fear in his eyes now.

"No. Not yet." Rodric wanted to get away from this place now, this man. He rose from his chair and said, his voice quiet, "I'm going to leave now but, if you supplied my wife with that drug, I expect you to go to the police and tell them you did."

Parker jumped up, stumbled into speech. "But I didn't, I told them–"

"Oh, shut up, man," Rodric said, deep contempt in his voice. "Do it, or I'll tell Delma she has to go to them, and, the way I feel now, I will do so, believe you me."

He left the room, head held high, fully expecting Parker to come after him, but he didn't. He got back to the Land Rover and sat for a moment with his hands on the wheel, heart hammering, feeling dazed; then he manoeuvred the car from its parking space and, hardly aware of what he was doing, began the drive back down the valley to the Abbey.

* * *

Fabia was determined to get some work done when she got home. She still hadn't arranged to collect the paintings that hadn't sold. She also needed to get her brain round the commissions that had come out of the exhibition. At least all this would take her mind off Matt and the troubles at White Monk Abbey, wouldn't it? She smiled to herself, ruefully, as she pulled up in front of her house. Probably not was the answer to that question.

As she opened her front door, the house seemed strangely empty. Over the last few days she'd got used to having company. Although she relished the peace and quiet, part of her, the part that had nightmares, was afraid of the loneliness. She went straight through to the kitchen and turned on the radio, then through to her dining room and did the same there, hardly registering what the programme was, but glad of the voices rumbling away in the background. She made herself a mug of instant soup and carried it into the dining room, sat down at her computer and began to go through the list of commissions.

A couple of hours later she had e-mailed everyone involved, made a couple of appointments with those who wanted portraits painted, and then she phoned Cath.

"Hallo, love." Cath's warm voice lifted Fabia's spirits. "I've been wondering how you were getting on. How's Anjali?"

"She's gone up to London for the weekend, but John's asked her to come back on Monday, he needs her here when he goes through the details of the will with the family."

"Ah, that's not going to be easy for anyone."

"No."

"Is there any more news, from Matt I mean?"

"About the murders?"

"Murders plural? Oh lord, don't tell me there's been another one."

"I'm afraid there has, at least, that's what it looks like. I'd forgotten I hadn't spoken to you for a couple of days." She told Cath about Mike's accident, and Garan's possible involvement. "Poor Bella is so worried, and so's Sheryl. It's awful for them all, in fact."

"And for Delma Mansell," Cath said.

Fabia grimaced. "I'm not so sure about that. I don't think there was much love lost between sister and brother; he was a very nasty piece of work. I have a feeling she might be quite relieved he's out of the way."

"Do you think she was the one who drugged him?"

"I don't know, Cath. It's all a bit of a mess. This morning I took some notes I'd made about the family into Matt's office, but I'm not sure they're going to help much."

"You went to the station?" Cath said, sounding as if she could hardly believe it.

"I did, and it was all very strange, and rather disturbing. People were watching me out of the corner of their eyes, probably speculating on why I was there, and when I left, Matt said he'd have to escort me downstairs for security reasons, that really got to me."

"I'm not surprised." But then she added, in what Fabia thought of as her 'must be fair' voice, "I suppose he has to obey the rules."

"But that's the problem with Matt," Fabia protested, "he's always obeying the rules and refusing to look at things from a wider perspective. For instance, I had another of those nightmares the other night." She heard Cath make a small sympathetic sound, but went on before she could interrupt, "And I'm sure it was, sort of, telling me something, but when I told Matt all about it, he just laughed at me."

"Actually laughed?"

"Well, no, but grinned. Sometimes I think I really don't like him, and I told him so."

"Good for you, but you know you love him really."

This echoed what Matt had said so closely that Fabia found it quite disturbing. "No, I–"

But Cath wasn't listening. "I've just had a really good idea. Since Anjali is away, why don't you ask Matt to come around, say tomorrow, for a meal? I'm sure it'd do you both good to have some time together. The two of you really need to talk, Fabia. And you can use those notes you did for him as an excuse – phone and ask what he made of them, then segue neatly into asking him for supper. Brilliant! What do you think?"

Fabia poured cold water on this idea but, an hour later, found herself scrolling down to Matt's number on her phone and, slightly nervous, waiting while it rang.

* * *

As Rodric walked into the hallway, Nonna hurried from the kitchen.

"Rodi! Where have you been? I've been searching for you. We have a real problem now."

"A real problem?" Rodric said, shaking his head in disbelief, "I thought all the problems we have at the moment were pretty real."

"Yes, yes, of course, but this just adds to them. Delma's gone."

"Gone? Where?"

"I don't know, I've just been up to your room and found this note on the bed." She held out a sheet of paper.

Rodric snatched it from her and began to read.

'Dear Rodi, I can't stand this anymore, I've had enough. I'm going up to London to stay with a friend for a few days, don't try to contact me. I've arranged for Paula and her brother to come in and look after the horses. I'll let you know when I'm coming back, Delma."

He looked up at Nonna. "You've read this?"

"Well, yes, it was just lying there, no envelope, nothing."

"This, about contacting her," he muttered, "how the hell can I? The police still have her mobile."

"Do you know what friend she could have gone to?" Nonna asked.

"No, I don't. There's that uni friend she sometimes visits, and there's Hannah who was a witness at our wedding, but I don't know how to get hold of either of them."

"Oh Rodi." She gave him an agonised look. "What if the police come asking to speak to her again?"

"Nonna! Why should they?"

"Why not? They're going to come back again and again until they find out who killed your father, or until they give up."

"We'll just have to put them off."

"No. It'd look better if we told them immediately. We can't leave it until they come and ask for her."

"You mean tell the police my wife has done a runner in the middle of a murder investigation?" he asked, incredulous.

She put her hand on his arm, her eyes full of sympathy but determination too. "It'd be much better if we did."

"Not yet. I'm sure Delma kept an address book, an actual one, not just stored on her phone. It's probably in the stables' office. I'll go and have a search for it."

"Good idea, I'll come with you."

"No," he snapped, then added, "Sorry, Nonna, but I'm sure you have other things to do. Don't worry, I'll find it if it's there."

He strode off, relieved that she didn't persist. He really didn't want anyone else hanging over his shoulder while he searched through his wife's desk. God knows what he might find. Best to keep it all to himself and pray that he didn't find anything more incriminating than the note and Delma's sudden decision to run away.

Chapter 20

Halfway through Friday afternoon, Dave Parry appeared in the doorway of Matt's office.

"I went to the brewery and had a word with the blokes who deliver to the Mynach Arms," he said. "I asked them about those two thugs, and they bear out what Garan Price said in his statement. I've got a good description of them, one particularly, who had a distinctive tattoo of a swastika on his neck and a slight cast in one eye, which matches up with one of that bunch of fascists Tom Watkins was monitoring. I ran it past Tom and he recognised the description, so we went through some mug shots and came up with a match. It's that Wayne Shuttleworth alright. Do you want me to have a word, like? Better me than Tom, since they might recognise him."

"I don't think I can spare you at the moment, but we'll keep them in mind. What with Cotter being out of the way, I think they might lie low," Matt replied.

"I suppose." Dave sounded disappointed. "Pity. I'd have liked to have a go."

"I'm sure you would, Dave," Matt grinned at him. "I'll keep you in mind if we decide to go after them."

They were interrupted by Matt's mobile. He took it out, looked at the screen, and said to Dave, "I'd better get this." He waited till he was alone before replying. "Fabia, hallo, I was going to give you a ring. I'm sorry about this morning."

"Sorry? What for particularly?" she asked, her tone cool.

Matt felt wrong footed. "Well, it must have been difficult for you, coming back here for the first time since you had to– were forced to retire. I should have accounted for that."

"I'm tougher than you think, Matt."

"Of course," he said, then added, "but you're still having nightmares."

There was a pause. Matt waited, wondering if he should have mentioned the nightmare. When Fabia said nothing, he went on in a rush. "Anyway, how can I be of service, madam?" he asked, hoping the silly phrase would lighten the atmosphere.

It didn't. Her tone was still coolly business-like when she went on. "I was just wondering if the notes I made were proving useful."

"They are. I'd like to go through some of the points with you."

"Oh? Okay." Now she sounded hesitant.

"Are you home a bit later?" he asked. "I could come over, use it as an excuse to leave the office at a reasonable time. Say about 8.00?"

Fabia agreed to this and said she'd make him supper, he said he didn't want to put her to any trouble, and she, sounding irritated, said don't be silly. When he ended the call he sat back, puzzled and a little worried. He felt there'd been a lot going on under the surface that she wasn't telling him. Maybe it was all about those nightmares. He still hadn't asked Hari Patel about what to look for in people suffering from PTSD. He searched for Hari's number on his mobile, but it rang and rang and then went to voicemail. Frustrated, he left a brief message. Hopefully Hari would get back to him.

* * *

Fabia had barely ended the call with Matt when her mobile rang again. She grabbed it up and answered without looking at the screen, wondering if it was Matt calling back to cancel, but it wasn't.

"Fabia? It's Megan." The breathy voice was hard to hear.

"Hallo, Megan." Fabia found herself talking louder than she'd normally do, as if somehow it would persuade Megan to speak up a bit. Strangely it worked.

"I was wondering, could I speak to Anjali?"

"I'm afraid not. She's in London."

"Oh no! She's not left for good, has she?"

"No, she'll be back on Monday. Hasn't John Meredith told you she has to be here when he goes through the will with all of you?" Fabia said.

"No– yes– I don't know. He might have spoken to Rodi."

"I would imagine he'll be talking to all of you, not a reading of the will as such, I don't think they do that nowadays, but just going through it. After all, Anjali has to decide what–" Fabia pulled herself up short. She really shouldn't interfere.

"I was so hoping she'd come and spend some time with us," Megan said, "particularly as Delma has gone to stay with a friend for a bit."

"Oh?" said Fabia. That was odd at a time like this, she thought. "How come?"

But Megan didn't seem to have heard the question. "What's Anjali doing in London?"

"She's visiting some buyers who've shown an interest in her designs."

233

"Of course, I'd forgotten about all that." There was a pause. "Nonna, I'm on the phone – sorry, Fabia, I won't be a minute."

Fabia could hear a muttered conversation going on in the background. At last Megan came back to her.

"Nonna asks if you can give us Anjali's mobile number. Then I can contact her and maybe arrange for her to come to us for a couple of days next week. Do you think that would be a good idea?"

"I'm sure it'd be fine, but you'd have to ask Anjali. I can't speak for her. I'll text you her number."

"I still haven't got my old phone back from the police. Let me give you the new one."

"It's okay, it came up on the screen," Fabia said.

"Yes, of course, and thank you *so* much," Megan said. "Nonna says thank you too."

As she texted the number to Megan, Fabia wondered if she was doing the right thing. Would Anjali want to be interrupted by Megan's constant phone calls? Too late now, she'd pressed send.

* * *

"Sir." This time it was Dilys at Matt's office door. "A call just came through about Delma Mansell, on the Crimestoppers line."

"Oh? Who was it?"

"Anonymous, a man I think, it was a bit hard to tell."

"And what exactly did he have to say?"

"It wasn't all that clear, he had a very quiet voice. He said she'd run off to London and gave the names of two friends she might be with, and their addresses. I've made a note of them." She passed him a piece of paper.

"It rather begs the question, how did they know?" Matt said.

"Surely it must have been someone at the Abbey or, at least, someone who knows the family well," Dilys pointed out. "I listened to the recording a couple of times, but I couldn't work out who it was."

"Could it have been Garan Price? Or the vet perhaps?"

"Both are a possibility, but why? And another thing the caller said was did we know Delma Mansell was terrified of her brother and would have been happy to see him dead."

Matt gave her a sharp look. "Do you think it could have been one of Mike Cotter's pals?" Then Matt shook his head. "No, why would they?"

"I think it's more likely to be someone close to the family in one way or another."

"Let me come and listen to it." But Matt was none the wiser after playing the tape over several times.

"This is such a pain. If it's true we'll have to go after her." He looked up at Dilys. "Of course, it could be a load of bollocks. Have you checked at the Abbey?"

"I'll do that now," said Dilys. She was back within minutes. "I phoned them and asked to speak to her. I got the aunt, Mrs Giordano, who just said Mrs Mansell was out and she didn't know where she'd gone, which doesn't really tell us anything. I thought it better not to mention the anonymous call at the moment, just left a message asking that Mrs Mansell phone us back."

"I'd rather not wait. Send Chloe out to speak to them, find out if those two addresses ring any bells with the family. When she gets back, I'll get on to Charlie Brewer at the Met and ask him to have them checked out. If necessary, we can have her escorted back home."

* * *

Fabia rummaged around in her fridge, trying to decide what to cook. She knew all Matt's favourites and one way she could think of to show him she cared about him – not loved him, she told herself, but cared – was to feed him. It had always been a part of her, this need to cook for her friends and family.

235

In the end, she took out some cod steaks. She'd make fish in a pesto crust, do some spinach with garlic to go with it, and a couple of baked potatoes. When Matt arrived, dead on eight, the fish and potatoes were in the oven and all she had left to do was the spinach.

He looked tired and dishevelled as he followed her into the kitchen, hands thrust deep in his pockets.

"You need a haircut," she told him, then wished she hadn't – it sounded too intimate.

"I know, but I haven't had time to do anything about it."

"That's hardly surprising."

She put a bottle of white wine on the table. "Can you open that?" she said to Matt, handing him a couple of glasses. "It's an Austrian white I found the other day and, since we're having fish, I thought it'd be a change from the usual red."

"Sounds good," he said, glancing at her with a touch of amusement in his eyes.

She felt her cheeks warm. "What are you grinning at?"

"You, behaving as if you're getting ready for a dinner party."

"I am not!" Fabia exclaimed, "But there's no harm in being civilized."

"None at all." Matt said as he poured wine into the glasses and sat down. He sipped at his wine, said, "Nice," and then stretched his long body back in the chair. "Dave Parry found out who those two thugs were, the ones that were threatening Garan Price."

"Good, are you going to tackle them?"

"I can't spare anyone just now, but we'll keep an eye on them. I've spoken to the chaps in Swansea and they've got them on their radar. I hope we can collar them at some point – they're a nasty bunch."

"You said those notes of mine have been useful," she said tentatively, her back to him as she pressed spinach leaves down into the olive oil and garlic.

"Yes indeed, they were certainly detailed. It's a pity, in a way, that Caradoc Mansell wasn't there when you went for the weekend. It would have been interesting to know about the dynamics between them all when he was around. In the circumstances, I'd particularly like to know what he thought of Mike Cotter."

"I did include some bits about that, but I couldn't say with any certainty how he reacted to Delma's brother because I never saw them together. I'd guess they didn't get on one little bit – chalk and cheese – and Caradoc used to be very rude about the English, particularly Londoners for some reason. Bella told me that when Rodric and Delma first got married he used to refer to her as 'your London floozy'. Bella told him off about it and he stopped. By the way," she added, "Megan said something about Delma going to stay with a friend, did you know about that?"

"Yes. She went screaming off to London. We got an anonymous call telling us she had. We still haven't worked out who that was from, so we sent Chloe out to check with the family and they admitted she'd done a bunk."

"Who did Chloe speak to?"

"Megan Mansell and Mrs Giordano, Rodric wasn't there."

"Are you going to fetch her back?"

"Yes, I've got it organised for first thing tomorrow morning."

Matt changed the subject. "We're getting on quite well with checking all the devices," he told Fabia. "We're pretty sure now that the old man knew things were going missing from the Abbey."

"How come?"

"We found a list on the computer from his study that matches up with our estimation of what's missing. I can't see any reason for anyone else to have made it, although anyone could have used the machine; he wasn't exactly careful about his privacy settings – didn't have any, in fact."

"I wonder what he was planning to do about the missing items?" Fabia asked.

"That I'd love to know. From what you said in your notes, he and Bella Price seem to have been close, at least until she moved up north. Do you think he might have spoken to her about it?"

"I've no idea. Do you want me to ask her?"

"Yes, if you would. She might tell you more than she'd tell me," Matt said. "Of course, he could have tackled Rodric, or Delma, which would give them a motive, don't you think? I mean, apart from the change in his will. Or maybe he spread it a little further. If the vet, Stewart Parker, thought his career was going to be threatened, there's a chance he could have taken action."

"That's a bit far-fetched, isn't it?" Fabia suggested. "How would he have got access to Caradoc in order to inject him?"

"I don't know, but he's been there quite regularly, looking after the horses and having an affair with the lady of the house."

Fabia smiled at this old-fashioned phrase, as Matt had intended her to do.

"I suppose it's worth investigating," she said. "Now I come to think of it I did get the impression people wander in and out of the Abbey without so much as a by-your-leave. The front door never seemed to be locked, nor the back."

Silence reigned while Fabia took the fish out of the oven and placed the dish on the table, decanted the spinach into a bowl and put the baked potatoes on to plates.

"Wow, this looks good," Matt said.

As they began to eat, Fabia said, "I've been thinking, Mike Cotter's death cuts the field of suspects down by one doesn't it? When it comes to Caradoc's death, that is."

"It does. Dilys pointed that out."

"Did she?" Why did he always have to mention what Dilys said or thought? Fabia was aware, too late, that her tone was a little sharp, but Matt didn't seem to notice. "But it doesn't cut him out entirely," Fabia pointed out, "it just means you might have more than one murderer on your hands."

"I'm an idiot. That hadn't actually occurred to me." He glared at her. "Oh, wouldn't that be great! Trust you to point out something that's going to make more work."

"Don't blame me."

"You might have mentioned it before."

"Why should I? It's not my place," she said, glaring at him.

"That's a ridiculous thing to say, you could have said something."

"Well! First you imply that I should butt out because I'm no longer in the force, and now you're having a go because I'm not interfering. I can't win."

"That's not fair. You know I value your input."

"Do you, Matt?"

"When you're behaving yourself, yes."

"Thanks a bunch!"

"Teasing." He held up his hands in a gesture of surrender. "Only teasing."

"Not funny, you horrible man."

"For goodness sake, Fabia, since when have you been so touchy?"

Their eyes met and what he saw in Fabia's pulled him up short. Suddenly, he looked stricken. "I'm so sorry." He stretched out and put a hand over hers. "I'm being stupid, I obviously didn't mean it. It's no wonder you're a bit sensitive."

She snatched her hand away. "What do you mean?"

"Well, it's only been six months since you came out of hospital. Things like that take a while to recover from, and it was only last night you had another nightmare."

"Yes, and you told me this morning it meant nothing."

"No, I didn't," he insisted, frowning across at her. "It's just that I'm not sure I believe in premonitions, and that was what you were suggesting, wasn't it? I'm willing to admit things can bubble up from our subconscious, things we might not realise we remember, but I just don't think what you suggested is likely. I will, however, think more about it; I promise."

"Forget it." But, like a dog with a bone, she didn't want to let this go. "You've made it clear you think what I suggested is nonsense."

"No," Matt said, trying to hang on to his patience, "just unlikely."

Fabia put down her knife and fork, very deliberately pushed her plate away and leant her elbows on the table. "Why did you ask me to make those notes, Matt, if you're not going to take what I say on board?"

"Oh, for goodness sake, Fabia, I am. You have great perception and your take on their relationships is invaluable. You've also filled in a whole lot of blanks when it comes to their motivations and the family history, which shines a spotlight on the behaviour of the different family members, all of that; but I have to work with facts, facts, facts." He thumped the table in time to the words. "I can't very well barge in and say, I'm arresting you because Fabia Havard had a dream."

"Do you think that's what I'm suggesting? Don't be stupid," she snapped. "But you could bear it in mind when you're questioning people."

"What makes you think I'm not going to?"

"Well, are you?"

The silence stretched out, the atmosphere thick with misunderstanding. Fabia got up and began to put their plates and cutlery in the dishwasher. She felt a little sick. This was going so wrong; it wasn't what she'd intended. She told herself she was being stupid. Matt was right, why did she have to be so touchy? But she couldn't think of a way out of the maze they seemed to have got themselves into. She turned and looked at Matt. He was staring straight ahead, his expression full of anger and frustration.

"Perhaps," he said as she came back to sit opposite him, "I shouldn't have involved you. It wasn't really fair of me, I'm sorry."

"What do you mean, not fair?"

"Well, you've had such a hard time over this last two and a half years, coping with being vilified, knowing that you'd been stitched up and unable to do anything about it, all that, and making a new life for yourself with your art, followed by– well, it must have put a hell of a strain on you."

"I can accept that, but I'm absolutely fine now." She tried to instil as much conviction into her voice as she possibly could.

"Are you? What with the nightmares and everything?"

"What everything?"

"You told me, a while ago, that you had panic attacks."

"Only the one, and that was months ago," she said.

"I still think I'm expecting too much of you. It's not as if I was asking for help from someone still in the force. It's not your job anymore."

Fabia felt a tide of anger rising up inside her. "That's a bit of an insult," she said, her voice a little unsteady.

"No, it's not," Matt insisted. "It's just a fact."

"Don't I know it," Fabia said bitterly. "But I haven't forgotten all my training. It doesn't mean I'm a different person to the one who used to be your boss. Why ask me to help when this is your attitude? I just– I just don't know what you want from me," Fabia said, a crack in her voice.

"I want your expertise, your perception, your wisdom, but I don't want to stress you out by asking too much," Matt told her, "and I also want your friendship."

"Is that all?"

"What do you mean? Isn't that enough?"

"Oh Matt, I don't know."

He pushed his long fingers through his hair, making it into even more of a mess, then he stretched a hand out and took hers. This time she didn't draw away. His thumb stroking the back of her hand set up a tingling in her skin.

As he began to speak again, he didn't look at her but down at the table. "Do you remember," he asked quietly, "years ago, must be about five years now, just after you moved in here after your aunt left you the house, I came to help you decorate this kitchen?"

Fabia nodded but said nothing.

"And I told you I wanted more out of our relationship, but you said no because we were colleagues and you knew how disastrous those relationships could be. You said you loved me, as a friend, a brother." There was self-mockery and a touch of bitterness in his voice. "You told me the age difference didn't matter, but there was no chance of anything more."

Still, she said nothing.

Matt looked across at her and there was determination in his eyes. "I seem to remember telling you at the time that I wouldn't give up hope." The grip on her hand became tighter. "Fabia, I care about you. I want more than just this friendship, and that's one of the reasons I keep coming back to consult you. I suppose it's an excuse to see more of you."

"So, it's not because you feel I have any particular expertise," she said, and immediately regretted it.

"Fabia! I'm trying to tell you I love you, that I want to be with you, and all you can do is go on about work and whether or not I respect your opinions!"

Matt jumped up, grabbed her arm, pulled her up out of her chair and close against him, close enough for her to feel his breath on her cheek. For a moment they were both absolutely still, then he put a hand to the back of her neck, feeling the soft curling hair wrap around his fingers. Slowly he bent his head and, for the first time since they'd met all those years ago, when he'd been a lowly sergeant and she his inspector, their lips met in a kiss that was very far from a friendly hallo or goodbye. It was an exploration, gentle, tentative at first, but it didn't stay that way. The kisses became deeper and more urgent and Fabia felt Matt's hand slide up inside her jumper, move up her back, warm on her bare skin. For a while there was silence except for an occasional murmur, and then she came to her senses.

"Matt–"

"Can I stay?" Matt whispered.

"No, no, I can't–"

"Please, Fabia."

She leant away from him, said more firmly, "No, love, not tonight."

He tried to pull her back close, but she said softly, "Matt, please, stop."

They broke apart, both breathing rather hard. Fabia leant her forehead on his chest. "Oh lord," she said, her voice shaking. "That was not – um – not what I was expecting to happen this evening."

Matt gave a gurgle of laughter. "Nor me." Then he added, "You said not tonight, does that mean another night you'd say yes?"

She pushed him gently away. "Give me time to think, Matt, please."

"I feel as if I've been doing that for a very long time," he said wearily.

"I know, I know." She took his hand, lifted it to her lips and kissed it. "And I promise I'm not just stringing you along. Look, can we just get through this case–"

"We?"

"You've asked me to talk to Bella. I can keep my eyes and ears open when it comes to the family, and I was planning to see if I can get proof of what I suspect."

"Oh no. Come on, Fabia, don't start putting yourself in danger again." He pulled her back into his arms. "I couldn't bear it."

"Don't be silly, Matt, that's not going to happen. Who do you think is going to beat me up this time?"

"If you don't promise me you'll be sensible, it may well be me!" he exclaimed, exasperated.

"Then I'll just have to report you to Dilys, and your career will be ruined."

He grinned and hugged her so hard that she thought her ribs would crack. Then, abruptly, he let her go.

"If I don't go now, I don't guarantee being able to leave at all." He took a deep, shuddering breath and stepped away from her. "I absolutely still want your help, understand?"

"Yes, I do. I'll speak to Bella tomorrow."

"Good, and let me know when Anjali gets back, I need to speak to her."

"Will do."

For a moment they stood there, uncertain of this new dynamic between them, then Matt put out his hands and clasped Fabia's arms. "At least now you know I love you, and not just as a friend." He gave her a quick, hard kiss and before she could respond he strode down the hall and out of the front door, closing it firmly behind him.

It was a long time before Fabia felt calm enough to go up to bed and, even then, she lay awake until the small hours thinking about what had happened and wondering why on earth she hadn't allowed Matt to stay.

Chapter 21

On Saturday morning Dilys arrived at work not long after Matt. She had become used to his moodiness lately and hadn't been expecting anything different today, so being greeted with a broad smile and a cheery, "Hallo, Dilys, how are you this morning?" was something of a surprise.

"Morning, sir." She grinned. "You've got your happy face on today."

"What?"

"Just saying," she added.

"Yes, well, I suppose I have," he said, and returned the grin.

Before she could enquire further, they were interrupted by Chloe Daniels.

"Sir, something's come up on the stuff stolen from White Monk Abbey. A dealer in Cardiff, a man by the name of Carey Hutchinson, says he was offered what the customer said was a Fabergé egg, green and blue, gold embossed, about the size of a hen's egg with a gold four-pronged stand," she said.

"Have you checked up on this dealer?"

"Yes, sir. He hovers on the edge of what's legal, known to us but not for anything in particular. I think he might want to get some brownie points. He says he was suspicious because the person who brought it in didn't appear to realise the value of it. It's not one of the originals, I did some research and they go for silly money, but he says it is pretty valuable. Apparently, the man told him he'd inherited it, but the dealer didn't believe him."

"Did he say why not?" Dilys asked.

"He said the man 'wasn't the type to own such a thing', but I'm not sure how he could tell. He told the bloke he had a collector who might be interested, said he'd get back to him, then he phoned us."

"And did he describe this 'type'."

Chloe glanced at some notes she'd made. "Male, around six feet tall, shaved head, snake tattoo on the back of his hand, well spoken with a Swansea accent."

"Observant, your dealer. Get Tom to bring up the mug shots of those pals of Cotter's in the Welsh Dragon Soldiers outfit, then contact Cardiff. Ask them to go round and check if this dealer recognises any of them," Matt said.

"Will do, sir."

"They're going to love us, giving them more work," remarked Dilys.

"Maybe," Matt said, "but I'm sure we can return the favour some time."

* * *

Saturday breakfast at White Monk Abbey usually saw all the family gathered in the kitchen, it was another of Nonna's little rules, and it didn't occur to Megan and Rodric that this Saturday should be any different.

Nonna was already busy preparing the meal when Rodric came into the kitchen, dressed and ready for work. He was followed by Megan, looking exhausted and still in her dressing gown. They helped themselves from the old French coffee pot which, as usual, was keeping hot on the Aga, and Nonna put a plate of toast on the table.

"Who wants what?" she asked, and added, without waiting for an answer, "you need to keep your strength up, Rodi, so you'd better have a proper breakfast, there's bacon and lava bread keeping warm and I'll do you a couple of eggs."

He didn't argue.

"Megan, *bach*, how about you?"

"Just toast for me, Nonna."

"I'll do you some scrambled egg to go with it. You need some proper food inside you as well."

Megan didn't argue either.

"You said you found Delma's address book, Rodi," Nonna said as she broke eggs into a bowl. "Have you found those phone numbers?"

"Yes, but neither of them is picking up."

"I can't understand why she went off without a word," Megan said, "it makes it look as if she was responsible for–"

"Let's not go there, Megan," Rodric said, his voice sharp.

"But why not, Rodi," Nonna said quietly as she ladled scrambled egg on to toast and broke two more eggs. "I have to say it does make it look bad for her, running away like that."

"Look. I don't want to talk about it, okay?"

Both women, with a quick glance at each other, subsided without another word. With a sideways look at her brother, Megan changed the subject. "I managed to get hold of Anjali last night," she told her brother, "and she's going to come for a couple of days when she gets back from London on Monday."

"For goodness sake, Megan, isn't that a bit hasty?" Rodric said, frowning. "I know we've got to have that meeting with John about the will, and obviously she'll have to be included, but we don't have to have her come and stay do we?"

"I want her to come," Megan said, digging in her heels. "She's our niece and I think we should get to know her, and Nonna agrees. I've spoken to Fabia and she's offered to pick her up from the station and bring her to us Monday morning. It's all arranged."

"You might have asked me!" Rodric protested. But, before he could go on, Nonna intervened.

"I think Megan's right. It only needs to be for a couple of days. She'll probably be going back to London soon anyway. I think your father would have wanted us to welcome her."

Rodi looked surprised at this reaction but didn't comment further, he just added, "Delma said we should try to persuade her to reject her inheritance, are you thinking we could do that?"

Megan shook her head. "I don't think that would be right, it wouldn't be what Da wanted."

"Let's leave it for now. Eat your breakfast," Nonna said as she sat down, took some toast for herself and spread it with butter and marmalade. "That's settled then. Hopefully John will arrange that meeting soon. Has he suggested a date yet, Rodi?"

"I've got to get back to him about it." He glanced at Nonna. "It's even more difficult now, with Delma not here. She should be there, she is my wife, after all."

"Well, since Anjali has to be there, and Garan and Bella as well, of course, you'd need to consult them. And, as you say, Delma should be included. You should keep trying to contact her then maybe leave it to John to organise. At least that takes the pressure off you," she said.

"I'll do that." A few minutes later he pushed his plate away, drained his coffee, and got up. "Thank you Nonna. I'll go and call those two numbers again."

Megan and Nonna watched him leave but neither spoke.

* * *

Having slept for a few short hours, Fabia woke just after eight and lay there going over and over the events of the evening before. Deep down she felt a warm glow when she thought back, but overlaying that were doubts. Did she really want to sacrifice her independence? Her past experiences of being tied into a relationship had not been good. Wasn't it safer to go on as they were? But she knew that wouldn't be possible now. They'd taken a first step into the unknown, there was no way they could turn the clock back. And the thought of losing Matt made her feel sick. After a while she told herself to stop fretting about it, just get up and do something useful.

As she threw the duvet back, her mobile rang. Her heart leapt, it might be Matt, but it wasn't, it was Bella. "Hallo, love," Fabia said. "How are things?"

"Not so bad," she replied, but her tone gave the lie to her words.

"Have the police been back to talk to Garan again?"

"No, and the uncertainty is really getting to him, but I suppose there's nothing we can do about that. Look, Fabia, I really need to talk to you. I've been thinking back to conversations with Caradoc over the years and, well, there are things he told me that might be relevant to all this. I may be letting my imagination run away with me, I don't know. I just need you to tell me if I am. Can I come around?"

"Come now if you want. I was intending to give you a ring today anyway."

"I will. I'll borrow Sheryl's car."

"Okay, see you in about half an hour."

Forcing herself to push Matt to the back of her mind, Fabia had a quick shower and threw on some clothes. When she got downstairs, she lit the fire in the sitting room, and she'd just finished checking her e-mails when the doorbell rang.

Fabia opened the door to Bella whose eyes were shadowed and her face paler than Fabia had ever seen it.

She took her friend's hand and pulled her into a hug, then released her and said, "Come on, we can sit by the fire, have some coffee and you can tell me what you need."

Once they were settled, Bella leant back in her chair and sighed. "It's great to get away for a bit. I've been helping out in the pub and the gossip is off the scale. Sheryl and I are trying to protect Garan from it because he gets so angry. We keep telling him flying off the handle won't help at all, but it's so difficult for him."

"And for you and Sheryl too. You're right, it'll be much better if he keeps as cool a head as possible," Fabia said.

"That's what I keep telling him. The police have told him not to leave the area, which was a bit worrying, as if he's going anywhere when he's got a pub to run!"

"I know, but they do have to warn people, they would have said the same to the rest of the family."

"I suppose." Bella sounded unconvinced.

"Some would do a runner no matter what responsibilities they had," Fabia told her, then thought it best to change the subject. "You said there were things Caradoc told you – what exactly?"

"Well, one thing he mentioned, and this was only a few weeks ago, was that he thought Delma was pinching stuff from the Abbey and selling it on. He said he was going to tackle her about it, and I wondered if that could be a motive, if he threatened to tell the police. Do you think she might have been responsible for killing him?"

"It's possible, and she of all of them at the Abbey could have had access to that tranquiliser. As it happens, Matt wanted me to ask you if Caradoc knew things were disappearing. Did he say exactly when?"

Bella frowned. "It was around the time Delma's brother turned up. He told me about that too. He was so angry, fuming about the fact she'd invited him without consulting anyone, and he loathed the man."

"Did he suggest that Mike might have been involved in the disappearances?"

"Yes, he did."

"But if Mike or Delma killed Caradoc, why did someone kill Mike?"

"Well, that could have been Delma too; if he threatened to turn her in, that'd be reason enough, wouldn't it?"

Fabia frowned. "I suppose. But I've just got this feeling we're missing something."

"What particularly?"

Fabia didn't give her a direct answer. "I had one of those nightmares the other night," she said.

"Oh, poor you, I thought those had stopped."

"So did I, but this one was a bit different. There was something about it that made me feel, well, that it was a message."

Unlike Matt, Bella didn't pour scorn on the idea. "What sort of message?"

"I felt as if it was something I should have known or suspected about Caradoc's death, about who killed him I mean."

"What?" Bella sat forward. "Do you mean you know who—"

"Not know, but I have a very strong feeling about it."

"So, who do you think it was?"

Fabia told her, and Bella didn't pour scorn on this idea either, but she did say, "I really don't think that's very likely, Fabia."

"I suppose you're right. It'd be totally out of character, wouldn't it?" She grimaced. "I find it so frustrating that I have no right to investigate this as I want to. I have to rely on setting up conversations with people, picking over what they say to me, or don't say for that matter, or relying on what Matt chooses to tell me, but I no longer have any right to get in there and use my training."

"I can understand how you feel. But Matt does come and talk things through with you, doesn't he?"

"Yes, he was here last night." Fabia could feel her cheeks becoming warm and bent to pick up her coffee mug. Too late, Bella had noticed.

"Was he?" she asked, smiling. "All night?"

"Bella! Of course not."

"There's no 'of course' about it. It's about time you two got together. And something's been going on, I can tell."

"God! You're worse than Cath."

"Come on, tell me, tell me. I need cheering up."

"We, just– well, we talked about our relationship a bit, that's all."

"Talked about it? Or did something about it?"

Fabia couldn't stop herself smiling, but the smile didn't last. "He wants that bit more from me than I feel I can give."

"Why can't you, Fabia?"

"My history with relationships is pretty dire."

"So, you've been unlucky with men in the past," Bella said, "but it doesn't mean that'll always be the case. It's bloody obvious you're fond of him; more than fond."

"How do you know?"

"It's the way you talk about him, rather a lot in fact. Cath and I have both noticed it."

"Are you two ganging up on me?" Fabia protested.

"No, darling, but we both care about you and want you to be happy, and we're both convinced that Matt is the man for you."

"Oh, I don't know. It's complicated. After all that's happened over the last few years, I'm not sure I can trust him." As she said it, she knew it was no longer true. Had Cath been right when she'd suggested Fabia get out of the habit of being angry with Matt and learn to trust him again? Maybe she'd done so without even realising it.

"I'm sure you can, but I won't nag you. All I can say is, take the plunge, you deserve a bit of fun and I think Matt

Lambert could certainly provide it. I wouldn't say no!" Bella grinned at her and Fabia laughed.

"You're incorrigible."

"That's me," Bella said, but a moment later she was serious again. "Thanks for cheering me up, but there's no escaping for long. I must get back. Sheryl will be needing her car."

* * *

Fabia spent the rest of the day unable to concentrate on anything useful. She couldn't get Matt out of her mind. After a scrappy lunch, she made herself go out for a walk, but halfway across Gwiddon Park she realised she'd left her mobile on charge in the kitchen and turned to hurry home. But when she got back, there were no missed calls and no texts.

Throughout the afternoon she kept checking her mobile again and again, but still there was nothing from Matt. Around four o'clock she was beginning to feel desperate and she'd just picked up the phone to text him when it buzzed.

At last, and it was from Matt. "Meant to text before, it's been frenetic here, just to remind you that I love you. Last night was not one of your nightmares, xxx Matt."

"Cheeky bugger," Fabia muttered to herself, then she grinned with relief. "Idiot." Then her fingers hovered over the keys, what to say next? She decided to keep it cool and just asked if they'd managed to locate Delma.

"Yes," he responded. "We're having her escorted back and Dilys is meeting them off the train, we're going to question her before we take her back, if we don't arrest her."

That should be interesting, thought Fabia. She sent another text. "Am picking Anjali up and dropping her off there on Monday morning, worried about that."

"You worry too much. How long is she staying?"

"A couple of days so will be on my own." She pressed send. Oh lord, should she have said that?

A response came back from Matt in no time at all. "Is that an invitation? Thought you said you needed time to think."

Fabia bit at her bottom lip. What was she doing? But she found her fingers tapping out, "Been doing that most of the day, not sure that's what I need most at the moment."

Matt's response took a little longer to come through this time. "I'll phone later. I love you, xxx."

A few times, through the evening, Fabia's phone rang, but each time she was disappointed. It wasn't Matt.

It wasn't until she was getting ready for bed that he finally called, and he didn't have good news. "There's been a serious incident, a knifing, in a night club in town, that dump called the Blue Banana. I'm the only one available to deal with it, so I'm not going to get to you tonight, or tomorrow either at this rate. You know the drill."

"Don't worry, I understand. I remember what it's like." In spite of her disappointment, she could cope with work getting in the way.

"You'll not change your mind, Fabia? About us?"

"I– we need to talk."

"I know, but please don't start having doubts. Don't start telling yourself you shouldn't have sent me that text."

Since this had been exactly what she had told herself, she wasn't sure how to respond to this.

"I know you," Matt went on. "If you have too much time to chew things over, you'll decide your text was a mistake and go back to keeping me at arms' length."

"Matt, let's talk about it when we actually have some peace and quiet."

"And time," he said. "Fabia," he sounded anguished, "you know how I feel about you, please don't change your mind."

Fabia could hear voices in the background. She heard him say, "Okay, Dilys."

"Matt, love, we'll talk soon," she said. "It sounds as if you need to get back to work."

"I'm afraid so. I'll– I'll see you soon." And he was gone.

Chapter 22

On Sunday Fabia was relieved that she'd invited friends for lunch. At least it kept her occupied and her mind off Matt. But once they were gone, he was back in her mind. Several times during the evening she picked up her phone, but each time she put it down again. Best not to bother him. In the end, she sent him a quick text, "Hope the nightclub case isn't too shitty, saw something about it on the news, love F". But there'd been no response from Matt. When she finally went to bed, she was feeling thoroughly miserable and a little annoyed with Matt, which she told herself was completely unreasonable, particularly as she'd told him she understood.

On Monday morning there was still no news from Matt, and Fabia was glad when she had to get going for the station to pick up Anjali.

"I'm glad I made the effort to visit those buyers," Anjali told Fabia as they left the station car park. "They seemed really interested in my designs. One of them is definitely going to put in an order, and I think the other might as well."

"That's good news."

There was silence in the car while Fabia negotiated two roundabouts and turned for the motorway, then Anjali said, "I'm not really looking forward to this visit, but I promised Megan so I must go ahead with it. However, I'm still going to make an excuse and tell them I have to go back to London in a couple of days. And I'll have to come back to your house first. I've left some of my stuff in your spare room, I'm sorry about that."

"No problem," Fabia said. "I can be your chauffeur again."

"You are so kind."

Anjali sounded a bit choked up, so Fabia went on quickly, "I think that's sensible. It'll put a sort of limit on it. And it's not as if you can't come back for John's meeting about the will."

"We've been talking a lot over the weekend. I really like him. He told me all about his family, and about his wife and her illness, and we talked a lot about Mauritius too. He says he'd like to visit."

Fabia smiled. This was good news, but all she said was, "Has he told you when the meeting will be?"

"No, not yet. He says he'll have to sort things out with Rodric and Megan first."

"I think it may have to wait until Caradoc's killer is found."

Anjali didn't respond, just turned to look out of the window. The weather had turned and, as they drove along the narrow, tree-shaded lane to the Abbey, dappled sun made patterns on the road.

"This is beautiful," Anjali said, sounding a little more cheerful now.

"It is, in this kind of weather." Fabia didn't tell her how gloomy and threatening it could be in October storms or January snow.

They turned in between the stone dragons and Anjali craned her neck to look up at them, remarking on how impressive they were. "The Welsh dragon is a good deal more fierce than our poor dodo at home," she said.

"Ah, but at least the dodo was real," Fabia said.

Fabia parked in the courtyard and, as they got out of the car, Anjali looked up at the house, eyes wide. "Wow!" she said. "What a place?"

Fabia pointed to the ruined chancel with its gaping windows. "I think that part goes back to the thirteenth century, and this–" She indicated the middle section of the house. "–is seventeenth century. The wing is Victorian. A complete mixture of styles and periods, but it seems to work."

"It does, but in a way it's a bit scary. I expect there are lots of ghosts." Anjali grimaced then gave Fabia an apologetic smile. "Don't take any notice of me. I'm being silly." She took a deep breath. "Well, let's go."

As they mounted the steps to the front door, it opened, and Megan came rushing out. "Welcome!" she exclaimed. "Come in, come in." She grabbed Anjali's hand and pulled her into the hall. Fabia followed.

"This," Megan said, arms flung wide, her voice high and excited, "is the great hall, and that up there, she waved hands above her head, "is the gallery. In the old days, musicians used to play up there while the family had banquets down here, but that stopped when the dining room was built. Do you want me to show you round the house?"

None of them had noticed Nonna join them from the kitchen. "Megan, *bach*, give the poor girl a chance to get her breath," she said, smiling.

"Oh, sorry," Megan said, blushing. "I'm just so pleased you're here. Anyway, this is our aunt, Rhiannon Giordano, but everyone calls her Nonna."

Anjali turned and held out her hand. "I am pleased to meet you," she said, very formal, her accent more obvious than usual. Fabia had noticed before that this happened when she was unsure of herself.

Nonna smiled and took Anjali's hand in both her own, "We're delighted you've come to visit us. It's what your grandfather would have wanted."

Fabia was relieved at this apparently positive reaction. Two down, two to go, she thought. So far it was going better than she'd anticipated. She told herself she'd been worrying unnecessarily.

"And hallo again, Fabia," Nonna said, "It's good to see you. Come on, let's all go into the kitchen and have some coffee, it's warm in there. This hall is always so chilly, except for when we have the yule log in the fireplace at Christmas."

"Yule log? What is that?" Anjali asked.

As they followed Nonna to the kitchen she explained the tradition: that a large log would be cut down from the copse at the top of the estate and brought in, then the fire would be lit on Christmas morning to warm the room throughout the day.

Anjali's eyes lit up. "That sounds beautiful. I wish I could be here to see it."

"Well," Megan said, her smile wide, "maybe you will be. If you're still in the UK come Christmas, you must spend it with us. After all, you're a member of the family now."

They all sat round the scrubbed pine table while Nonna prepared coffee.

"I'm really sorry I have to desert you tomorrow morning, Anjali, just after you've arrived," Megan said.

"Fabia told me about your meeting with her agent. It's very important, you mustn't miss it."

"But still, it does seem a bit rude," Megan said, "although I'm sure Nonna will look after you."

"Of course, I will," Nonna said, smiling. "Since the weather is so good this afternoon we can go for a walk, show you the farm and the village. Then tomorrow, while Megan is out, I can show you round the house and the rest of the Abbey – give you the guided tour – would you like that?"

"I would. It's an incredible place. I've never been anywhere like it before."

"It's just home for us, but perhaps we're inclined to take it for granted. It'll be interesting to see it through someone else's eyes."

"And Nonna knows all the history, every detail," Megan said, "so she can tell you all about it."

As Nonna was pouring the coffee into mugs, there were sounds of an arrival at the back door. A moment later Rodric came into the room, the lurcher, Mabel, at his heels. He stopped dead at the sight of Anjali and frowned, but Megan didn't give him the chance to say anything.

"Anjali has come to visit us for a few days," she said, her voice high pitched and nervous. "You know I told you she was coming?"

"You did," he said as he turned to Anjali. "Welcome to White Monk Abbey. I hope you enjoy your stay with us." The tone was coolly formal, as if she was a visiting stranger or some business associate.

A shadow passed across Anjali's face and the colour came up into her dark cheeks as she held out her hand and shook Rodric's. Fabia felt a flash of anger on Anjali's behalf and decided to intervene. Eyebrows raised, she said, in a tone reminiscent of the one she used when dealing with a cocky subordinate, "Good morning, Rodric. I'm just here as chauffeur to bring your niece," she emphasised the word, "to visit you."

He flashed her a dark look, but then he sighed and turned back to Anjali. "Yes, well, I can't hang around, I'm afraid, I've got to get back to work. Megan, do you know where Delma is? I've just come from the stables and Moonlight's clattering around in his stall. I think she needs to see to him."

Nonna looked at him, the expression on her face sombre. "She's in her room. She said she's not feeling well.

She was going to get hold of one of her regular girls to see to Moonlight."

Rodric frowned. "I'll go and check that she's done so."

Quickly he left the room and all four women watched him go, differing expressions of worry and irritation on their faces.

Anjali stumbled into speech. "I feel I'm intruding, so much has happened and I'm sure you don't want me here at such a time."

"Nonsense," Megan said, "having you to stay will cheer us all up, won't it Nonna?"

"I'm sure it will," Nonna said calmly. "We want you to get to know us. It's not your fault that these terrible things have happened. We'll just have to hope this awful business is sorted out by your friends in the police, Fabia."

"I'm sure they're doing their best," said Fabia, slightly defensive.

"Hopefully they are," Nonna said. "And we're a strong family. We'll survive."

A few minutes later Fabia got up to go.

"I'll see you tomorrow at Sheena's office, Megan," she said.

"Yes, yes, I can't wait."

"You are sure you'll be able to find it?" Fabia asked her. "It'll be best to park in the Adam Street car park, then it's only five minutes' walk from there."

"It's fine. I know the area. I'll see you there at half past nine."

Anjali came to the front door to see her off and Fabia gave her a hug. "You're doing the right thing," she told her, trying to sound convincing.

"Do you think so?" Anjali asked anxiously. "I wish you weren't going."

"Nonsense. You'll be fine."

"I've made sure my phone is well charged so I'll give you a ring later and let you know how I'm getting on, and

I'm going to skype Maman this evening to tell her all about it."

"You do that, and I'll see you in a couple of days."

As Fabia drove away, she found it hard not to stop and turn around. She wanted to go back and take Anjali away from the sombre Abbey, but she couldn't.

* * *

Fabia spent the rest of the day swinging between wondering when she'd hear from Matt and wondering how Anjali was getting on. She didn't hear from Matt, but she did get a call from Anjali later in the evening.

"How's it going?" she asked.

"Alright," Anjali said, but she didn't sound very sure. "Megan and Nonna have been very sweet. I haven't seen much of Rodric, though when I do he's polite but not friendly; and I haven't even met Delma, she's stayed in her room. Megan says she's been there since she got back from London. Rodric says she's got a migraine."

"If the truth were known, that's probably made it easier for you."

"Yes, maybe. We went for a long walk earlier, it's beautiful countryside around here, and then, before dinner, Megan and David Harris took me down to the pub, in spite of protests from Nonna."

"Protests?"

"She said it wasn't appropriate for us to go to the pub because of all the gossip, but I got the impression Megan just wanted to get out of the house."

"I suppose you can understand her feelings about gossip."

"Perhaps, and I think she thought it might be awkward for me. But Megan was insistent, and it was fine. I met Garan and his wife, and Bella, she's lovely."

"Yes, she is. She's a great friend of mine, and she was a very good friend to your grandfather. I bet you attracted some attention from the locals."

Anjali laughed. "A bit, I think. I managed to persuade Megan not to introduce me as her niece, thank goodness."

"That's just as well."

There was a pause, then Anjali rushed on. "I'm sorry, Fabia, but I don't think I can cope with more than a couple of days staying here. I really want to come back to your house on Wednesday, before I go back to London."

"Of course you can," Fabia assured her.

"And we'll speak tomorrow, won't we?"

"Absolutely, I'll phone when I get back from the meeting with Megan and my agent."

"Please do. I think you're my *doudou* at the moment. What is it called in English? Security blanket?"

"I'm flattered," Fabia said, smiling, but for a while afterwards she sat frowning at the screen of her phone. The sooner Anjali came back to Pontygwyn, the happier she'd be.

* * *

The following morning, Megan was late leaving for her meeting with Fabia's agent. Fabia had arranged for the manuscript to be downloaded onto her own laptop, since Megan's was still with the police, but Megan wanted to take a hard copy with her. The trouble was she couldn't find it. After a frantic search, Nonna ran it to earth on the sideboard in the kitchen. After that Megan couldn't find her new mobile, and another search ensued. She finally discovered it in the pocket of her coat. Then she wanted to go over how Anjali would occupy herself while she was out.

"I'm sure you'll enjoy going around the house, and I'll get back as soon as I can," she assured her.

At last, just before nine, she got going.

As Anjali went back into the house, Nonna was waiting for her. "Would you like to do that tour of the house now?"

"Yes, I would," Anjali said, feeling that it would fill the time until Megan got back.

"Well, let's go, I'm looking forward to it," Nonna said.

Anjali glanced at her, a little surprised. The older woman sounded so enthusiastic. She'd prepared herself for an unfriendly attitude from Nonna, given what Fabia had told her, and this wasn't at all what she'd expected. She felt relieved.

An hour later, having been shown all the rooms on the ground floor and been given a detailed history of their contents, had the identities and life stories of the people in family portraits described to her, and been shown most of the rooms off the gallery, they came back downstairs. As they made their way along to the kitchen, Nonna stopped.

"I'll show you the cellars, they're really interesting." She fiddled with a piece of the panelling then pushed and it swung open.

"Wow!" exclaimed Anjali. "I didn't expect that."

Nonna smiled. "This panelling was put in by an ancestor of your grandfather's, at the time of the Civil War; he wanted to be able to hide from the Roundheads."

"Who were they?"

"The Roundheads? They were followers of Cromwell who fought against Charles I, the rightful, anointed King." Nonna's tone of voice showed which side she'd have been on and Anjali noticed that, as she spoke, she stroked at the large crucifix hanging from her neck. "He was murdered by them, and those who'd supported him had to go to ground. Gwilym Mansell, who owned the Abbey in the seventeenth century, was faithful to the King. He was persecuted by the Cromwellians, which is why he created this secret entrance to the cellars, so that the family could hide. Come, I'll show you."

Immediately in front of them Anjali could see a steep stone staircase. Nonna flicked a switch and a naked bulb in the passageway below dimly lit up cobwebs hanging down on all sides. Reluctantly, Anjali followed her down. She didn't like spiders, nor did she like the atmosphere in this dank place. At the end was a door with heavy iron hinges and an iron ring for a handle.

"This is the oldest part of the Abbey. We very rarely come down here, in fact I can't remember the last time any of us did," Nonna told her. She pulled at the ring and the heavy door quietly swung open.

"What a place," said Anjali as she peered into the dark room stretching away in front of them. The only light was from the passageway they stood in, although there was a slight greying of the darkness at the end. There was a steady drip of water and the smell was of damp stone and decay.

From behind her Nonna pointed. "Can you see over there, to the side where there are small alcoves? It's believed they were monk's cells. I expect your grandfather would have known all about it."

Anjali leaned forward to look then shuddered and, as she began to step back, away from this awful place, there came a sudden violent blow between her shoulder blades. She fell forward on to the stone floor, hitting her head on the door as she went. For a second, she blacked out, then, as she came to her senses, the slam of the heavy door echoed around her and she was plunged into darkness and complete silence.

Head ringing and dazed, she crouched there for what seemed like an age, then she pushed herself up and tried to stand, but her knees buckled under her. "Nonna! Open the door!" she screamed, "Nonna! Nonna!" But her voice just echoed eerily around her, and the door stayed firmly closed.

Chapter 23

Megan had arrived a little late at Sheena Matthews' office, but Fabia felt the meeting had gone well. She hadn't expected Megan to be at all business-like but, as it turned out, she was, and Fabia could tell that Sheena was impressed. After a successful meeting, they emerged into a sunny Cardiff at half past ten.

Megan gave Fabia an impulsive hug. "Thank you so much. Having the book to think about has really helped over the last few days; it's kept me from thinking about Da and everything."

"I'm glad," Fabia said.

"I must get back," Megan said, "I feel I've been neglecting Anjali."

"I'm sure she won't mind, but you get going. I've got some shopping to do."

Megan strode off toward the multi-storey car park, giving a wave as she went, and Fabia made her way to the city centre in search of a coffee and a bit of retail therapy. On the way she tried Anjali's phone, but all she got was an automated voice telling her the number wasn't recognised and suggested she try again later. Fabia frowned, puzzled, then remembered that Megan once said that reception at the Abbey was sometimes patchy. She sent Anjali a quick text and decided she'd try phoning again when she got home. As she put her phone back in her pocket, a text came through, but it wasn't from Anjali, it was Matt. Her heart leapt, but then plummeted a moment later as she read, "Sorry not to get back to you, v busy, will try to phone later, xxx M."

Bugger, she thought, but she'd told him she understood, hadn't she? She tapped out a quick reply and, no longer interested in coffee or shopping, she retraced her steps through the crowds to pick up her car.

* * *

The traffic was unexpectedly heavy, and it took Megan an hour to get home. As she pushed open the front door she called out, "I'm back. Anjali? Nonna?"

There was no reply, so she made her way to the kitchen, thinking it the most likely place to find them at this time of day, but it was empty. Megan frowned, wondering why there was no sign of preparations for lunch, and where everyone was. Then it occurred to her there'd been no car in the courtyard. Maybe Nonna had taken Anjali out. Feeling a little put out that she hadn't been included in these plans, she was about to go back along the corridor when she heard footsteps approaching. A moment later, Nonna walked into the room.

"Oh, there you are, Megan. Have you been back long?"

"No, only just this minute. Where's Anjali?"

"She's gone, Megan," Nonna said quietly. "I've just got back from taking her to Newport station."

"What? Why?"

Nonna put a hand on her arm. "Megan, love, sit down, I'll explain."

Megan subsided into a chair and Nonna sat down beside her. "It was all rather upsetting. Just after you left, Anjali had a call from her mother to say her father's been taken ill. I texted you, didn't you get it?"

"No. What do you mean, her father's ill?"

"Just that. Her mother asked her to come home immediately."

"But–"

"She was so worried that I suggested she check flights to Mauritius on her laptop. I thought maybe she'd be able to get one in the next couple of days. It turned out the only one with space before next Wednesday was leaving at ten tonight, and we worked out that if she got a train immediately, she'd be able to make it, so she booked it and I took her to the station."

"Oh dear, oh dear," Megan said. "Did she leave a note for me or anything?"

"No, love, she didn't have time, but she asked me to tell you how pleased she was she'd met us all."

"What about the meeting with John? And the will?"

"I'm sure John will contact her and sort that out."

"Do you think so?" Megan shook her head, completely phased by this development, then she brightened. "She'll still be on the train, won't she?"

"Yes, I suppose."

"I'll phone her now."

Megan thought Nonna was going to protest, but then she said, "Good idea."

But Anjali didn't pick up, then or later when Megan tried again, and again. In the end, she phoned Fabia.

Megan poured out her news at such speed that it took Fabia a while to work out exactly what had happened. Finally, she understood and asked, "So she's on her way to London?" Fabia was finding the whole thing hard to believe.

"She should be there by now. Has she contacted you?" Megan asked.

"No, I tried her earlier but I couldn't get through. I've heard nothing from her since last night."

"Maybe her phone's playing up," Megan said. "I'm not sure she'd have time to go back to her friend's flat in

Streatham. I don't know London well enough to work it out."

"Her friend might know what's going on," Fabia said, feeling a little more hopeful, then her heart sank once more. She had no way of contacting Anjali's friend. All she knew was that her name was Tania and she lived in Streatham.

"I think Nonna said the flight leaves from Gatwick, but not until quite late."

"She might have contacted John. Do you want me to give him a ring?"

"Yes please, Fabia. He might know more. I so want to speak to her and make sure she's planning to come back."

"Okay, leave it with me," Fabia told her, trying to sound calm, but deep down she didn't feel calm at all.

It took her a while to get hold of John, but when she did, he said he hadn't heard anything from Anjali either. In fact, like Fabia, he was completely taken aback by her sudden departure. "What was wrong with her father?" he asked.

"I don't know. John, have you got a number for her friend, she's called Tania, but that's all I know."

"I have, actually. We– er– Anjali gave me Tania's number, as a sort of– I'll get on to her."

"Please, and get back to me as soon as you can."

"Will do."

Half an hour later he was back. "Tania says she hasn't heard from Anjali, and she's puzzled. She says she spoke to Anjali's mother early this morning, apparently their mothers are close friends, and nothing at all was said about Anjali's father being ill."

"I've got a really bad feeling about this, John."

"What do you mean?"

But Fabia didn't give him a direct answer. "You keep trying to get hold of her, and I'll tell Megan to do the same, but I'm going to get on to Matt. I'll get back to you as soon as I can." She ended the call before John could ask any more.

* * *

"Right," Matt said to Dilys as they sat in his office. "Now we've got a confession out of him, that about wraps it up, lousy little toad. What is it with these kids and their knives?"

"They think they need them, for protection," Dilys said.

"Protection, my arse!"

"I know, sir. Don't let it get to you."

"Okay, back to the Mansells." His mobile rang and he snatched it up and barked, "Lambert," without looking at the screen.

"Matt! Thank goodness," Fabia said. "I need you–"

"I'm delighted to hear it," he said, smiling.

"No, that's not what I meant."

"Oh?" Matt said.

"Matt. Listen. It's Anjali, she seems to have disappeared. I'm really worried."

"What do you mean, seems?"

"She went to stay at the Abbey and now she's gone off back to London, but I don't think she has."

"Fabia, you're not making sense," he said, all the amusement gone from his voice. "Slow down. Just tell me what's up."

She took a deep breath then launched into an explanation, ending with, "And none of us can get hold of her, her father appears to be fine, and we can't work out where she is. Do you remember what I said about my dream? Well, Anjali was alone at the Abbey with Nonna all morning. I'm so afraid something awful has happened to her."

"Okay. We can go up there and ask a few questions."

"Would you?"

270

"Of course. We're still on the case when it comes to the Mansells. And you think Mrs Giordano has something to do with all this?"

"I don't know, Matt," Fabia said, her voice agonised. "I know what you mean about my dreams and all that, but I have such a strong feeling about this. Can you do another search?"

"We can, but I doubt that it'll turn up anything useful."

"Matt!" Fabia exclaimed, frustrated.

"Alright, leave it with me. I'll take a team up there now."

Fabia found waiting for Matt to get back to her incredibly difficult. She paced about the house, unable to settle to anything, and when he finally rang back, she snatched up her mobile and nearly cut off the call in her haste.

"I'm afraid we found nothing, and they were none too pleased that we turned up again. Megan Mansell is worried, but accepts that Anjali had to go home; Delma Mansell has taken to her bed with a migraine and didn't even meet Anjali when she was there; her husband was out, and Mrs Giordano stuck firmly to her story. She was very haughty, all lady of the manor about it all, but she did express a wish that Anjali would come back soon. There's not much else we can do," Matt said.

"Did you search the whole Abbey?"

"Yes, including the stables."

"What about the cellars?"

"Cellars? What cellars?"

"Didn't you know about them?"

"No. Where the hell are they?"

"Megan showed me where the entrance is when I was there" Fabia told him. "I think they extend under the oldest part of the Abbey. Megan hates them, that's why we didn't go down there."

"How do you get to them?"

"There's some panelling in the corridor to the kitchen, the central part is actually a door. Some secret mechanism opens it."

Fabia could hear Matt take a deep breath. "Right, I'm sticking my neck out for you here, Fabia, you owe me."

* * *

Matt and Dilys had parked at the pub while he phoned Fabia. He ended the call and turned to Dilys.

"She says there are cellars. Why didn't we know about them?"

"I don't know, sir. How do you get to them?"

Matt told her what Fabia said. "I've told her we'll go back."

"Okay, sir," Dilys's tone was completely neutral but she said, "they were none too pleased when we turned up again this morning, sir."

"I know. But I think Fabia might be right."

"About Mrs Giordano?"

"Yes."

"Are you sure?" She sounded dubious.

"No, I'm not," Matt snapped, "But I'll never forgive myself if she's right and I didn't do anything about it."

"Okay, sir. Do you want me to ask Dave and Chloe to join us?"

"Yes, just in case. They'll only be halfway back to the station."

Dilys made the call and Dave told her they'd meet them at the pub. Matt hoped they'd get a move on as their car was attracting attention from the pub's customers. Although no-one had approached them or tapped on the window to ask why they were there, several people had lingered in the car park, giving them curious glances. Matt was relieved when, ten minutes later, Dave's car pulled up beside theirs. Quickly he brought them up to date and they drove in convoy up to the Abbey once again.

This time it was Rodric Mansell who opened the door. At the sight of them he scowled. "What the hell are you back here for? I was told you'd done another search this morning. This is bloody harassment."

"I'm sorry, sir, but I'm afraid it's necessary," Matt said. I hope to God I'm proved right, he thought.

For a moment there was a stand-off, then Mansell opened the door wider and they all trooped into the hall. A minute later they were joined by Megan and Nonna.

"What's going on?" Megan cried.

And Nonna demanded, "Haven't you done enough?"

Matt was firm. "When we were here this morning, we searched the house and the stables, but none of you mentioned the cellars and we were not aware they existed."

"Well, of course there are cellars," Rodric snapped, "this is an old building."

"You can't go down there," Nonna insisted. "You mustn't go down there! They're not safe."

Matt caught a strange glance Rodric shot at her, saw Megan open her mouth to speak, then close it again. He decided to probe. "In what way are they not safe?"

"Well, there's damp down there, the stairs are very slippery, and the brickwork is very old: crumbling, unstable."

"Nonna, why haven't you told me about this?" Rodric said.

"I didn't want to worry you. Last time I went down there, oh it must be months ago, a brick fell – it's not safe." She was gabbling now.

"Be that as it may," Matt insisted, "we need to search them. We'll be careful." Matt gave Dave and Chloe a nod, they'd know what to do if things kicked off. "I'll leave my two constables with you, ladies, and perhaps you, sir, would show my sergeant and I how to get to these cellars?"

"No!" Nonna screamed. The contrast to her usual calm and measured tone was stark. "You mustn't go down there, I tell you. It's dangerous!"

"Nonna! What is the matter with you?" Megan exclaimed, alarmed.

"We'll take great care," Matt repeated firmly. "Please, Mr Mansell."

Leaving a cacophony of voices behind them – Nonna shouting, Dave and Chloe attempting to calm her, and Megan joining in – they followed Rodric Mansell to the kitchen corridor. Here he stopped in front of the panelling Fabia had described. Matt watched him closely as he put up a hand to a narrow, embossed strip, twisted it sideways, and pushed against the central panel. A section swung open revealing a dark doorway with stone steps descending into the gloom. Rodric put a hand to the side and flicked a switch. A dim light came on at the bottom of the steps. At the end of a short passageway was a door. Matt and Dilys made their way carefully down the stairs, followed by Rodric Mansell.

When they got to the heavy wooden door Dilys asked, "Is this locked, sir?"

"No," he said. "You just turn the handle and push. We were always told not to go in there because it's very difficult to open from the other side."

Matt gave Dilys a sharp look, then put out his hand and turned the handle. It struck him that it moved too smoothly, he thought the handle and the hinges must have been oiled recently. As the door swung open, they heard a scrabbling noise inside and a hoarse voice said, *"Merci bon dieu, merci bon dieu!"*

On the floor in front of them a woman was huddled, blinking in the light. Her nails were broken and bleeding and her forehead and cheek were grazed and bruised.

"Anjali!" Rodric gasped.

Dilys rushed forward to crouch down beside her and put a comforting arm round her shoulders. Matt came to her other side.

"Are you able to stand?" he asked.

"I– I think so," she croaked.

Between them they helped her up. "She pushed me in."

"Who?" asked Matt.

"Nonna." She shuddered as they supported her out of the room. "Nonna did, she pushed me."

Rodric stood on the sidelines looking stricken.

"I shouted for help, and I tried to get the door open, I tried and tried." Anjali subsided against Dilys and began to sob.

Chapter 24

Fabia felt as if she'd been on the phone for hours.

First it had been Matt. "You were right," he said, "I just don't know how you do it. Mrs Giordano shut Anjali in the cellar. The poor girl was in a dreadful state when we found her."

"How awful. Where is she now?"

"She's been taken to hospital, the Royal Gwent. The ambulance has just left, and I've texted Hari Patel, asked him to make a point of seeing her if he can. She'll probably be kept in overnight."

"So, you've arrested Nonna?"

"Oh yes, initially for false imprisonment."

"What was her reaction?"

"Hardly anything. She just stared straight ahead when I cautioned her and didn't resist when she was taken out to the car," Matt said.

"What on earth did she expect to achieve?"

"God knows. Hopefully we'll find out soon."

"And what about Caradoc and Mike?"

Fabia could hear voices in the background. "Sorry, Fabia, I've got to go. I'll get back to you later."

Next it had been John to tell her he'd heard from Matt. "Anjali asked him to phone me. I'm going straight to the hospital. I want to know what's happening."

"Ask for Dr Hari Patel," Fabia suggested. "Matt's asked him to look after her, he's a friend."

"I'll do that."

"I'll come now."

"Fabia." His tone was slightly apologetic. "Can you leave it to me for the moment? Do you mind?"

"No-o," Fabia said, a little unsure what he meant.

"Anjali probably won't be allowed that many visitors, at least, not until they've checked her over."

"But she'll need some toiletries and stuff if they keep her in."

"I'll get them, don't worry."

"Are you sure?"

"Fabia, I care about her, let me do it."

"Of course, John, you go ahead."

"Thank you. I'll get back to you later."

Fabia smiled as she ended the call. This was a pleasant development.

Then Bella had phoned. "What's going on, Fabia? I saw a police car go past and I could have sworn Nonna was in the back."

"You probably did, she's been arrested."

"Good God! You were right then."

"I don't know. At the moment it's for what's called false imprisonment." Fabia told her what had happened to Anjali.

"I'll send Garan up to the Abbey," said Bella. "They'll need support."

Fabia knew her friend too well. She guessed that this was also a way for Bella to make sure she was kept in the loop, but Fabia understood entirely.

And then Megan had phoned, in floods of tears, and poured out the events of the afternoon. When she could get a word in, Fabia asked, "Is David with you?"

"Oh yes," Megan said, "I don't know what I'd do without him."

"You make sure he stays, Megan."

There was a little silence then Megan said, her voice stronger now, "You know something, I'm going to do that."

Fabia guessed that David staying at the Abbey had not been allowed by Nonna. She was delighted that Megan sounded so determined. But Megan was soon back to saying how awful it all was and wanting Fabia to explain Nonna's behaviour, which she couldn't. "You'll just have to be patient. I should think the police will be questioning her for quite a while. Try not to dwell on it too much." As she said it, she knew it was a pointless suggestion.

She'd been rescued from this call when her landline rang. It was Cath, who was unaware of all these dramatic events and had to be brought up to date as well; then she went on to what she considered most important in Fabia's life. "And how are things with Matt?"

"Cath! He hasn't exactly had time to pay me any attention, what with all this going on," Fabia protested.

"I suppose, but don't lose sight of your goal."

"My goal! Yours and Bella's more like. I gather you two have been discussing my supposed love life."

Cath laughed, then told Fabia she'd have to go on with this conversation another time as there was someone at the door.

An hour later John had phoned back. "I was able to see Anjali. Christ, Fabia, if I could just get my hands on that Giordano woman!" Fabia had never heard him sound so angry. "The poor girl thought she was going to die in there. Her hands are all bandaged up because she tore them to shreds trying to get the door open, and she's got grazes and bruising from when she fell. Nonna pushed her from behind and she must have knocked her head as she went down. They're keeping her in overnight and they've sedated her so she can get some sleep. Matt's doctor friend

278

says physically she'll be fine in a few days, mentally it might take a little longer."

"I know what that feels like," Fabia said.

"I remember, bless you," he said, then went on, his voice decisive. "But I'm going to look after her."

Fabia smiled. "You do that, John, and I'll help too."

"Before I left, she told me she wanted to come back to your house when they let her out. Would that be okay?"

"Of course."

"She was rambling a little, the sedative I think, but she did say something about going to meet Branwyn Pierce in Swansea. I think that'd be a good idea."

"So do I."

"And she's given me her mother's mobile number, asked me to contact her. What do you think I should say, Fabia?"

"Would you like me to phone her?"

"Oh please, I think it'd probably come better from you, as a woman."

"Fine," Fabia said, smiling a little. Now he was back to the quiet, reticent man she was used to. "I'll just tell them the bare bones, say she's had a bit of an accident and she'll speak to them tomorrow. I suppose she'll be able to by then?"

"I think so."

Fabia had managed to get through to Anjali's mother quite easily and found herself going into more detail than she'd intended. Sabita Kishtoo had been politely determined to be told all the details.

"Anjali has told me about this woman," she said. "She has told me also about Rodric and Megan, I suppose they are my half brother and sister. I would like to meet them."

"Megan has been very kind to Anjali," Fabia assured her.

"Good. And so have you, I hear. I thank you so much for this."

"It's been a pleasure," Fabia told her. "I'm only sorry she's been put through this awful business."

"But she will be fine now," Sabita said firmly. "And this John, she has talked about him a lot; I think she likes him, yes?"

Fabia didn't quite know what to say in response. "I believe so," she said, smiling.

"I will check on him when I come."

Fabia wondered if John was prepared for being scrutinized by Anjali's mother. Ah well, that was up to him and Anjali.

Sabita told Fabia she would book a flight to the UK immediately, thanked her again for looking after her daughter, and asked Fabia to text her details of hotels in Newport. Fabia came to the conclusion Anjali's mother was a force to be reckoned with. It sounded as if Sabita took after her father, Caradoc.

For the last half hour, the phone had been quiet. Fabia glanced at her watch. It was half past six. She was sure that Matt would be continuing with questioning Nonna for ages yet. What would she say? How would she explain what she'd done? Fabia was desperate to hear from him, but she knew she'd have to wait as patiently as she could.

* * *

Fabia was dozing in front of the television when the doorbell finally rang. She jumped up and rushed to the front door, pulled it open and there was Matt in his familiar stance, leaning against the side of the porch with his hands thrust deep in his pockets.

"What time do you call this?" she said, but she was smiling.

"Half past ten, I think," he said. "Can I come in?"

"Of course," she said, opening the door wide. "I've been waiting to hear what's happened."

"And you were sure I'd come around?"

Fabia gave him a straight look. "No. I just hoped."

He put out his hands, cupped her face and kissed her deeply. At first, she responded, but soon she pushed him away.

"Matt, wait." She leant back. "Please. I want to know what's been happening."

"And that's more important than this." He traced a finger round her mouth.

Fabia shivered then sighed and he gave in. "Come," he said, taking her hand and pulling her along to the kitchen. "I'm ravenous and I need a drink. Then I'll bring you up to date on the whole bloody business."

She poured him a glass of wine and got cheese, cold meat and a tub of potato salad out of the fridge. "This is quicker than making you something hot, do you mind?"

"That's perfect," he said, taking a sip of his wine.

Fabia added bread and pickles to the feast and sat down opposite him. "Now, tell me."

He got busy filling his plate to overflowing, then began to speak. "At first she clammed up completely, wouldn't say a word. She refused the duty solicitor, and we obviously couldn't contact John Meredith because he'd be conflicted."

"He's dancing attendance on Anjali."

"Is he now?" Matt said, and grinned. "Anyway, that meant we had to do without. Made it a bit easier, actually."

Fabia nodded. She understood this all too well.

"She just sat there staring at some point above Dilys's head, fiddling with her rosary and that crucifix she wears, and muttering to herself."

"A rosary? Oh yes, of course, she's Roman Catholic, isn't she?"

"So it seems," Matt said, through a mouthful of ham and potato salad. "This went on for about half an hour, so I decided to change tactics and started asking her about the family. When did her sister die? When did she come to live at the Abbey? I also asked about her relationship with the rest of them, things like that. I just rambled on a bit."

"I used to use that technique."

"I probably learnt it from you."

"Did it work?"

"Well, she did start to look at me rather than at the wall, and she stopped muttering."

For a while Matt concentrated on his meal, but Fabia was getting impatient. "Did you manage to get her to open up?"

"Hold on, I'm coming to that."

"Sorry."

Matt pushed his plate away. "Thank you. Much better." He picked up his glass and drained it. Fabia refilled it.

"What next? Oh yes. When I mentioned Anjali and how delighted her grandfather must have been to discover her, she glared at me and spat out, 'That black heathen!'"

"Good lord!"

"I know. I'm not sure what she feels is worse, the black bit or the heathen bit. She insisted she had to protect the family from Anjali's influence. What was it exactly? She had to protect the integrity of the family. She kept using that word, integrity. I think Dilys was getting a tad frustrated as she snapped out, 'Does that entail knocking her over, locking her in the cellar and leaving her there?' Well, that opened the floodgates."

"Well done Dilys."

"She ranted on and on about Anjali not being a fit person to be part of the Mansell family. She kept talking about the purity of the family's ancestry, which, since she's not blood related, I find pretty weird. It's an obsession with her. She called Anjali and her mother and grandmother every racist name in the book, went on and on about the evils of Islam, in spite of the fact Anjali's family is Hindu."

"Did you point that out?"

"I tried, but she wasn't having any of it. Said it was all the same, they were all unchristian devils. She said Caradoc had brought disgrace on his ancient name having a relationship with 'that black woman', and she insisted Anjali had stolen Megan and Rodric's birthright. She also said something about 'that gypsy and her bastard', I probed a bit and realised she was talking about Bella Price and Garan. She said Caradoc had betrayed them all and he had to pay for his sins. I managed to interrupt at this point and ask her direct if she'd poisoned him and she said, 'But don't you understand, I had no choice, I had to protect my children.' *My* children mark you. It was really coming home to me that we were dealing with serious mental illness here, and a completely warped view of the world. I think she'd stepped over some kind of line between sanity and– I don't know, some kind of mania, but I'm no expert."

"At the very least she has to be mentally unstable, surely," Fabia insisted.

"Well, let's just say the psychiatric reports on this one are going to be fascinating reading."

"I'll say. Did you ask her about using Caradoc's computer?"

"Yes, and that was quite disturbing too. She suddenly went all coy and asked me if I knew what a silver surfer was?"

"What on earth?"

"I know. She was very proud of herself, said she'd done a computer course in secret and now she knew all about them; not that she'd have had to be that savvy, given the old man's casual attitude to online security. She told us she'd read every e-mail sent between 'that heathen' and Caradoc, and the e-mails about the will between him and John Meredith. Then she said, 'But I didn't know he'd changed the date for signing it, he really shouldn't have done that without telling me'. She sounded seriously angry about that."

"What date?"

"Originally Caradoc was going to go into John Meredith's office and sign the new will on the 29th, but he changed his mind and went in on his way back from London on the 23rd. She didn't know he'd done so and that it was too late to stop the changes going through, so killing him was pointless in the end."

"What a waste," Fabia said, shaking her head.

"I know." Matt sipped at his wine and frowned. "We obviously had to press her on how she killed him."

"Did she actually come right out and say she was responsible?" Fabia asked.

"In the end, yes, and how she did it. Apparently, she always made him a hot toddy last thing at night. This time she put a load of crushed up sleeping tablets into it."

"Ah. Same as with Mike."

"Yes. Then, when Caradoc was unconscious, she injected him with the tranquiliser, which she'd found in the stables. She said it was hidden behind a skirting board."

"Who by? How did she know to look there?"

"Apparently, she knew that was a place that Delma had hidden things she'd taken from the Abbey, small stuff. She'd seen her do it, so she checked. She told us she was only looking for what belonged to them, the sainted family again I suppose, and she found this phial of stuff. I think that was probably the point when she decided to use that way of killing the old man. I asked her how she knew what it was, and she told me that she knew a drug when she saw one, then she looked it up online just to be sure. We think she used the computer in the stables to do that, another way of pointing in Delma's direction."

"And you'll have to have another go at Delma, won't you, and that vet?"

"Yes, Fabia, we will," he said, eyebrows raised.

"I know, sorry." She grinned. "I'll shut up. Go on."

"Nonna – I can't think of her as anything else – obviously felt she'd planned it all rather well. She seemed to think it would be a perfect solution for Delma Mansell to be accused of the killing, to punish her for helping her brother steal 'our precious possessions', and she insisted that Delma had never been 'one of us' as if that made it okay."

"And what about Mike?"

"He told her he'd seen her with the tranquiliser. There's no knowing if he actually had, but I think he was shrewd enough to suspect she might be involved, maybe he saw her searching around the stables' office and chanced his arm. He tried blackmailing her, said if she paid up, he'd keep quiet about it all. She was certainly vocal about that, what an insult it was and how he deserved everything he got. We haven't managed to get her to confess to drugging him yet, but the use of sleeping tablets on Caradoc as well should give us something to work on there. I don't think it'll take long before she's boasting about getting rid of Mike Cotter as well. It'll probably be manslaughter in his case, but I'd say we can get her for first degree murder when it comes to the old man. It was premeditated and well planned."

Fabia gave a gusty sigh. "So Garan is in the clear?"

"Looks like it."

"Bella will be so relieved. She was convinced he was going to be arrested for drugging Mike."

"I certainly thought he was more deeply involved at one point."

At last there was silence in the kitchen. Matt leant back in his chair, pushed his hair off his forehead, and looked across at Fabia, his eyes intent and full of warmth. Glancing away from him, she got up rather quickly and took another bottle of red wine from the rack, twisted it open and refilled their glasses. He smiled and kept looking at her.

"Is that displacement activity?"

"What do you mean?" She could feel her cheeks getting warm.

"You always have to be doing something when you're embarrassed."

"I'm not embarrassed."

"Well, unsure of yourself."

"Shut up."

But he was serious now. As if to give himself courage, he took a generous gulp from his glass, then he took a deep breath. "Fabia. You're pouring a lot of wine down my throat."

"You're doing that, not me."

"Okay, but it was you that opened another bottle. There's no way I can drive tonight."

Fabia said nothing, just waited.

"Since Anjali's not here," Matt said, "I could sleep in your spare room, or on the sofa." He got up, came round the table, took her hands and pulled her into his arms. She didn't protest. "But Fabia, my love," he said softly, "I'd much, much rather sleep with you."

He didn't try to kiss her, just studied her face as if he was trying to commit each feature to memory. The minutes ticked by, then Fabia smiled, kissed him and, taking his hand, she led him up the stairs.

Acknowledgements

A few thank-yous, to my writing gurus, Jeannie and Dallas, and to all in the Guernsey Writers' Group, particularly Linda for her help with getting the Welsh place names right. To all at The Book Folks for their eagle-eyed editing and sticking with Fabia, Matt and me. And most of all, yet again, thank you to Niall for listening and contributing, for his unfailing encouragement, and for never grumbling when he's left with all the shopping and cooking.

If you enjoyed this book, please let others know by leaving a quick review on Amazon. Also, if you spot anything untoward in the paperback, get in touch. We strive for the best quality and appreciate reader feedback.

editor@thebookfolks.com

www.thebookfolks.com

Also by Pippa McCathie:

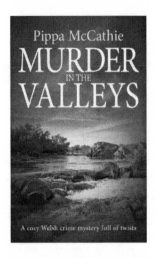

MURDER IN THE VALLEYS

The first book to feature Fabia Havard and Matt Lambert

Having left the police following a corruption investigation, ex-superintendent Fabia Havard is struggling with civilian life. When a girl is murdered in her town, she can't help trying to find the killer. Will her former colleague Matt Lambert stop her, or realize the value of his former boss to the floundering inquiry?

Available in paperback, audio and FREE with Kindle Unlimited.

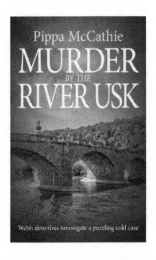

MURDER BY THE RIVER USK

The third book to feature Fabia Havard and Matt Lambert

Almost ten years after he went missing, a student's body is found. Forensics show that he was murdered and a cold case is reopened. But when detectives begin to investigate his background, many people he knew are found to be keeping a secret of sorts. Faced with subterfuge and deceit, rooting out the true killer will take all their detective skills.

Available in paperback, audio, and FREE with Kindle Unlimited.

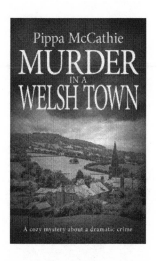

MURDER IN A WELSH TOWN

The fourth book to feature Fabia Havard and Matt Lambert

Hopes for a town pantomime are dashed when a
participant is found murdered. The victim was the town
gossip and there is no shortage of people who had a
grudge to bear against him. Detective Matt Lambert leads
the investigation but draws on the help of his girlfriend,
ex-police officer Fabia Havard. Can they solve the crime
together?

Available in paperback and FREE with Kindle Unlimited.

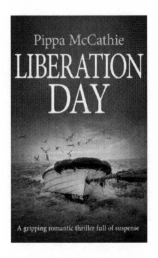

LIBERATION DAY

A standalone romantic thriller

Having become stranded in the English Channel after
commandeering her cheating boyfriend's boat, Caro is
rescued by a handsome stranger. But when the boat is
impounded on suspicion of smuggling, she once again
finds herself in deep water.

Available in paperback and FREE with Kindle Unlimited.

Made in the USA
Columbia, SC
02 August 2021

42840505R00178